Prized
Possessions

Also by L.R. Wright

THE SUSPECT
SLEEP WHILE I SING
LOVE IN THE TEMPERATE ZONE
A CHILL RAIN IN JANUARY
FALL FROM GRACE

Prized Possessions

L. R. Wright

DOUBLEDAY CANADA LIMITED

Canadian Cataloguing in Publication Data

Wright, L. R. (Laurali Rose), 1939-
Prized possessions

ISBN 0-385-25416-4

I. Title.

PS8595.R566P75 1993   C813' .54   C92-095532-0
PR9199. 3.W68P75 1993

Jacket illustration by Adam Niklewich
Printed and bound in the USA

Published in Canada by
Doubleday Canada Limited
105 Bond Street
Toronto, Ontario
M5B 1Y3

This book is for Dorothy Kea—my Aunt Queenie

Author's Note

There is a Sunshine Coast, and its towns and villages are called by the names used in this book. But all the rest is fiction. The events and the characters are products of the author's imagination, and geographical and other liberties have been taken in the depiction of the town of Sechelt and the city of Vancouver.

Chapter
One

She awakened from an uneasy sleep feeling cool around the shoulders, not cold, but not cozy, either. She pulled up the quilt and felt a chill upon the side of her face. She lifted her head from the pillow and saw that the French doors were wide open, and the drapes too—they were moving slightly, in the breeze that drifted into the bedroom. She looked back over her shoulder. The other side of the king-size bed was empty: this didn't surprise her. He'd be out on the patio, probably, smoking a cigarette. And thinking. She turned onto her back, holding the quilt snugly at her throat.

The bedroom was filled with moonlight, and the scents of cherry blossoms and cedar. She heard the shushing of the nighttime breezes and imagined the muted sound of the sea. She lay drowsy and witless under the quilt, having exhausted—perhaps forever—her ability to make decisions.

She heard a scraping sound from the patio.

She imagined him getting up from the padded chaise, stubbing out his cigarette in the black plastic ashtray that was kept out there...and now he would appear in the wide-open doorway to the bedroom, slippers on his feet, his robe wrapped around him, ready to talk some more. She watched through slitted eyes, concealing their gleaming; watched, watched...but he didn't appear.

1

She imagined him at the back fence, leaning his arms upon it and looking unseeingly across the lane and over the park to the houses on Hudson Drive, and behind them, the sea, which would be ink-black, moon-splotched, moving, restless, like a great black being.

He didn't come, and he didn't come...he's looking up, now, she thought, up into the enormous soft-hanging branches of the cedar tree that stood in the back corner of the yard; a tree so huge he couldn't stretch his widest embrace around half the circumference of its trunk; a tree whose lowest limbs he could not reach without a ladder.

Now he will come back into the house—now, she thought, regulating her breathing, making it slow and even. But the drapes at either side of the French doors stirred not at the touch of his hand but in a current of night air that wafted, curious, toward the bed.

She turned on her side, her right hand under the pillow, her left hand clutching the quilt. She wasn't cold, but she didn't like the feeling of the blind breezes fumbling at her face, and she would have liked to close the door. She realized that she had gradually begun to breathe faster and lighter. She was acutely aware of sounds and shadows, warily alert to a myriad of possibilities. She glanced at the clock on her bedside table, and wondered how early the sky began to lighten, in April, and when the birds awoke.

Her eyes were wide in the almost-dark of the bedroom. The moon had shifted in the sky and now tossed cedar-bough shadows upon the floor and she wanted that door closed, and the drapes pulled firm and fast against the night.

Her heart was high in her throat, and she couldn't understand this. She let go of the quilt for an instant, to blot the palm of her hand. It was a very simple life she wished to live, not at all complicated, an utterly straightforward life...

He came through the other door, not the open one she was watching but the other door, the one from the hallway. She heard the sound of it opening, like an inhalation of breath, and quickly closed her eyes, smoothed the skin of her face from the inside, relaxed the hand that gripped the quilt, and breathed once more like a person asleep. It wasn't unusual to pretend to

2

be asleep. People did it all the time. Everybody did it. There were times when you simply didn't want to talk, and it was more polite to pretend to be asleep than to say to someone, I'm sorry, but I really do not want to talk to you anymore right now.

She could hear nothing, nothing, except the sound of her heart, trapped in the hollow of her throat, trying to find its way back down into her chest; and so she opened her eyes a little bit because she had to know where he was—and she saw his legs, bare in the moonlight, and watched a restless cedar shadow shudder across them, saw that he was wearing the plaid robe she'd given him, the one that came to his knees, and the plaid slippers that matched. He was making no sound. He was moving slowly toward her...and now he was right beside her, standing no more than two feet away from her.

For a long time he didn't move. He just stood there. He was close enough for her to smell him.

Finally she could stand it no longer and she stirred, slowly, as if in her sleep, and placed her head sideways upon the pillow, and blinked her eyes, and left them open; she would pretend to be awakening, she thought.

He was taut and motionless, his face utterly unreadable.

She smelled the cherry blossoms and from the early morning darkness heard two slow, clear notes of bird song.

Her husband lifted his right hand, slowly, and aimed his revolver at her head.

One Year Later

Chapter Two

On the first Monday in April, Eddie Addison mounted the steps of a three-story house near the corner of Fourth Avenue and Alma Street on Vancouver's West Side. He was young and bulky, tall, with carroty red hair. He crossed the wide porch, knocked on the door, and waited. He cast small, uneasy glances from side to side, not looking for anything in particular, just keeping his eyes open, keeping his smarts at the ready.

He heard a muffled cry from inside, and for a second the hairs stood up on the back of his neck. Then the door flew open and she was standing there smiling at him, small and blonde-haired, wearing a pair of jeans and a T-shirt with the sleeves ripped out of it.

"Here," he said, thrusting the package at her.

"Oh, thank you. Come on in," she said, stepping aside, "and wait, while I..." She left the door ajar and hurried off down the hall.

He went inside reluctantly. Warily. God only knew what kind of stuff went on in this house. He didn't want to have anything to do with the place.

Eddie knew she was going to get him a tip. Of course, she should have had it ready, so as to be able to give it to him gracefully, not saying anything about it, just handing it to him at the same time she took the package. That's how Mrs. Holden on Mackenzie Street did it, when he delivered. This girl had no class, he thought disapprovingly, despite the fact she went to the damn university.

He stood there feeling more and more awkward, waiting while she hustled off to rustle him up a tip, filling the whole damn hallway up with his body. It wasn't hardly wide enough for a person of a decent size to turn around in. And then they had these bikes in it too, lined up against the damn wall, two of them, one behind the other.

To Eddie's right was a door with a glass doorknob and a little window in the top. He peered through it—well, it was right there, wasn't it? Right in front of his eyes, pretty hard to ignore—and through it he saw a bedroom that was the biggest mess he'd ever seen in his life. He couldn't believe his eyes at first. He thought something must have blown up in there, throwing this person's clothes to kingdom come. The bed, which was not really a bed at all but only a big mattress with a couple of quilts and a couple of pillows on it, was totally covered in pieces of clothing. And there were stacks of books on the floor, and a dresser with hundreds of bottles and jars sitting on top of a big lace doily thing. Stuff was draped over the mirror too—necklaces and scarves—and there were photographs shoved in between the mirror and its frame; and more clothes were on the window seat, piles of sweaters and a couple of purses; and shoes were all over the floor, which was covered by a big rug with Indian stuff woven into it, a huge black raven, stuff like that.

"I gotta go," Eddie muttered. He wasn't going to stand here all damn afternoon while she looked for her damn purse or whatever she was doing.

"Oh, no, don't go," she called out, and stuck her head into the hallway from a room a little way down, past a big bookshelf thing that was packed with clothes instead of books. She must have seen him looking at it, because she said, like she was apologizing. "That's mine; my room doesn't have a closet." So somebody else lived in the mess across the hall then, Eddie thought. She popped her head back into her room, and he heard her talking to herself, her voice coming out into the hall in little swoops and swirls, like a bird ducking back and forth in the air. He heard little bits of what she was saying: "...know I put it...*think*, Melanie..." and then a flurry of laughter. "Here it is!"

Eddie took a step down the hall. And it was because he was so big that it seemed like only one step brought him right to the doorway of her room.

It was a very wide doorway. At first he thought maybe it was meant for a wheelchair—this was because of Mr. Bacon who came to the drugstore every day, and it was Eddie's job, one of Eddie's jobs, to hold the double doors wide open for Mr. Bacon's wheelchair. And then he saw that this was one of those sliding doors that came out of the wall, half from one side and half from the other. Which was a pretty dumb kind of a door to have on a bedroom.

But it didn't look much like a bedroom in there, he thought, staring. There was a fireplace, for pete's sake. And the bottom half of all the walls was paneled in wood, an effect Eddie found pleasing, but weird. So it wasn't a bedroom at all but a living room, he decided. Except there was a bed in it, and a chest of drawers, and a mirror, just like in the other room he'd seen.

He was about to say something to her; maybe, "This is an interesting room" or "Did this used to be a living room?" or "Do you ever light that fireplace?" thinking it'd get pretty damn hot in her bed if she did. But then she glanced up from the purse she was rummaging around in, and she happened to look right into Eddie's eyes at exactly the same second that he happened to look right into her eyes.

Eddie felt a jolt go through him, like he'd been electrocuted, and changed into a statue.

Her eyes were brown, mostly brown, with something shiny and gold about them; the same color, Eddie thought, as tea or maple syrup. But these comparisons dissatisfied him. He thought harder about where he had seen that particular amber-brown color before, all warm and sparkly and beautiful, and he still couldn't move, but he was very content to stand there, looking at the color of her eyes, until she let him know what to do next.

Finally, she stood up, very slowly, hanging on to the strap

of her handbag, and Eddie, his penis stirring, waited without breathing to hear what she was going to say.

"Please don't come into my room," was what she said.

His surprise was immense. He toppled from his dreamlike state into mortification, and felt his face get hot and red. He took a step backward and bumped into the edge of the door. "Fuck you," he said, and it came out all hoarse and trembly. "Fuck you," he said, loud and strong this time.

"I'm sorry," said the girl named Melanie, stammering. She brushed some hair out of her face.

"Yeah, sure," said Eddie bitterly, "you're sorry, sure, right, I just bet you're sorry," he said, backing into the hall.

"I am, really I am," she said. "Here. Please." She held out some money. "Take it. Please."

Eddie stared at it, then at her. His face flushed even redder—he felt it heat up like a stove burner somebody'd turned on. "Fuck it. Fuck you."

"Oh, please, don't—don't—"

He wondered if she took drugs.

Eddie looked hard at her chest, and then he deliberately looked farther down, right at her crotch. Now he looked back at her face. "Fuck you," he said again.

She stood there with her white face hanging out, clutching his tip, with her shoulders hunched, now, not all straight-backed and cocky like before. "You'd better go," she said.

He didn't like what was in her voice, or in the expression on her face. But he didn't know what to do about it. So he turned himself around in the narrow hallway and went back to the front door, and slammed it behind him, and stomped across the porch and down the steps, and all the way back to the drugstore he imagined himself doing things to her.

Chapter
Three

The Sunshine Coast is what British Columbians call a southernly stretch of their coastline that is reached by ferry from Horseshoe Bay, just north and west of the city of Vancouver. It extends from Gibsons in the south to the village of Lund, eighty miles and another ferry ride to the north. At Lund, the highway comes to an end; the rest of the thousand-mile Pacific coast is accessible only by boat or float plane.

There are numerous towns and villages scattered along this eighty miles of coastline.

Among them is one called Sechelt.

Charlie and Emma O'Brea unloaded grocery bags from Charlie's Honda Accord and took them into the house. It was a mixed-up spring day, full of cloud-glower and sporadic sunshine. A chilly day; unfriendly, Charlie thought.

He deposited two bags on the kitchen counter and went into the bedroom to change into his gardening clothes—old jeans, baggy at the knees and in the seat, and a big old sweatshirt that said "U.B.C.," which stood for the University of British Columbia, on the front. He was hanging up the pants he'd taken off when Emma came in. She wasn't carrying anything; Charlie didn't know what her purpose was in coming into the bedroom at that particular moment.

"Oh, leave that, Charlie. I'll do it for you," she said.

"Thanks, hon," said Charlie, picking up his blue sweater and putting it on a hanger, "but I've got it."

She came close to him, placed the palms of her hands flat against his chest, and smiled up at him. Her blonde hair fell back from her face. There were tiny crinkles around her eyes, which were hazel. Charlie could see brown eyeliner on the top lid, and brown eyeshadow like bruises, and brown lashes lengthened and thickened with mascara. She was looking at him questioningly. He kissed her forehead, squeezed her shoulders and released them, and headed for the back door.

A few minutes later, standing in the middle of the backyard, he saw her through the kitchen window, putting the groceries away.

The tune that had been spinning around in his head for the last several days made its way into his throat, asking to be sung, but he only hummed it, as always: "All around the mulberry bush, the monkey chased the weasel; the monkey thought 'twas all in fun—pop! goes the weasel." There was a game that went with the song. Charlie dredged about in childhood memories but couldn't find it.

He stood in the middle of his backyard with his hands in the pockets of his jacket, and he had to laugh, because there was nothing whatsoever to be done out there, he realized, now that he had had a good look around. The lawn didn't need cutting. The hanging baskets Emma had planted earlier in the week didn't need watering. The bed of tulips didn't need weeding. And it was too early in the season to deal with the raised bed, where he grew heat-loving things like tomatoes and cucumbers and peppers.

He walked around to the front of the house, in case something had been left undone there. The early blooming azaleas under the living room window had finished flowering. He began removing the dead blossoms. But Charlie was extremely restless this Saturday afternoon. He had wanted to expend some serious energy out in his garden, not pass the time doing finicky stuff like deadheading the azaleas.

He found a few weeds and pulled them, and decided some ground cover was called for under the azaleas. But that was finicky work, too.

He'd clean the garden tools, he decided. Clean them and oil them. The shovel, the spade, the fork, the rake, the clippers. And he'd take the electric mower apart and clean that, too, and see if it needed oil.

He returned to the backyard and opened the door to the tool shed. He stood there staring inside, not really surprised by what he saw; Emma's sticky invisible webs were everywhere. The garden tools beamed at him, shining, from their hooks on the wall. The mower sat contentedly on the floor, throwing off a dull glow. Charlie closed the door on all of it.

He went back into the house, took off his jacket, and sat down at the kitchen table. "Thanks for cleaning up the gardening stuff." He heard the warmth in his voice; you'll go far, Charlie, he told himself.

"You're welcome," said Emma, folding paper grocery bags. She made a neat pile of them and tucked it in between the refrigerator and the wall. "Would you like some coffee?"

Charlie looked at his watch. "What time do we have to be next door?"

"Six o'clock."

It was now three. Three hours. It loomed before him like a great black hole in his day—in his life. A hole he'd have to either fill up or jump over. And if he leapt and didn't make it, if his jump fell short, where the hell would he end up? Maybe it's worth having a look, he thought, but the idea created such terror in him that he felt physically sick.

"Charlie? What's wrong?"

"Nothing. I just need—yeah, coffee. Coffee would be great." He got up and went into the dining room, and looked through the window into the backyard. The sun had gone behind another cloud, and the wind was gusting. Keep the lid on, he told himself. But it was hard. Very hard. He couldn't believe how hard it was.

"Charlie," said Emma behind him.

He nearly jumped out of his skin.

"Sorry. I'm sorry. I didn't mean to startle you."

"It's okay. I've, uh, got a headache, I think."

"I'll get you an aspirin," said Emma. "Come on. Sit down

in the living room with me. Have your coffee."

She continued to glance at him worriedly, even after he'd taken the aspirin and drunk a cup of coffee and then another, even though he assured her he was feeling better now, his headache was gone now.

"You've been jumpy lately," she said. "I think you should see Dr. Sawatsky."

"I may do that," said Charlie.

She got up and came over to his chair, and placed her hand across his forehead, seeking a fever. Charlie smelled her perfume, or maybe it was hand lotion. Whatever it was—the fragrance, or the coolness of her hand, or her lips, pouty and seductive, or the rise of her breasts under her cotton sweater— for whatever reason, Charlie surprised himself by placing his hands on her waist (ah, such a slim waist) and pulling her sweater free from her jeans. A shudder went through him when his hands touched the smoothness of her skin. He reached behind her to undo her bra, and then took her breasts in his hands. Emma removed her sweater, and her bra, and slipped into his lap. Charlie held her breasts and sucked them, felt the nipples erect in his mouth. He undid her belt, and the button and the zipper in the front of her jeans, and got out of the chair, pushing her into it.

He knelt in front of her and pulled down her jeans, and her panties. It was important not to look into her face but he wanted to taste her lips, so he closed his eyes and pulled her toward him, and covered her lips with his open mouth, gnawing gently, licking, sucking at the undersides of her lips. He felt the tune in his throat, humming there like a living thing—"Pop! Goes the Weasel."

Charlie pulled away from her and opened his eyes. He stood up and took off his clothes. Emma lay sprawled in the chair, her legs spread, and in his peripheral vision he saw that she'd flung one arm across her eyes. Charlie got down on his knees in front of her again, between her legs. He wanted her to talk to him. He wanted her to say, "Do it to me, Charlie, do it to me." He imagined that he heard her saying it: "Do it to me, Charlie, fuck me, Charlie, oh yes do it to me do it do it." He put his hands on her hips and drew her closer.

And then a venomous flicker of memory occurred. He saw her face in the light from the streetlamp at the end of the alley, and he felt like a fool again, and he lost his erection.

He wondered how much of the three hours had passed.

He sat back on his heels. Keep the lid on. You can do it.

"That's too bad, Charlie," said Emma, her voice clear and calm.

"Yeah," said Charlie. But—it's just as well, he thought.

He stood up and pulled on his underwear, and his jeans, and his sweatshirt. He looked at his watch. Three forty-five.

He went into the kitchen to get his jacket. He'd mow the damn lawn, front and back, whether it needed it or not.

Chapter
Four

"I ought to be out at the marina on my day off," R.C.M.P. Staff Sergeant Karl Alberg grumbled, turning off the highway. "Looking at sailboats to buy. Not having dinner with somebody I see every day at work."

"You're right," said Cassandra Mitchell agreeably. "Where are we going, anyway? Do they live on the water?"

"Near it. Not on it. How come I don't have any friends except other Members?"

"Maybe nobody else likes you. Maybe you're a miserable person."

Alberg brooded on this. "Well?" he said finally. "Am I?"

They were traveling slowly along a crooked street. Clouds swept across the sky, restless and glowering, shifting size, shape, and color as they went. Cassandra clutched her sweater around her. "No, Karl. And you do have friends who aren't cops. I mean, police officers. There's Alex Gillingham, for instance."

"Jesus, Gillingham."

"And there's me."

He glanced at her, pleased. "Yeah. True."

"I want it to be warm again," said Cassandra, shivering.

"When it comes time to trade in my Olds," Alberg mused, "I think I'll get one with air."

"With air?"

"Yeah. Air-conditioning."

"Karl, we get a summer like last year's about once every century. You don't need air-conditioning here."

"You're right," said Alberg, nodding. "I need a boat. That's what I need." He pulled up in front of the Sokolowskis' house and turned off the engine. "Well here we are. Christ."

"Oh for heaven's sake, stop complaining," said Cassandra, exasperated.

"I've never been here for dinner before. Maybe I'll have to invite them back." He stared at the house, which was set back a considerable distance from the street. It was such a small place, for a man as large as Sid Sokolowski. Alberg looked at his watch and wondered aloud how long they'd have to stay.

"You aren't a very sociable person, are you," said Cassandra pityingly.

"I'm damned hurt you should say such a thing," said Alberg.

He got out of the car and moved quickly around to the passenger door but Cassandra had it open before he could get there, as usual.

"Well I'm not going to sit there like some potentate waiting for you to do something I'm perfectly capable of doing for myself," she said.

He followed Cassandra through the gate and up the walk, admiring her legs. "Is it okay to admire your legs?" he said as they reached the front porch, and she said it was.

Sid came to the door wearing a yellow shirt and a pair of khaki pants and brown leather sandals. Alberg thought it was early in the season for sandals. He also found the sight of the sergeant's naked toes embarrassing. And he felt overdressed; he was wearing a jacket and a tie, for god's sake. He couldn't remember if it had been Cassandra's idea or his. It must have been Cassandra's, he thought, loosening the knot in his tie, unbuttoning the top button of his shirt.

"Come on in," said Sid, and they trotted after him dutifully, down the hall and into the living room. Through an archway they could see the dining table, set for more than four. "Let me get you a drink," said Sid, and took their orders.

His wife, Elsie, came into the room, smiling. She deposited

a tray of vegetables and dip on the coffee table and shook hands with Alberg and Cassandra. "Sit down, please," she said, but then Sid returned with glasses of wine and as he handed them over, he invited Alberg to go outside and look at his new fence, and they ended up all four of them going outside.

"That's a lot of work," said Alberg admiringly. He walked to the east side of the yard and looked across at the next property, which was unfenced.

"That place is a disgrace," Sid muttered, his bare toes curling in disgust. "Look at the damn dandelions, will you? They're gonna go to seed, all the damn fluff's gonna blow over here."

Alberg knew Sid hadn't been keen to buy this house, which he and Elsie had occupied now for five years. The Sokolowskis and their five daughters had lived in a big place over near the high school, a house on a straight street, with a straight lane behind it, and houses on either side that looked straight ahead, like houses should. "A street on parade, you might say," he'd said to Alberg, who sometimes had difficulty deciding when Sid was joking.

When the last of the girls left home, Sid often wandered wistfully through the place looking into his daughters' abandoned bedrooms—they'd all left stuff behind, for various reasons, and sometimes, he confided to Alberg, he pretended for a minute that they still lived there. Elsie, on the other hand, upon finding herself alone so much of the time, decided to take control of her life.

"She tells me, 'I don't want to drift, Sid. I mustn't start drifting.'" Sokolowski reported this to Alberg with a pained expression and a helpless shrug of his enormous shoulders.

One day she announced that she'd gotten herself a job managing a dry cleaning establishment. Her husband, who had expected her to have considerable difficulty finding employment, was shocked. But Elsie pointed out that running a seven-person household was excellent training for practically anything.

Next, she wanted them to move. It took her several months to persuade Sid that this wouldn't be the end of the

19

world as he knew it.

They put their big house on the market and started looking around for a smaller one, and eventually they'd ended up here, on Persimmon Drive.

Hudson Drive ran west of Persimmon and parallel to it, tracing a gentle curve around a small bay. Houses had been built along this street as along any other, upon rectangular lots that stretched from the sidewalk to the edge of a low bluff that overlooked the water. "Now you'd think," Sokolowski had complained to Alberg, "that the next street up would do the same, maybe be a little bit straighter, even. But no." Persimmon had been laid down in two exultant swoops that formed a reverse S. To Sokolowski, this made absolutely no sense. The lots were pie-shaped, and they didn't fit together particularly well. Some were much bigger than others, and some lay sideways to the lane. Between this lane and Hudson was a park, with a couple of houses on ordinary lots at either end.

Sid Sokolowski's house was the second from the western end of Persimmon. The lot on the corner was also fenced and snuggled neatly against the Sokolowskis'. The one on the other side, however, was, Alberg admitted, peering over the fence, truly a mess.

"Although there's a certain charm to the place, Sid," he said, studying the automobile carcass through which tall grass was growing, and the thicket of wild yellow broom at the edge of the lane, and the bright golden dandelions scattered across the shaggy lawn.

Sid just looked at him, and Alberg knew he was thinking about Alberg's own backyard and realizing that on this particular subject he was talking to the wrong guy.

"We'd better go inside, Sid," said Elsie, who had thrown a sweater over her shoulders before leaving the house. "Cassandra's freezing out here." Cassandra murmured a polite denial but headed quickly for the back door.

Sid gestured toward the fenced yard to the west. Alberg glanced over there and saw cloud shadows racing across the lawn, and a human shadow caught his eye, too, as it moved quickly away from a window in the back of the house. "There's another couple coming, too," Sid was saying, as they followed

Elsie and Cassandra. "We owe them. Because he threw in with me on the fence."

Alberg turned this remark over in his mind until he knew what was wrong with it, which was the phrase "another couple," implying that he and Cassandra were a couple. Which they were, he supposed. But not a married couple, which was what Sid and Elsie were, and probably their neighbors, too. Alberg felt a sting of nostalgia; for a moment something in his body hurt.

The other couple arrived a few minutes later. They were introduced as Emma and Charlie O'Brea.

Again, Sid offered drinks. "Emma? Charlie?" As he turned to Cassandra she said, "I'm fine, thanks," interjecting quickly so he wouldn't have to fumble around trying to decide how to address her. She'd told him to call her Cassandra, but he seemed to think that inappropriate, for some reason. Alberg wanted to grin at her, but he didn't. He sneaked a sideways glance, though, and saw that she was tense in the company of these several strangers.

He felt the need to say something to her in private. It didn't matter what. It wasn't the message, it was the conveying of it, in private, but among other people, that was important. He would touch some part of her and whisper something to her that nobody else could hear, and either he wanted nobody else to notice him doing this, or else he wanted everybody to notice it, he wasn't sure which. For the moment, though, he would let there be space and distance between them, as if they were estranged.

Politely, he turned his attention to the newcomers. They sat side by side on a long sofa, Charlie at one end, his wife in the middle. Charlie, Alberg had been pleased to notice, was also wearing a jacket and tie. He was in his early forties, Alberg figured, tall, with dark brown hair, graying: its tight curls were controlled by a very short haircut. His shoulders were broad, and his hands were large and square, with spatulate fingers. His eyes were blue and the bones in his face—cheeks, forehead, jaw—were prominent.

"I'm in insurance," he said when Alberg inquired, and looked amused when Alberg expressed surprise.

"What would you have guessed?"

"Something—I don't know. Something outdoors," said Alberg with a grin.

Charlie laughed. "Insurance salesmen spend a lot of time outdoors. On the road. Going from client to client."

"I guess they do."

"He isn't a salesman," said Emma, placing her hand on her husband's sleeve. "He's a partner in a consulting group." She looked up into Charlie's face and smiled. "In West Vancouver."

Emma O'Brea was quite a lot younger than her husband, Alberg decided. Her blonde hair fell from a center part just short of her shoulders. It was sleek and shiny, and when she shook her head, it didn't fly off in all directions but kept its shape. She had a slight lisp and spoke very softly, so that Alberg's eyes went to her mouth when she talked; her lips were so full as to look almost swollen. Her hazel eyes were carefully made up, her skin glowed, and her body was positively voluptuous, sheathed in a short black dress. She seemed utterly at ease. But her tranquillity felt to Alberg shielded and private, as if she were keeping it to herself, like a secret.

"West Van," he said. "You commute, then."

Charlie nodded. He stretched out his long legs, cradling his wineglass in both hands. Next to him, Emma sat sideways on the sofa, one arm along its back, the skirt of her black dress pushed several inches above her knees.

It was revealed that Emma had a degree in art history. She had married Charlie right after graduation. She didn't have a job, and didn't want one.

"That must be very very nice for you, Charlie," Sid began, nostalgic.

"Things change, Sid," Elsie interrupted briskly. "Life changes. People change."

Alberg noticed with interest the rapid pulse in Charlie's throat. His heart's going like a sonofabitch, he thought. Yet there's nothing on his face but blandness.

When they stood to go in to dinner, Alberg caught Charlie's eye. His gaze was so guarded, thought Alberg, that looking into his eyes was like looking into an anteroom. Alberg was intensely curious, and he thought Charlie knew this, for he held Alberg's gaze while he reached for his wife and pulled her close to him and smiled. Alberg could feel Charlie's body willing itself to relax, and accomplishing this.

After dinner they returned to the living room for coffee, and the conversation turned to neighborhood matters, and Alberg's attention wandered. At the dinner table he had been seated next to Cassandra, and had become acutely aware of her physical presence—the rustle of her clothing, the smell of her perfume, the gleam of her hair, the sound of her voice. Now he felt an ache in his body because she was too far away from him. He got up and moved an ottoman next to her chair, and sat down on that. He looked at her face, in profile, for what seemed a long time, and finally she turned her head and looked back at him, smiling a little. He reached over and picked up her hand and held it with both of his. He turned it over and brought it to his lips and kissed the palm. He let his eyes move to her face again and saw that she was blushing. But he kept looking at her, and knew that the longer she returned his gaze the weaker she felt in the middle of her, as if she were melting, as if her muscles were dissolving. He bent toward her and put his lips against the side of her throat, below her ear.

When he lifted his head, Emma O'Brea was staring at him, her serenity shattered, her face contorted with rage. Alberg turned away, got up from the ottoman and returned to his chair. He took his time picking up his coffee cup, taking a sip, replacing it. When he looked again at Emma she was talking to Elsie, and she was once more rosy and serene.

Chapter
Five

*E*ddie hadn't forgotten about the girl called Melanie, but at least he'd stopped looking for her all the time. For the first couple of days he'd looked for her everywhere: on the street, in the drugstore, in the café where he almost always had lunch, everywhere he went. This wasn't because he wanted to see her—hey, not on your life. What he wanted was to *not* see her. Or rather, to see her first, before she saw him, so he could make sure not to meet up with her, look her in the face, have to say any words to her. There was no way he wanted her in any part of his life, even in the smallest part of it.

And then on Saturday he looked up from the shelf he was loading up with antiperspirants and there she was. With her back to him. Looking keenly at the jars of nail polish in the next aisle over.

Eddie ducked his head a little and peered more closely from between the antiperspirants. It was her, all right. He'd recognize her anywhere, even from behind. He didn't know what the hell to do, so he called in his mind upon his sister Sylvia, who obliged him promptly, as she always did: *Ignore her, Eddie,* he heard Sylvia tell him; *you've got your dignity to think about.* Yeah, right, Eddie said to himself, concentrating upon the antiperspirants. He was lining up the roll-ons now, each one in its own little box: What a waste of cardboard, thought Eddie, and he snatched another glance over the top of the rack of shelving. He was a whole head taller than the shelves. He noticed that the girl was a whole head shorter.

She'd moved up the aisle a bit and was now looking at the hair stuff—brushes and combs and barrettes and stuff like that, the stock replenished that very day by Eddie himself. He saw her take something off one of the racks—he couldn't see what it was—and he watched closely, imagining for a second that she was going to stuff it into her pocket and walk out without paying for it. He had a little fantasy about chasing after her, out the door and onto the sidewalk, and then he'd put a big hand on her shoulder and say, *hey, lady,* all full of sternness, *let me see what you've got in your pocket there.* But she put it back, like he knew she would—she was a bitch, but she was probably no thief—and went on up the aisle. What is she *doing* here, Eddie muttered to himself.

And then it occurred to him that she might have come to the drugstore to make some trouble for him.

His fingers got suddenly big and clumsy and several boxes of deodorant toppled over. It took him a few seconds to straighten that up, and when he peeked again into the next aisle, she was gone. He was partly relieved and partly disappointed.

He thought about her a lot during the rest of the day: while he was loading up the shelves, and unpacking boxes in the back room, and having his coffee break, and cleaning up after some kid whose mother let him tear open a bag of nuts and spill them all over the floor.

All he thought about her while he took off the blue drugstore jacket he wore over his own clothes, the one with *Eddie* sewn onto the lapel in red writing.

And he thought about her while he drove home, too, until finally he heard Sylvia in his mind admonishing him not to brood. So while he cooked his supper he turned on the hockey game, and then he forgot about her for once and for all because the play-offs were on.

And then two days later, what happened but she came into the store again.

This time he was stocking the magazine racks. It was a job

he particularly enjoyed. In fact he enjoyed it too much, really. Harold, the manager, had had to speak to him a couple of times about not letting himself get too absorbed in the covers. He didn't get mad at him; Harold never got mad. He'd just give him a friendly word. "No reading on the job, Ed," he'd say, giving Eddie a clap on the shoulder as he passed. So Eddie tried to be very conscientious now. He'd look quickly at the magazines and the paperback books, but he wouldn't let himself read the words on the covers. Some, of course, he had no trouble ignoring: the crossword puzzle magazines, for instance. But he found most of the others very interesting, for one reason or another. He got to take some of the magazines home whenever the new ones came out.

On this Monday afternoon, he dug into the box he'd just opened and reached up to put a handful of copies in the *Maclean's* rack—and there she was. Just like that. She just materialized, like from black magic or something.

Eddie felt like some kind of fool squatting down there, squinting up at her, while she stared down her nose at him.

His mouth opened. "Hi," he said.

Right away he could have kicked himself for being the naturally polite kind of person he was. But what could he expect? Of course he was automatically going to say, "Hi," to a person he knew—well, sort of knew—when she was looking straight into his damn face.

But *she* wasn't a naturally polite person. Oh no.

"Hi," he said to her.

And she turned around and flounced away. That's what she did. He didn't get a damn word out of her. Not a "Hi," not a "Howdoyoudo," not a "Kiss my butt." Nothing.

He watched her go and he was steaming, just steaming. Of all the nerve, of all the damn nerve, that was all he could think of, that was the only thought in his head: of all the damn nerve.

He finished the magazines and picked up the empty boxes, to return them to the storeroom. This required that he pass the prescription counter at the back of the store, and he saw the girl standing at the end of the lineup. Probably getting penicillin or something, he thought. Probably she's got some sexually transmitted disease. He shivered at the thought and stared at the

27

back of her head with distaste as he passed her, and he let the box he was carrying bump her, real gently, in the ass as he went by. "Oh, sorry," he said, and she glared at him so hard that he could just barely hold in his laughter until he got into the storeroom, where it was okay to let it out.

Chapter Six

O n Friday afternoon Emma was out in the backyard with a long-handled pruner, snipping branches from the cherry tree to bring them indoors. They were already in bloom, so they wouldn't last long, but she only wanted them for today, for tonight.

Today was her sixth wedding anniversary, and her twenty-ninth birthday.

The neighborhood in which she and Charlie lived was west of town, south of the highway, half an hour's drive from the Langdale ferry terminal and five minutes by car from what would have been called downtown Sechelt if Sechelt had been a bigger place. Their house, which faced north, was about a city block from the sea. Emma could see the ocean, and hear it, from the backyard when she was outside working in her garden. She could see it by standing on her tiptoes and hanging on to the fence and stretching her neck to look over the top; it was downhill to the ocean from her backyard.

A breeze came tumbling in from the sea, and white petals filled the air from a moment, then fluttered down; some of them caught in Emma's blonde hair. The breeze made her shiver because it was a spring day; yes, she could see that, in the grass that suddenly needed another mowing, and in the tulips growing next to the fence; but it was an unpleasant spring day, blustery and petulant and much colder than it ought to be. She shivered in the cold breeze from the ocean but took pleasure in its salty fragrance—and tucked that away in her head to pass it on to Charlie: the rough cold touch of the breeze on her face and the salty smell of it.

Indoors again, she plunged the cherry boughs in hot water and arranged them in the tall heavy glass vase that she'd bought to replace a similar one that had gotten broken last year.

"What do you want for dinner?" she'd asked him.

He'd pretended to think about it. He was very polite; it was one of the things that pleased her about him. But she knew it wasn't a question that interested him.

"How about if I surprise you?" she said, and he agreed to this, smiling. On past anniversaries he had suggested that they go out for dinner, but Emma always said no. The day was a gift she gave herself, and making dinner was its centerpiece.

Always, in Charlie's absence, Emma conjured him up, moving through her day as if he were with her—or, rather, she ordered her motions, and, as best she could, her thoughts, so as to delight him should he be there. She looked upon this as preparation for his death. She could continue doing it after his death, she thought, and in that way keep him alive for her.

She liked observing the world for Charlie, those parts of it he was too busy to notice for himself. The palms of her hands recalled the texture of the bark of the cherry tree; she had memorized the limpid green of its new-springing leaves. She captured these things, interpreted them, and passed them on for his enlightenment.

When Emma was about ten years old, she had had a dog that got killed by a car. She lived in a small town, and everybody knew which dog belonged to whom. A little boy came running into her yard yelling at her that her dog, whose name was Pat, was hurt. She followed him, running, and when they approached the street that went past the park and the flower shop, she saw Pat, a golden cocker spaniel, lying by the side of the road. She got close enough to see that he was perfectly still. She'd never seen him motionless before; even when he slept, he twitched. Then she turned around and ran home, pelted home, her legs going very fast, and she was screaming for her mother when she was still half a block away.

Emma took the silver candlesticks into the dining room. She spread newspaper on the table, got polish and rags from the kitchen, and sat down to clean them. Through the window she saw a blue jay strutting the length of the front yard fence, looking in at her with sharp metallic eyes, a blue jay wearing a black hood, with pencil strokes for legs.

Emma at twelve had come home from school one day to find her mother sitting all by herself in the kitchen, without a coffee cup, without even her cigarettes and ashtray; just sitting there as if turned to stone, not hearing Emma when she spoke. It turned out that her mother's sister had died. Emma remembered that there was an echo in the kitchen. Something had been sucked from the air, leaving a hollowness into which Emma's voice plunged and then caromed around. Her mother looked at her, finally, and at first Emma thought she didn't recognize her, and then she realized that her mother didn't even see her standing there. Maybe she saw her sister, Emma's aunt. Anyway, she began to cry.

Emma was going to cook a filet of beef, with asparagus, and Yukon gold potatoes. And she had already made the meringue for a Pavlova.

The sun suddenly wrenched clouds from its face and fell upon Emma's carpet in a sullen sprawl. Emma stopped in her housewifely duties and moved across the living room to stand in the sunlight for a moment, letting it warm her face.

Her mother died when Emma was twenty-two and about to get married. One minute she was in Emma's life and the next—gone. Her father had died years earlier, when Emma was still a baby, so now she was an orphan. Emma in her wedding gown began to wonder if God had it in for her. She deeply mistrusted His having given her Charlie to care for.

It was six o'clock when Charlie pulled up in front of the house. He sat in the Honda for a moment, looking at the front door, but it didn't open. Yeah, ground cover would be good under those azaleas, he thought.

He was very conscious that it was the third Friday in April, that a certain kind of time was running out. So he concentrated on the bare earth beneath the azaleas, imagining periwinkle there, or creeping Jenny. After a while he picked up the package lying on the passenger seat and collected his briefcase from the floor and got out of the car.

The house could use a coat of paint, he noticed, opening the gate in the fence. He'd mention it to Emma. "The house could use a coat of paint, hon," he'd say to her, and that same afternoon the yard would be swarming with workmen.

"Emma," he called out as he opened the door, "I'm home." She arrived in the hall as he was hanging up his raincoat and gave him a hug and pretended not to see the package sitting on top of his briefcase. He didn't want to drag things out, though. "Let's have a drink," he said. "I want to give you your present."

In the living room he poured two glasses of scotch, then had to take them into the kitchen to get ice. He returned to the living room and handed one of the glasses to Emma.

"To us," said Emma, smiling, raising her glass.

"To us," Charlie agreed. They drank. "Sit down, now, and open this." He gave her the package.

It was wrapped in paper that said Happy Anniversary! all over it, and it was tied with silver ribbon and topped with a silver bow that was bigger than the box itself: the store had done this for him. Emma opened her present carefully, easing the invisible tape away from the paper without tearing it, revealing a blue Birks box inside. She looked at Charlie with raised eyebrows and parted lips.

"Yeah," he said. "I think you've guessed it."

Emma removed the lid and pushed aside a layer of cotton wool. She plucked from the box a wide silver bracelet, hinged. "Oh, Charlie," she breathed. She slipped it onto her wrist and closed it; held her slim arm up and moved it into the sunlight, so that the bracelet flashed. "It's beautiful." She got up to thank him with a hug and a kiss. "You just sit there and enjoy your drink," she said, "while I finish up in the kitchen."

Charlie downed his drink, poured another, and turned on the television news.

"This is wonderful," said Charlie, at dinner.

Emma smiled upon him, content.

Over the Pavlova she said, "I'm taking more lessons." She'd just completed a course in gourmet cooking.

"Good," said Charlie. "What is it this time?"

"Piano."

He smiled at her. "Good."

She refilled their coffee cups. She was so sharply aware of the difference between this anniversary and their last one that she knew he must be also. She got up and stood behind him, her hands on his shoulders, and gently kissed the side of his face.

She tried never to think about it. The only reason it had crept into her mind now was, obviously, because it had happened exactly one year ago. Six years ago she and Charlie had gotten married. One year ago she had woken in the night and found him standing over her, pointing a gun at her head.

Poor Charlie, she thought.

"I love you," she said, squeezing his shoulders.

He patted her hand. "Thank you, Emma, for a terrifically good anniversary dinner."

She sat down again and gazed at him across the table. The candlesticks gleamed. The cherry boughs cast a pale fragrant glow in the corner of the room. "Isn't this better," she said softly, "than last year?"

Charlie nodded, slowly, his face tipping in and out of shadow.

Chapter
Seven

*E*ddie worked only a four-hour shift on Friday, so when he got to his sister's place, it was early in the afternoon. "Where are the kids?" he said, looking around.

"Play school," said Sylvia, who was cleaning the big front-room window.

"How come they're there on your day off?"

She flicked him an exasperated glance. "I need to clean the house in peace once in a while," she said, rubbing vigorously at the glass, "without them getting underfoot."

"It sure looks clean, all right," said Eddie, trying to get in her good books. He sat down on the sofa, keeping his back straight, his feet flat on the floor, his hands quiet in his lap.

After a few minutes Sylvia gathered up the paper towels she'd used on the window and took them and the spray bottle into the kitchen. "Want some coffee?" she called out to him, and Eddie said loudly that he did.

He got up and joined her in there and sat at the kitchen table, which was under a window that looked out into the backyard. Eddie had hung a tire from the big maple tree out there, for the kids to swing on.

Sylvia made coffee in her glass percolator. "Have you had any lunch?" she said, washing her hands at the kitchen sink while the coffee pot burped and bubbled.

Eddie shook his head. "I'm not hungry, though."

Sylvia ignored this and fixed them both lettuce and tomato sandwiches and put out a plate of her homemade peanut butter cookies too. All this time she had the radio on, way down low. Sylvia almost always kept the radio on just low enough so you couldn't hear anybody's words. This was okay when there was music playing, but when it was a talk show, like now, it was very irritating. Eddie wanted to ask her to turn up the volume or else turn off the radio altogether. Finally, as if she could read his mind, she reached over and switched it off. Eddie felt a lot more relaxed then. He ate his sandwich and drank his coffee and had three cookies, all the while listening to Sylvia talk about her job and the kids...and this was good, this felt good; it was family stuff and family was very important.

After a while, though—well, it was like when you have to stop walking, because wherever you're going, you've all of a sudden gotten there. Eddie could feel Sylvia looking at him and thinking and wondering why he'd phoned her up and asked if he could come over. So, "Sylvia," he said, "there's something worrying me."

He knew he'd probably used those exact some words in the past. And this was good, because she sort of knew now what was coming. He looked up at her from the cookie crumbs he'd been moving around on the plate. She was looking straight back at him, her face calm and even. The day was soft and bright, with a thin gray veil of cloud over the sky, and the light was tender upon Sylvia: Eddie could see no worry lines, no roughness; and her brown hair, drawn back in a businesslike ponytail so it wouldn't get in her eyes while she cleaned, was clean and shiny. Eddie almost got tears in his eyes gazing at Sylvia; he was so thankful she was in his life.

She nodded at him, and he went on.

"I didn't do a thing to her," he said. His hands were flat on his thighs, and he was leaning toward her earnestly. "There was a misunderstanding." He looked down again. Sylvia waited. "I swore at her," Eddie muttered.

Sylvia lifted her coffee mug, black with an elaborate design of flowers all over it, and sipped. She was wearing jeans and a long-sleeved T-shirt with no collar. There was a short little opening at the throat, with four tiny buttons that she had left undone. She was sitting sideways on her chair, with one arm over the back of it, and her legs were crossed. Now she uncrossed them and put both hands on the table in front of her, pushing her coffee mug aside. "What was the misunderstanding?" she said. Her voice was calm too, just like her face.

Eddie told her about delivering the parcel. "I didn't know it was her bedroom. It didn't look like a bedroom. I was just looking in there, thinking about how it didn't look like a bedroom. That's all. That's all, Sylvia."

"How come you didn't wait by the front door, though?"

Eddie shrugged. "I don't know. I don't remember. I think she said something to me. Called me. I didn't think anything of it," he protested. "I just went down there. I knew she was getting me a tip. I wanted to get going, get out of there." He felt his blood moving faster and figured his face was probably getting red. "She got it all wrong for god's sake."

"Eddie," said Sylvia; a warning.

"Well, she did. 'Don't come in my room,' she says." He said it again, "'Don't come in my room,'" putting on a high, petulant voice. "As if I'd want to go in her damn room."

"Eddie," said Sylvia sharply.

"So 'fuck you,' I told her."

"Eddie!"

"'Fuck you lady.' That's what I said." He slumped back in his chair.

After a while Sylvia sighed. It sounded big and wistful, like the wind just before rain starts to fall. Then she got up and went to stand behind Eddie's chair, and began massaging his shoulder muscles: he hadn't known they'd been hurting, until then. For a while they hurt more, but by the time she moved away and sat down again they weren't hurting at all.

"You've gotta apologize," said Sylvia.

Eddie groaned.

"Eddie," she said quietly. Reluctant, he looked at her. "It's the only thing that works. You know it."

"I feel like I've been apologizing my whole damn life," he said resentfully.

"And whose fault is that?"

"Well it's not entirely my fault, Sylvia, not entirely." He badly wanted a smoke, but Sylvia didn't allow cigarettes in her house. "I gotta stand up for myself. A man's gotta stand up for himself."

"Get real, Eddie. Shoot." She pushed her chair away from the table. "You'd think by now—" She tore the elastic band out of her hair and shook it free. "After all the times—" She grabbed a hairbrush from the windowsill and brushed her hair furiously. "And all the people—" She grabbed her hair, gathered it up at the back of her neck and wound the elastic around it again. She rested her elbows on the tabletop, staring across at him, and leaned into the sunlight that was suddenly shining down through a ragged hole in the cloud cover. Eddie felt bad, because there were lines across her forehead now, and a pair of them, like brackets, from the bottom of her nose to the edges of her mouth. "Remember that girl when you worked for the post office?"

"I don't wanna go through it all, Sylvia," said Eddie wearily. "I don't."

"First they warned you. Then they fired you."

"I told you, Sylvia—"

"You almost got fired from McDonald's, too."

Eddie shifted in his chair. He craved a smoke so bad....

"And Eddie, for pete's sake if it hadn't been for that nice cop up there on the campus, two years ago you would've been in the slammer."

He put his hand over his eyes. He'd got her started, now she was going full bore; there was nothing to do but wait for it to be over.

And this, surely, was why he'd come, wasn't it?

Chapter Eight

*T*he next day was a harbinger of summer. The grass was long and thick and fragrant, the rosebushes were laden with buds, and the air was warm enough for shorts and T-shirts.

In Sechelt, Karl Alberg prepared a platter of food and took it out to the sun porch, along with mugs of coffee and a pot of strawberry jam.

"It's so beautiful, let's eat out on the lawn," said Cassandra. So they moved a card table and two chairs outside, and began to eat.

Cassandra, tearing a croissant in half, looked around her and frowned. Alberg's backyard wasn't designed to sit in. It was a yard you walked through on your way to the garage. "You should get a patio put in here," she told him.

"Good idea," he said contentedly. "I'll do it."

She smiled a little, realizing how much she liked the look of him: tall, broad, too thick around the waist, fair-haired, blue-eyed, with a face ageless and enigmatic—she continued to find him attractive and was glad of that. And glad that he found her attractive too. She glanced at him frequently as they ate. It was good to see him happy and relaxed.

"Karl," she said, licking strawberry jam from her thumb, "do you remember how we met?"

"Yeah," he said, grinning. He pushed the platter closer to her. "Have more."

"Did you answer a whole bunch of ads? Or only mine?"

"Why?" he said cautiously.

"I was just wondering." She helped herself to a bagel and smeared it with cream cheese. "Do you remember *when* we met? I mean, how long ago?"

He cocked his head, looking thoughtful. "Boy, it's got to be—three years? Four?"

Cassandra's lips settled into a thin line. "We met in June of 1984."

He was clearly astonished.

"Almost eight years ago," she said.

"No. Really?"

"I was forty-one years old."

"Uh huh," said Alberg.

"On my next birthday, Karl, I will be fifty."

"You've never looked better, Cassandra," he said sincerely. "And I can tell you from personal experience, being fifty isn't so bad. Me, I was dreading it, but—"

"Karl," she said, interrupting him, "are you up to having a serious talk?" She watched his eyes and waited for the shutters to drop, and they did. Wham. No access.

He did this at will. She associated it with his being a cop and wondered if it was one of the reasons he'd become a cop, or if he'd got like that only after he became a cop.

Cassandra suddenly felt unutterably weary. She tossed her napkin on the table and got up.

With her hands in the pockets of her shorts, she made a slow circuit of his yard, looking at the rosebushes that swarmed over the fence, and through the grimy window into the garage, at Alberg's Oldsmobile, and along the opposite fence, also smothered in rosebushes. One fence separated the backyard from a lane; across the other was a well-tended yard with a brick patio near the house and a vegetable garden at the back.

"You haven't finished your bagel," said Alberg.

"I've had all I want."

He joined her at the fence. "What do you want to talk

about?" He was standing near enough to touch her, but he wasn't touching her.

Cassandra shook her head.

"Come on," he said softly. "Let's go inside. Have another cup of coffee. Talk."

She let her body list slightly to the right, until her shoulder brushed against his arm. Alberg's arm came up and around her, pulling her close to him, holding her firmly. She rested her head on his shoulder and sighed.

"Come on," said Alberg.

They took the dishes inside. Alberg poured more coffee and led the way into the living room. "Okay," he said. He put his feet up on the hassock and spread his hands on the arms of the wingback chair. "Go ahead."

"I resent that," said Cassandra, who was still standing.

Alberg lifted his shoulders and donned an expression of helplessness.

"I haven't got a speech to make," she said. "I don't want *me* to talk—I want *us* to talk. About us. About the future. As I'm sure you've guessed."

Alberg put his hands behind his head. "Okay. Where should we start?"

She sat down on the sofa. "Let's start with you and your job."

"What about my job?"

"When are you going to retire?"

"I don't know. I haven't thought about it."

"You could do it now, couldn't you? Because you've got your twenty-four years and a day, right?"

"Yeah. I'm not ready to retire, though."

"How much time do you figure to put in?"

"I don't know, Cassandra. I told you, I haven't thought about it much."

"I don't believe that, Karl. Listen." She got up and went over to him. She sat on the hassock and put a hand on his ankle. "Do you resent my asking you about this? Because if you do—if you think it's none of my business—then just say so."

He reached to take her hand. "No, of course I don't resent it. You have every right to know what I plan to do. But the thing is—I don't have a plan."

"What are your alternatives?"

He sighed. "I hate this. Okay, okay. I've got twenty-eight years. If I stay in until the thirty-five-year mark, I can retire with seventy percent of my pay. That's probably worth doing."

"In seven more years you'll be almost sixty—"

"Fifty-nine. I know how old I'll be, Cassandra."

She withdrew her hand and went back to the sofa.

"I don't have to quit then, either," he said. "I can stay in until I'm sixty-five."

"Wonderful."

"What's this got to do with anything, anyway?" he said angrily. "How about your job at the library? When are you going to retire from that?"

She gazed at him evenly. "We'll get to me in a minute."

He dropped his feet to the floor and pushed the hassock to one side.

"Don't get defensive, Karl," she said softly. "Please."

"I'm not defensive," he snapped. He shook his head. "Okay I'm defensive." He sat forward. "Look. I don't like to think about it, okay? I don't like to think about leaving the Force."

"But aren't there other things you want to do? You're still young, Karl."

He laughed.

"—youngish. You *are*. There are all kinds of things you could do with your life, if you retired early."

Alberg imagined himself a bearded seafarer, exploring the coast of British Columbia in a thirty-foot sailboat. He looked at Cassandra, earnest and loving and afraid of the sea. "Like what?" he said dryly.

"You could set up an investigation business."

He stared at her.

"You know. Become an investigator. A private investigator."

"In Sechelt."

"Well, in Vancouver, then," she said, flushing.

"Cassandra—" He shook his head. "Listen. I don't want to live in Vancouver. I don't want to be a p.i. Jesus Christ." He stood up. "Look. I like what I'm doing. I don't want to do anything else. This is it. You want to know what I want out of life? I'm doing it. This is what I want."

She looked at him, looming angry and intense above her. "But what about when you can't do it anymore?" she said quietly. "What about when your job is just a desk job?"

He said nothing for a moment. The cats emerged from the bedroom. One arranged herself in a neat triangle and began washing her paws. The other sloped over to the scratching post and stretched, and scratched.

"I'm not prepared to talk about this any longer," said Alberg.

"Will you think about it?"

He looked at her for a long time. Then he reached down, took her hands, and pulled her to her feet. He put his arms around her. "I don't know."

Chapter
Nine

*W*eekends had become the worst days of all. Charlie had learned to structure them, to stuff them full of planned activities, events that possessed a remorseless momentum that would grind him through Saturday and Sunday despite himself.

He'd planned this weekend, too, just like the rest, but it turned out not to be necessary. Once the anniversary dinner was out of the way, Charlie found himself feeling astonishingly at peace. He was looking at things, at people, differently. He discovered within himself an attitude of generosity and tenderness that surprised and pleased him. He was stronger, perhaps, than he had known.

He and Emma went out for breakfast, Saturday morning, and then did the grocery shopping. When they got home, Emma changed the sheets on the bed and did a load of laundry while Charlie worked outside. Again, there wasn't much yard work to do, so when Sid Sokolowski invited him next door for a beer, he went. Sid spent most of their time together complaining about his other neighbor, whom he blamed for the dandelions he'd had to dig out of his lawn. Charlie listened to all this as if in a dream, conscious of the half-smile upon his face, and the ache in his heart.

He went out to rent a movie, later, and Emma ordered Chinese food.

Charlie was able to sleep almost as soon as he closed his eyes that night, and if he dreamed, he couldn't remember his dreams in the morning.

He moved through Sunday slowly and attentively, observing the cleanliness of the house, and the greenness of the lawn, and Emma's beguiling grace. He sat still for long periods of time, watching his wife preparing their Sunday brunch, or curled up in an easy chair reading a book, or stepping outside just before dinner to cut some tulips, one hand holding her hair back from her face as she bent over to look for flowers not yet fully opened.

It was as though he had been seriously ill, and was now convalescent. There was the same distant appreciation for small things. He knew it was temporary—but what a relief, what a joy to have this unexpected hiatus, these two precious days of tranquillity.

"You're very quiet today," said Emma, when they sat down to eat dinner. "Aren't you feeling well?"

"I'm feeling great," said Charlie.

He would have said more, but couldn't: he'd been struck by a feeling of déjà vu so intense that he suddenly wanted to weep. He put down his knife and fork.

"Great," he repeated, looking down at the chicken breast in lemon sauce that occupied his dinner plate, along with a scoop of mashed potatoes and some glazed baby carrots.

Was it the sight of the food? The smell of the coffee drifting in from the kitchen? Emma's blonde hair and rosy skin? He lifted his head and looked at her. She was eating, calmly and neatly, cutting small pieces of chicken, pushing mashed potatoes onto her fork, lifting chicken and potatoes to her mouth. Her teeth chewed, calmly and neatly. She swallowed. Sipped from her water glass.

Charlie felt a thousand miles away from her.

"Yeah," he said, picking up his fork. He cleared his throat. "I feel great."

Chapter
Ten

ddie knew Sylvia was right, he had to apologize to the girl called Melanie, and he was just about ready to do this when another bad thing happened and sent all his best intentions flying into a cocked hat.

He finished work at noon on Monday. He left the drugstore through the front door, because of having to buy a pack of cigarettes, and went around the block and down the lane to where the Camaro was parked, behind the drugstore, right next to Harold's Volvo.

On the other side of the lane was a row of backyards, some with garages attached to them, and some not. And it was garbage pickup day, so people had put their garbage cans out. Eddie noticed a dog sniffing around one of them; a young, skinny dog with a long tail and middle-size floppy ears and no collar. He saw it get up on its hind legs and knock the lid off the garbage can, slick as anything. Eddie was admiring this when the next thing he knew the dog had knocked over the whole damn can. It started pawing through all the garbage, getting crap all over the lane right behind the drugstore.

Eddie shouted at the dog and waved his arms around. Right away the dog moved, so it could keep one eye on Eddie, but meanwhile the rest of its body was still busy strewing the damn garbage all over the place. Eddie started running toward it—and he felt the flesh on his body jiggling and thought about the gym, and how he had to work out more often: Gotta get my life more organized, he thought, lumbering toward the dog. When he got close enough, he aimed a kick, but he missed. The dog leapt back and immediately circled around and came right back at the garbage. Eddie saw that it had unearthed the carcass of a cooked chicken.

Eddie was hollering now and kicking out at the dog, and missing, and getting madder and madder, so that at first he didn't even hear her—and then he did.

He turned around, amazed. There she was, all right, coming out the back door of the Laundromat that was two stores up from the drugstore. Her purse was over one shoulder, and her arms were wrapped around a big black plastic bag. She was wearing shorts and sandals, her bare skin still spring-white, and sunglasses on her pale face.

He sure wished, at that moment, that he'd gotten around to apologizing to her. If he had, things would have been entirely different between them now and she wouldn't be so angry, which was bound to cause trouble—and it did.

"Stop that," she was shouting at him.

Eddie looked back at the dog, which was trying to get its jaws around the chicken carcass which Eddie decided must actually be a turkey, it was such a big bugger. He aimed another kick at the dog, and this time he connected, and the dog yelped.

"God damn it!"

Eddie turned to the girl. She flung the plastic bag onto the ground and her purse too and started striding toward him. Eddie thought this was funny, because what the hell did she think she was going to do?

"What're you gonna do, hit me?" he said, grinning, his hands on his hips.

She walked right up to him and slapped his face.

Eddie didn't even think. He grabbed her by the shoulders and wrestled her across the lane and slammed her against the side of the Camaro. He could see that the breath was knocked out of her.

"Bitch," he said. "Cunt."

He considered hitting her. He could feel it in his fist, hear the sound of her nose crunching, see blood falling down her white face from under the lopsided sunglasses. But he didn't do this. He didn't even come close. He'd scare her a bit, that's all, he decided.

"Don't you swear at *me*, bitch. Don't you smack *me* in the face."

And he dry-humped her.

That was all. That was all he did.

Then he stepped back, thinking maybe she'd hit him again, and he was ready for that. But she didn't.

She lifted a shaking hand to her face and straightened her sunglasses. Then she walked slowly back to where she'd dropped the plastic bag. Eddie watched uneasily as she pushed into the bag the clean clothes that had fallen out. Maybe I should help her, he thought. But then it was done, and she picked up the bag of laundry, and her purse, and walked unsteadily to the corner and around it, and then he couldn't see her anymore.

He turned back to the overturned garbage can. The dog was gone, and so was the turkey carcass.

Eddie went into the drugstore through the back door and got a broom, and swept up the garbage before he went home.

That evening, he sat at his kitchen table with a pad of lined paper and a pencil. He'd write it in pencil first, so he could erase mistakes, and then he'd do a good copy in ballpoint pen.

He didn't know for sure that she'd complain about him. In fact, she probably wouldn't. There was probably nothing at all for him to worry about. He knew he'd scared her, and she'd probably never set foot in the drugstore again.

But every time he got to this point in his thinking, the next thought he had was yeah, but she could phone up Harold or write him a letter. And he thought himself around that circle about a million times...until finally it occurred to him that he could do this too.

He could phone her up. Or write to her. Apologize. Like Sylvia had told him to do. It wasn't too late. He wasn't absolutely sure, come to think of it, what he was supposed to have apologized for before. It was the damn girl who owed him an apology, Eddie thought, for insulting him in her house like she'd done. But now, yeah, he had to admit, now he had something to apologize for, too.

He wasn't very good on the phone. He often got stammery, and couldn't think of stuff to say. Besides, what if she didn't answer? What if somebody else—the person who lived in the messy room—what if that person answered? When Melanie got to the phone, the roommate would probably listen in—he could just see them cackling away together, at his expense.

So it would be better to write her a letter.

It was tricky, though. He wasn't about to admit anything. Not in writing. He was no dummy.

He didn't know how to start the damn letter, either. What did he say to her—"Dear Melanie?" To hell with that. And he didn't know what the hell her last name was.

Eddie pushed the notepad away from him so hard it landed on the floor. He sat there looking at the table that he'd covered with red-and-white-striped oilcloth. After a while he got up and got himself a beer and picked up the notepad and sat down again. "Dear Melanie," he wrote, and then he crossed out the "Dear."

"Melanie." It sounded abrupt, but that was okay.

He thought for a long time. Then he wrote, "You were right. I shouldn't have kicked that dog." He read it, then read it aloud. It sounded okay. Except it was too short.

He thought some more. "I cleaned up the garbage," he added. He read it again, from the beginning, out loud. It still wasn't quite long enough.

"I should have helped you with your stuff." Now it was a decent-size letter. Yeah, that oughta do it, he thought, and he signed his name. "Eddie Addison." He liked his name. It was a good name.

He folded the letter and put it in an envelope and wrote "Melanie" on the front. That wasn't so hard after all, he thought, feeling a lot better, putting the envelope in his jacket pocket. He'd drop it off at her house before going to work tomorrow.

He poked around in his fridge, trying to decide what to

have for dinner. If she got it tomorrow, which was Tuesday, and answered it right away—well, it would depend on whether she mailed it or delivered it to the drugstore herself, but one way or the other he figured to have her answer by Friday at the absolute latest.

Eddie got out some leftover spaghetti, the spaghetti and the sauce all mixed up together, and dumped it into a saucepan.

He wondered what kind of paper she'd write it on. Maybe it would be perfumed—they sold perfumed stationery at the drugstore. Maybe it would have her initials on it. Maybe it would even have her whole name and address on it, at the top, and then he'd get to know her last name.

Eddie heated up his spaghetti and sliced two pieces of whole wheat bread to eat with it. He'd show her answer to Sylvia, he thought. It would please Sylvia a lot.

Chapter Eleven

"I'm sorry, Em, but I have to go in to the office for a while today."

Emma, looking up from her toast and marmalade, made a moue of disapproval. "Charlie. It's Saturday."

They were sitting at the dining room table in intermittent sunshine; the cutlery glinted, then the light rapidly faded and the silverware dulled, became pewter.

"I know. But we've got a big meeting on Monday. I want to be sure I'm ready for it."

"That explains the way you're dressed, then." Emma was in a pink quilted housecoat, and her hair was tied back from her face with a pink ribbon, and there were pink mules on her feet. But Charlie was wearing brown wool slacks and a cream-colored shirt, no tie, but his brown loafers were brushed, as usual (thanks to Emma), to a scintillating shine.

"Charlie." She put down her coffee cup. "Why don't I come with you? I could spend the day at Park Royal."

"Not much point, hon. I won't be long."

"We could shop together, then. When you're through. Or have lunch. Or dinner."

He tossed his napkin on the table. "I'm sorry, Emma, but this meeting is all I've got on my mind today." He looked at his watch. "Better get going. I want to make the eleven o'clock ferry."

She walked him to the door, where he slipped into a sport jacket and picked up his briefcase, which was waiting next to the umbrella stand.

"You're flushed, Charlie." She placed her hand on his forehead. "I think you're feverish again."

He removed her hand and leaned down to kiss her cheek. "I'm fine, Emma." He opened the door.

"When do you think you'll be home?"

"It depends," said Charlie. He went down the walk to his car, which was parked in front of the house, behind Emma's. She watched, shivering, while he unlocked the driver's door. He opened it and then stood still, looking at her across the roof of the car.

"Have you forgotten something?" she called out.

Charlie shook his head. He tossed his briefcase in the backseat and gave her a little wave.

Emma waved back and stood on the porch, half hidden behind the open door, until he'd driven off.

She wished he'd told her about this earlier. She was sure that if she'd been dressed and all ready, he would have let her go with him. She felt terrible, now. Pouty. Her day was all out of shape. Usually they went grocery shopping together on Saturday. And picked up a movie and some take-out food for the evening.

She cleared the table and washed the dishes by hand; there were too few of them to bother loading up the dishwasher. Back at the dining table, she leaned on her hands and looked out at the day. The sun had retreated, apparently for good. Cherry blossoms spilled their petals into the wind.

Emma roamed the house for a few minutes, then went into the bedroom to dress and put on her makeup. By the time she'd finished this, it was eleven o'clock. Charlie would be on the ferry. Probably in the cafeteria, hunched over a cup of coffee, absorbed in papers taken from his briefcase. She looked into the mirror, checking her makeup. Then she reached for her new bracelet and snapped it around her wrist.

In the kitchen Emma made a shopping list, checked her wallet to determine how much cash she needed, collected library books due to be returned, and put into a plastic bag two sweaters and a dress to take to the cleaner. Then she left the house, locking the door behind her, and walked out to her car. The day was cold and gusty, and Emma almost went back for her down jacket. But she was wearing jeans, and her dark blue sweater was thick and warm; she'd be all right.

It was almost noon when she parked in front of the supermarket that occupied one end of Sechelt's small shopping mall. Charlie would be in his office by now. He'd probably be the only one there; that company, she thought, would be ten times more successful if everyone connected with it were as conscientious as Charlie was. It was located in a building adjacent to the Park Royal shopping center and consisted of a small, tastefully decorated reception area, offices for each of the two partners, another for the secretary and the office clerk who worked for both of them, washrooms, a storeroom that also served as a work area, and a boardroom. Emma had often been there, of course; though not lately, she realized, laying claim to a shopping cart somebody had abandoned in the parking lot. She thought about the photograph of herself that stood in a leather frame on Charlie's desk. It had been taken three years earlier, when her hair was a lot shorter. Perhaps she'd give him a new one for his birthday.

The only reason she shopped on Saturdays was so that she and Charlie could do it together. The stores were far too crowded on Saturdays, even in Sechelt. Shopping on Saturday was not a pleasant occasion if you had to do it alone. She found herself flinging things petulantly into her cart, having apparently forsaken her grocery list. Cans of things, cuts of meat and poultry, frozen foods, dairy products, fresh vegetables and fruits—she kept tossing things in there until the buggy was half full.

She leafed through the new *Chatelaine* while waiting in line at the checkout counter but kept a wary eye on the toddler in the cart ahead of hers, who was clutching a chocolate bar and waving it around erratically. Emma was quite sure chocolate bars weren't good for children that age. His mother looked harassed—and Emma suddenly felt a flood of gratitude; when she and Charlie had a baby, she'd be able to hire somebody to help her. And she'd get right back to normal in her body too, she thought, watching the overweight mother load grocery bags into her cart, evidently unaware that her offspring was leaning over to watch and, in the process, smearing chocolate bar on his mother's shoulder. She'd diet and exercise, and soon you wouldn't be able to tell, looking at her, that Emma had ever given birth.

The wind was blowing strong when Emma came out of the store. People were hunching their shoulders against it and hurrying to their cars. Emma's hair blew wildly as she struggled to push the shopping cart to her car. When the groceries were stowed away in the hatchback, she got in, started the motor, turned on the heater, and sat there, shivering, for a few minutes, unwilling to drive until she felt warmer.

The thought of going straight home was not appealing. She'd have lunch out. She drove to a restaurant that looked out over the ocean and wondered what Charlie was doing for lunch. Probably he wasn't having any, she thought, watching the waves whipped up by the wind; he was careless about meals when he was absorbed in his work. But if he skipped lunch, he'd be finished sooner and home sooner.

She had a Greek salad, pushing chunks of red onion to the side; she didn't want to greet Charlie with onion on her breath.

It was almost two o'clock when she got home, but the day was so gray and threatening that she turned on all the lights in the house. She took her time putting the groceries away. Then she dumped the contents of the clothes hamper into the washer, added laundry soap, and turned on the machine. She watered the few plants the house contained, did some ironing, swept the kitchen floor, and emptied the wastebaskets. Finally, she had a long, hot bath, drowsing in the perfumed water.

He'd probably caught the three-thirty ferry, thought Emma, toweling herself dry, which would be pulling into the dock at Langdale just after four—right about now. She could expect him in about half an hour, then.

She put on her black lounging robe, made up her face, clasped the bracelet around her wrist, and stepped out into the hall.

She heard the wind, much stronger than before. And was amazed at the blackness of the sky. It had begun to rain too; she heard it on the roof, sharp and angry, like toenails scrabbling for purchase on the shingles.

Emma went to the phone and called Charlie's office—although he didn't like to receive personal calls at work—but there was no answer. She hadn't expected any, of course. He was almost certainly on his way home. He would drive slowly, because the weather was bad, and might take twice as long to get here as usual, which would make it five o'clock before she could start expecting him.

The road out of Langdale was narrow and twisty, and there was that terrible hairpin hill the other side of Gibsons.

She was worrying; of course she was worrying; it was perfectly natural to worry.

She turned on the television and made herself a pot of tea. She realized that she was shivering again and adjusted the thermostat.

Emma watched the news and drank her tea, and in the middle of the sports report the power went off. She was calm, though. She lit several candles and started a fire in the fireplace.

The unseasonable storm raged outside, and she was unable to do anything but imagine Charlie in a variety of road accidents. Halfway through the evening she called her friend Lorraine in Vancouver.

"Charlie hasn't come home," she told her.

Lorraine laughed. "Lucky you."

Emma waited, and in a moment Lorraine apologized.

"Those are gale-force winds out there," she said to Emma. "It's one of the worst spring storms in history. That's what they said on the news. He's probably pulled over somewhere, don't you think? Whatever else I may think of Charlie," she added, "the man's not a dunce."

"But he would have called me," said Emma. She was imagining Lorraine in her snug, ground-floor apartment on Dunbar Street.

"Did you phone him at work?"

"Yes. There was no answer." Lorraine would be slouched back in her Scandinavian chair, smoking a cigarette and probably drinking scotch. Emma focused all her concentration on this image, dredging up disapproval.

"Em. You're really worried, aren't you?"

"Yes. I am."

Lorraine was a junior high school teacher. She said her job fulfilled her almost completely. She said she was only a little bit resentful of Emma because she was married and didn't have to work. She always smiled when she said this, because they both knew that Lorraine had no desire at all to be married. She said she'd had enough of family life, growing up in a household with three older brothers.

"Phone the hospitals," said Lorraine. "As soon as they tell you he isn't there, you'll feel better."

So Emma did this, and Lorraine was right, she did feel better knowing that a person of Charlie's description had not been admitted to either the Gibsons or the Sechelt hospital.

She poured another cup of tea, put more wood on the fire, and curled again into the oversize easy chair, from which she could see outside through the window and the front door, with its glass pane at eye level.

But what if he'd had an accident on the other side of Howe Sound, between West Vancouver and Horseshoe Bay, she suddenly thought. He'd be taken to—where?

And then she thought, what if he was dead? What if the accident killed him? Where would they take him then?

She found herself standing up, rubbing the palms of her hands against her sides, staring outside at the black, blustery night. The candles flickered twice, in the living room and in the window glass. Emma pulled the drapes closed and picked up the telephone again. But this time it was dead.

"I'd like to know," said the civilian, "if you've had reports on any automobile accidents tonight."

"You got somebody out on the road in this weather?" said R.C.M.P. Corporal Ken Coomer sympathetically.

"Can you give me that information?" She smoothed her hand over her blonde hair, flicking rainwater onto the floor.

The phone rang. "Excuse me," said the constable, and he looked over his shoulder toward Corporal Sanducci, who got up from Sid Sokolowski's desk and approached the counter.

"Can I help you, ma'am?"

Emma leaned toward him, spreading her hands. The wide silver bracelet on her right wrist made a soft clunking sound as it struck the countertop. "I'm very worried about my husband. I don't know what to do." She was dry-eyed, but her voice trembled, and Sanducci figured she wasn't usually so pale.

He opened the gate. "First of all, come on through here and sit down, and let me get you a cup of horrific coffee. What do you take in it?"

"Nothing," said Emma. "Black."

Sanducci, handing her the coffee, noticed the bathrobe under her raincoat and the backless black slippers on her feet. She was wearing eye makeup and lipstick, though these had not been recently applied.

"My phone went dead," she said, holding the mug with both hands. "Or I would have called you, instead of coming down here."

"Sure," said Sanducci, nodding.

"He was supposed to be home for dinner. About four. Or five. He went to Vancouver this morning. West Vancouver. To his office."

Sanducci waited, but she had nothing more to say. "What with the storm and all," he said, "don't you think he might have decided to stay overnight?"

"He would have called me. He would have."

"But your phone's dead."

"Yes, it is now. But it wasn't. And the storm started earlier. If he'd decided to stay over there, he would have called me."

Sanducci nodded. "Well, first of all, you'll be glad to know we've had no reports of serious accidents. So you can put that out of your mind. But why don't you give me a description of your husband's car anyway, and I'll put it out on the radio."

Emma did this.

"Good," said Sanducci. "Now, if one of our patrol cars spots it, they'll pull him over and let him know you're concerned. Okay?"

"I knew he was going to die," she said. "It was only a matter of time."

"I beg your pardon? Ma'am?"

She was looking straight at him. Usually Sanducci liked it

when an attractive woman gazed into his eyes. He knew he appealed to women. But this woman wasn't actually seeing him at all. He didn't think she'd know him if she met him the next day on the street.

"I probably won't actually die of grief," she was saying, in all seriousness. "But I don't see how I can live, either."

"I think you're being unduly pessimistic, here," Sanducci protested uncomfortably.

"I mean, I guess I'll go on doing things. But once I've done them, will they really have been done?"

"Ma'am, we've got no reason to think that anything's happened to your husband."

"Do you understand what I mean?" She looked away, over toward Ken Coomer, manning the telephone.

"I can't say I do, ma'am, no," said Sanducci politely.

Emma stood up and held out her hand. "Thank you for your concern."

Sanducci shook her hand, which was small and cold. "Why don't I phone somebody for you." She was moving through the gate, toward the door. "A friend, or a relative. Ma'am? Ma'am?"

Emma sat in the easy chair all night.

When Sunday morning dawned, she put on her jeans and a red sweater, cleaned her face, opened the drapes. The storm had passed, but the power didn't come back on until early afternoon.

The phone was working again by evening.

But Emma didn't call anybody. She waited. Occasionally she took note of her calmness.

She put the washing in the dryer, and when it was ready, folded the clothes.

She made macaroni and cheese for dinner, and then scraped it into the garbage.

She left the porch light on. And every so often she picked up the telephone, to make sure it was still operating.

It rained all day, but there was no wind.

She spent Sunday night in bed, but she didn't sleep.

Monday morning Emma got up, drank some coffee, got

dressed, and made the bed. At exactly nine o'clock she phoned Charlie's office.

"I'd like to speak to Mr. O'Brea, please."

She thought for a moment that the phone had gone dead again. But was aware of sounds.

"Hello? Hello? Did you hear me? It's Mrs. O'Brea calling. I'd like to speak to my husband."

"Mrs. O'Brea," said the receptionist, breathless. "I'm sorry. Your husband—"

Emma closed her eyes and pressed her hand against her chest, trying to stifle the beating of her heart.

"I'm sorry. I thought you knew. Mr. O'Brea doesn't work here anymore."

Emma opened her eyes. She lifted her right hand and turned it, watching the bracelet gleam, a silver handcuff around her wrist. "I beg your pardon?"

"Friday was his last day," the receptionist stammered. "He quit. I thought you knew."

Chapter Twelve

*W*hen Friday came, Eddie still hadn't received an answer to his letter. And this made him totally fed up. Melanie was a girl with the manners of a pig.

But he couldn't afford to let himself get mad, even though he had every right to. He had to figure out what it meant, that she hadn't answered him. Did it mean she couldn't be bothered with him? Because even though this would be mortifying, and would make him mad as hell, it would be good, since it would also probably mean she couldn't be bothered to complain about him.

On the other hand, though, ignoring his letter might mean she was plotting something. She was spiteful enough to be doing that, all right—getting her revenge. He was sure of it. And you certainly wouldn't write a letter to a person you were plotting against.

He would have dearly liked to consult with Sylvia, and he thought he ought to be able to do this too—after all, he had apologized, just like she'd told him to do. But then he knew he'd have to tell her about what happened in the alley. And warning bells clanged and danger sirens went off whenever he thought about that.

So he ended up doing what he knew all along he'd do if things didn't straighten themselves out, and that was to call up Gardiner.

He'd gone to high school with Gardiner. They'd hung out together then, and they still did. Gardiner made Eddie nervous, but he was a comfort too, because he always knew what to do about stuff. Eddie sometimes didn't like the particular solutions Gardiner came up with, but they were sure as hell better than no solutions at all.

So he called him up, and Gardiner came over, and right away he turned on the hockey game. Eddie got them cans of beer, and he put out some chips and a thing of dip he'd bought at the Safeway, and they sat there drinking and eating and watching the game. Eddie figured he'd wait until the first period was over before bringing up his problem; it was a playoff game, and the Canucks were in the playoffs, and Gardiner was very hot on the Canucks.

At the first break, though, Vancouver was ahead by one goal and Gardiner was too wrapped up in the game to think about anything else.

"I gotta take a piss," he said when the commercials came on, and that's the only thing he said that wasn't about hockey. Eddie knew he might as well resign himself to sitting through the whole damn game before he got to talk about his situation.

Fortunately, the Canucks won. Gardiner could get in a hell of a rage if things didn't go right for him—or for his hockey team, or his football team. Or, sometimes, his friends.

As soon as he'd turned off the television, Eddie said, just blurting it out, "Gardiner, I got a problem."

Gardiner was sprawled out on the sofa, drinking his fourth beer. He was a tall skinny guy with so much energy it didn't matter how much he ate, he never put on a pound. It was like his motor was revving all the time, using up gas whether he was moving or just spinning his wheels. He had big teeth and very light-colored hair, so that when he didn't shave, there was no shadow on his face; it just looked dusty.

"What kind of a problem?"

"Kind of a woman-type problem."

Gardiner guffawed and put on a leer, and Eddie waited patiently while he joked around and offered various crude kinds of help. Then Eddie shook his head. "It's not that kind of a problem. This woman's giving me some trouble." And he told Gardiner all about it.

"And you sent her a *note*? You stupid weasel. What a dumb thing to do. You ain't gonna get no respect that way."

Eddie was pretty sure Sylvia would have approved of the note.

"She didn't answer it," he confessed.

"Of course she didn't answer it," said Gardiner. He squeezed up his eyes and looked at Eddie like he didn't believe what he was seeing. "You thought she'd *answer* it?" He clutched himself around the middle and fell off the sofa, laughing.

Eddie had had enough. He hadn't waited around all evening watching a damn hockey game while he was so worried it felt like there were big insects in his stomach, eating away at him, just to get laughed at. He stomped out to the kitchen and started throwing beer cans into a brown paper bag.

Pretty soon Gardiner came out there too and leaned against the edge of the doorway. "Okay, okay. So what do you want from me?"

"I want your advice. I want you to tell me what to do."

Gardiner heaved a sigh and pulled out a chair. "I don't get it. What're you scared of? What do you think's gonna happen to you for shit's sake?"

Eddie turned around from the sink, which he'd been cleaning with baking soda. He'd given up buying Old Dutch and stuff like that because of the environment. Though he hadn't been able to figure out exactly why Old Dutch wasn't as good for the environment as baking soda was.

"I think she might tell Harold," he said. "She could get me in a lot of trouble." He sat down across the table from Gardiner. "She could get me fired," he said heavily, rubbing at his right eye, where a sty was growing in the lid. "I can't have something else get on my work record, Gardiner. It'd be—I'd be, like—doomed. If that happens."

Gardiner looked at him thoughtfully. "Gimme another beer, willya?"

Eddie got him a beer.

"You oughta throw a scare into her," said Gardiner. He nodded. "Yeah. Show her not to fuck with you."

"Yeah, well, I already did that, didn't I?"

"You gotta do it again. Like a one-two punch, you know?" said Gardiner, jabbing at the air. "Scare the piss right out of her."

"Well, but how?"

Gardiner shot him a sly glance. "I'll do it for you, if you want."

"No," Eddie said quickly. "No, that's okay."

"You can't go through your life letting yourself get pussy whipped, Ed."

"I'm not. I don't," Eddie protested. Then he started getting angry again. "You know I don't, Gardiner. You damn know that."

"Yeah yeah. I know, I know. Sorry." He gave Eddie a wink. "We're buddies, right? So I gotta watch out for you. Gotta make sure you're on the straight and narrow." He was overcome by another fit of laughter, which made his face red and his eyes bright, and when it was over, he stood up, quickly, like he did everything, and slapped Eddie on the shoulder. "Come on. Show me where she lives. We'll work on a plan."

Chapter
Thirteen

*A*lberg's phone had awakened him at one-thirty in the morning.

He thought it was work. But as he picked up the receiver he thought, it might not be work, it might be Diana, or Janey. Or even Maura. The most likely thing of all never even occurred to him.

"Alberg," he said.

It wasn't work. It was his mother.

The skies over London, Ontario, were leaden when he arrived there late in the afternoon, and the white stuff drifting down the following morning wasn't the petals of cherry blossoms.

"It won't stick," said Alberg's mother.

"It's supposed to be spring," said Alberg.

"How quickly we forget," said his mother with a wry glance at him. "It *is* spring, Martin. In Ontario, sometimes, in springtime, it snows." She was the only person left in the world who called him by his first name.

Alberg's mother lived in a large, yellow brick house built in 1895 that still had its original woodwork. It was set at an angle on a corner lot where wide, treelined streets converged. Alberg had always loved it, even though he'd never lived there: his parents had bought it after he left home.

His father's death had been expected—and yet Alberg was

discovering that he hadn't expected it at all. He'd prowled the house, last night, looking into every room, as if hoping to find his father there. (He'd noticed while making his explorations that his parents had had a waterbed installed in their bedroom. He pondered it for quite a while and finally decided they had bought it for its salubrious qualities.)

Alberg was an only child, and he felt responsible for this event, his father's funeral. But he kept disbelieving it, the whole damn situation: his father dead, having to dispose of him somehow, the need to protect his mother from the armies of friends and relations who kept marching up the walk to pay their respects. He had been so clumsy and ungracious carrying out this last duty that his mother now wouldn't allow him to answer the door, or the phone, either.

"I wish you'd come back and live with me when this is over," he said to her. "You'd like Sechelt."

"I'm sure I would. I'm sure it's beautiful. But I don't want to live anywhere but here."

He was immensely relieved to hear this. What on earth would he have done with her, his elderly mother, if she'd said yes, I'll come and live with you?

"I'm prepared for this, you know, Martin. He's been sick for a long time. We talked about it, about what was going to happen when he died."

Alberg, sitting next to his mother on the window seat, shuffled his feet uneasily.

"I know what he wants to happen now, the funeral and the burial and all. And we talked about what's best for me now too."

"It's such a big place, though," said Alberg, looking around the spacious living room, squinting up at the ceiling.

"Somebody else cleans it. Somebody else does the garden." She put a hand over his. He looked down at it, gnarled and liver-spotted, misshapen by arthritis. "It's what I want, Martin. I want to stay right where I am."

The window looked out onto a veranda that encircled the house. In the summer a porch swing stood out there. His parents had liked to sit in it, side by side, gently swinging, watching the corner where two streets crossed, watching cars purr slowly along, watching people strolling, watching the squirrels and the birds and the evening light that slanted golden through the trees. Would she sit there alone, this summer? Would she trade in the two-seater for a single? Or would the veranda be empty in the summer evenings to come?

"Maybe you could visit me for a while in the summer. I'd like that a lot," said Alberg. And this he meant.

She squeezed his hand and patted it. "Maybe."

Maura and his daughters arrived the following morning, and Alberg picked them up at the Toronto airport in his rented car. He hadn't seen Maura since her remarriage the previous summer. He gave Janey and Diana a big hug each and offered Maura a friendly kiss on the cheek. "You've put on some weight," he said to her. "It suits you."

Maura apparently didn't think so.

"How's your mother?" she asked him while they waited for the bags.

"She's good. She's actually really good."

There was a small anteroom with three pews, one behind the other, and that was where the family was supposed to sit. Alberg stationed himself at the end of the first pew. He could see his father's casket through the archway that led into the chapel. His mother was next to him, then Maura, then Diana, and at the far end of the pew, Janey.

His father had been one of seven children, but he had outlived all his brothers and sisters. There were some cousins left; they sat behind Alberg, along with his mother's younger sister, June, and her two sons.

The chapel was packed with people. Alberg had been taken aback at the size of the crowd. He had forgotten, temporarily, his father's long history in this place. And Alberg's own, much shorter one, had come to seem almost irrelevant in the rapid sweep of his life toward Sechelt, and middle age.

Squeezed into the hard wooden pew, he felt resentful and disoriented. He folded his arms and let his head sink into his neck, willing his mind elsewhere, trying not to hear the organ music, the words of the minister, the occasional sniffles of grief coming from behind him.

His mother sat straight and still, wearing a black coat and a small black hat with a little veil. Somewhat to Alberg's surprise, she'd had her hair done the day before; it was white and curly. Her gloved hands rested quietly in her lap.

Alberg decided he ought to be remembering things about his father. He began ransacking his mind for memories and came up with bizarre, disquieting images: his father's face invisible behind a cloud of smoke from his pipe; his father stretching his arms into the branches of a tree, reaching for a bird's nest; his father's tall, lean frame disappearing into a hole in a frozen river; his father watching a porno flick, his face impassive... these were not memories. Then what the hell were they? Alberg tried to push his dead parent out of his mind. There was a zinging sound in his head; he wondered if he was getting the flu or working up to a heart attack. He wanted to hold somebody's hand.

Suddenly there was organ music again. People began standing up. Everybody in his pew was standing up now, so finally he stood up too.

"Follow me, Martin," said his mother.

Speechless, he did so.

He heard Diana whisper to Maura, "Do we have to go, Mom?"

"Yes," said Maura curtly, and they formed a line behind him.

Where the hell are we going? thought Alberg, trailing after his mother. This is how they got people into the gas chambers, he thought.

She was, he knew, leading him to the casket.

He trudged along behind her, out of the anteroom, through the archway, and onto the stage where the casket was displayed. At least it felt like a stage to Alberg; he was going onstage in somebody's goddamn play, but nobody had told him what to do when he got there. He waited while his mother said whatever she had to say to her husband and then she moved on and he found himself staring down at his father who was of course pale and waxen and not his father at all. He had nothing whatsoever to say to this apparition so he moved on, too, and retraced his steps back to the anteroom, where he waited for the rest of his family to file past and have a look.

After this we have food, he thought, visualizing the dining room table in his mother's house covered with a white linen cloth. There were a lot of people looking after that aspect of things; he didn't have to think about that.

His family was now reassembled in the anteroom.

"What's next?" said Alberg to his mother.

"We go out to the graveyard," she said, and turned to the door that led outside.

"Right," said Alberg, moving to follow her.

But all strength had left his limbs. He stumbled, clutched at the doorframe, and saw his daughters, his ex-wife, through a blur of tears. They were looking at him in shock. Diana shrank back, and Maura put a protective arm around her shoulders.

Then Janey rushed to him and took his arm. He would never forget the strength and confidence in her voice. "It's okay, Daddy. You're okay."

The next morning he drove them back to the airport and saw them off on the plane to Calgary.

He decided to spend a couple of hours in Toronto before returning to London and called his mother to tell her that.

The phone rang four times and he was about to hang up when the answering machine clicked on.

"You have reached the home of Eileen and William Alberg," said his father's voice. "Please leave a message, and we'll return your call as soon as possible."

Alberg listened to the silence that followed the beep. He was, for a moment, prepared to believe in anything.

Chapter Fourteen

*I*t was very early Tuesday morning. The day was already bright.

There was almost no traffic on Fourth Avenue.

The sky was absolutely clear, free of the yellow-brown haze that too often hovered over Vancouver.

Petals fluttered down from the double pink blossoms of the ornamental cherry trees that bordered this section of the avenue. They had collected thickly in the gutter; drifts of pink petals concealing whatever dirt and litter might be huddling there. They had scattered themselves along the sidewalk in front of the gourmet coffee store and the shop that sold nothing but buttons and the children's clothing boutique.

There was a thin layer of them, too, on the roof of the bronze Camaro parked in front of the bookstore.

It was just past six o'clock. None of the shops was open.

Several blocks away, Melanie Franklin emerged from her house, wearing a light jacket, black slacks, and a white shirt, with an enormous carryall slung over her shoulder. She closed the door softly behind her and hurried down the steps, along the cracked sidewalk, and through a gate in the six-foot high laurel hedge.

On Fourth Avenue, Eddie Addison, sitting in his Camaro, looked again at his watch. He had decided against the plan Gardiner had come up with Friday night, which was to spray obscenities on the front of the house Melanie lived in. Gardiner hadn't liked having his plan rejected. He'd become suddenly bored and gone home. And Eddie had thought very hard and finally, three days later, finally he'd come up with a plan of his own.

Eddie was hidden behind sunglasses and a straw hat with a wide brim. He planned to remove his disguise at the last minute, because he didn't want to disguise himself from the girl, only from anybody else who happened to be hanging around. But there wasn't anybody else hanging around.

Melanie walked quickly through her neighborhood, where the waxy white magnolias were in bloom, and the dogwood trees, too, and lilacs, and rhododendrons, and azaleas.

Eddie, sitting upright behind the wheel, his hands on his thighs, cleared his throat nervously. Occasionally a vehicle passed him, and twice during the hour and a half he'd been waiting, a bus had trundled by. But no pedestrians.

At a cross street, Melanie looked north to catch a glimpse of English Bay and beyond it, the North Shore mountains. The sea was very blue today. She took one more look—maybe she'd take her studying to the beach this afternoon—and turned south, toward Fourth Avenue.

Eddie turned the key in the ignition, glanced into his rearview mirror, and pulled the Camaro out into the street. He drove west, very slowly, barely moving, whispering to himself, fast and urgently. He had to time things just right. He'd worked it out in his head over and over again. It would be a maneuver like when the army was showing off and part of the show was the motorcyclists doing those crossover things, one line of bikes crossing through the middle of another line of bikes. It would need that kind of split-second timing. And Eddie knew he had it.

Two blocks ahead he saw her emerge from one of the cross streets. She looked casually left and right and started across the avenue.

The Camaro shot forward, gathering speed. He'd whisk past her real close, give her a little nudge, a little bounce off the fender...

She saw the car coming and hesitated, unable to decide

which way to run.

Everything was happening very fast—but Eddie's thinking was keeping up with it. As she loomed bigger and bigger in his windshield he knew she wouldn't just stand there forever, she'd break to one side or the other—he had to guess right here, or he was going to screw everything up—and although she was almost dead center in the road she was a little bit closer to the right-hand sidewalk than the left-hand one, and Eddie guessed she'd run to the right: he aimed a little bit to the left, just as she made her move.

The car struck her.

Eddie kept on going.

Melanie's body was flung into the air.

The street was quiet again, in the early spring morning. The breeze lifted a few stands of Melanie's hair, and rustled the pages of a textbook that had spilled from her carryall. Some of her blood trickled out from under her head, and moved hesitantly across the avenue, but it stopped before it reached the drifts of pink petals in the gutter.

Chapter
Fifteen

"It sounds like he's had some kinda breakdown," Bernie offered.

"Yes, that's what's in my mind too," said Emma. A breakdown. It sounded reassuringly ordinary. Some piece of the mental machinery had gone temporarily awry. They'd laugh about it later, when the appropriate repairs had been made.

"That's probably what it is," said Bernie, nodding. She was sitting very straight in a kitchen chair, with a mug of coffee steaming on the table in front of her. Bernie came on Tuesdays and Thursdays, for half a day, to do the heavy work.

Emma combed her hair back from her face with her fingers. "Whatever it is that's happened, Bernie, he needs me. He surely does."

Bernie's face, crisscrossed with hundreds of tiny lines, was full of worry. It was a comforting sight. Every time Emma thought of Bernie, the phrase "nut-brown maiden" flickered through her mind, even though Bernie, at fifty-eight, was far from being a maiden.

"Bernie, another thing's occurred to me. Maybe—what if he's got amnesia." This was a terrifying concept. Surely, he would then be truly lost to her.

Bernie drank some coffee while she thought this over. Emma watched her intently. She was tough and sturdy, Bernie was, incapable of being horrified.

"He'll have identification on him, though," said Bernie, with satisfaction. "So it won't matter if he loses his memory, he'll still be able to figure out who he is."

Emma nodded. "That's true." And once he'd found his way back to her, she would reclaim him, as she had once before, with love and unswerving devotion. Even if he never remembered the past they'd shared, together they'd make a new future for themselves. It wouldn't be the first time.

"When was the last time you ate?"

"I don't know."

Bernie stood up and went to the fridge. Emma didn't protest. She'd let Bernie fix her some breakfast. She'd even try to eat it, because it was important to keep up her strength.

"What should I do, Bernie? What would you do, in my position?" She played with the rings on her fingers, the gold wedding band and the jade ring she wore on her right hand. She'd picked them out herself. The silver bracelet too. All she had to do was ask for something, and it was hers.

Bernie put two strips of bacon on a double layer of paper towels and popped them into the microwave oven. "He's a missing person, your man is."

"Well, Bernie, I don't know if you could call him missing, exactly."

Bernie fixed Emma with her beady black gaze. "He ain't at his home. He's quit his work. He ain't phoned you. He's been gone forty-eight hours. That's missing."

Emma bent her head. Missing person. The poignancy of the phrase struck at her heart.

"I got a man I do for," said Bernie, dropping whole wheat bread into the toaster. "He's a policeman. He's the head man over there. He's the fella to see."

"Maybe," said Emma, pushing crumbs around on the table-top. Where had they come from, anyway, those crumbs? "Maybe he's in the crawl space." She looked up at Bernie. "I read a book once, about somebody who took up residence in a crawl space, and the people in the house didn't know he was there for ages."

"You got a basement here." She plucked the bacon from the

microwave and blotted it with more paper towels.

"Maybe he's in the basement, then."

Bernie poured a large glass of orange juice from a pitcher in the fridge. "Go have a look, if you think it's likely."

Emma shook her head.

Bernie buttered toast and made a sandwich with the bacon. She sliced it in half, put it on a plate, and set Emma's breakfast in front of her. "Eat."

To make her happy, Emma picked up the glass of juice. The first sip ignited hunger so intense it was intolerable. She drained the glass in a series of ravenous gulps, her mouth full of the voluptuous taste of oranges warmed by a summer sun. Her concentration on this sensation was absolute: when she set down the glass she was out of breath, almost dizzy. She licked her lips and turned to the sandwich and devoured it, chomping warm toast and crunchy bacon, pausing only once, to drink a glass of milk that Bernie set down before her.

When she was finished, she sat back and pushed the plate away from her. Butter was smeared on her mouth like lipstick. Bernie was nodding approvingly. Emma sat there trying to decide how she felt and whether there were any thoughts in her head.

"You live alone, don't you, Bernie?"

"I do."

"What's it like?"

"I like it." Bernie put Emma's dishes in the sink and turned on the water.

"Do you get lonely?"

Bernie considered this while squirting detergent onto the dishes. "Nope."

"Never?"

"Never."

Emma pushed herself slowly up from the table. "I'm going to town."

Bernie looked at her quickly. "To do what?"

"I'm going to Charlie's office."

"You should be going to see Mr. Alberg, my policeman, that's what you should be doing."

"I will, Bernie. I'll do it later." She tore off a square of paper toweling and wiped her mouth. "But first I have to see if he took my picture with him."

"And what'll it mean if he did, or if he didn't?"

Emma put her arms around Bernie and rested her cheek against Bernie's artificially auburn hair. "I don't know."

Chapter
Sixteen

"No no no no no no," said Eddie over and over. He sped along the street, and she vanished behind him, into his past—except that she didn't.

She hadn't looked like anything made of flesh; she'd bounced up into the air like a big doll, her arms flailing, and the bag thing she was carrying went one way and she went another, toppled down like a tree hit by an axe or a deer felled by a rifle shot, except not powerfully and prettily, like a tree falls, or a deer.

The Camaro had flung her into the air. He hadn't expected that, hadn't meant that. The Camaro had actually *hit* her, struck her with a force that he'd felt behind the wheel. He hadn't expected that. Now he was afraid she might be hurt, and he hadn't intended to hurt her, only scare her.

Yet he was—not exactly proud of himself—but satisfied with what he'd done. Because he'd done it on his own, solved his problem himself; he hadn't needed Gardiner to do it for him. He felt excited, and stern, and full of righteousness.

And nobody had seen him, either. Except the girl, of course. She'd seen his car all right...

Eddie pulled the Camaro over to the curb, because something was bothering him. She'd seen his car, yeah...

But she didn't know it was *his* car. How was she supposed

to know what kind of a car he drove?

He conjured up her face, turned toward the sound of the Camaro racing toward her, and saw it get bigger and bigger, and saw confusion on it, and then fear—but no recognition.

He banged the steering wheel and shouted. "She didn't know it was me!" He banged it again. And then he remembered his disguise, the sunglasses and the big hat. "Shit!" he said, and tore them off.

He threw the Camaro into gear and hooked a U-turn, heading back the way he'd come. He had to get to her before she limped off to call the damn cops. He had to let her know who it was who'd hit her, because unless she knew *who*, she wouldn't know *why*, and what was the point of *that*?

He saw her from more than a block away. She was still lying on the pavement. She wasn't moving. He stopped in the middle of the street and stared intently through the windshield. He thought he saw her begin to stir, and relief stood on tiptoe, waiting to take over, but it was only some pages of a book, ruffling in the wind.

Eddie turned right and drove slowly around the block. He felt dazed, bewildered. She must have been hurt worse than he'd thought. But why was she just lying there? If she didn't drag herself up off the street soon, some lunatic was going to come along and run right over her, squash her flat.

Now he was approaching from the east, like he had only a few minutes earlier, and he glanced to the north, as if expecting to see her emerge from the cross street. *Let's take this again*, he heard someone say, *and let's get it right this time*. But that was only in his imagination. In real life she was still lying in the street. He saw the bag with books in it. He saw one of her shoes—a black shoe; a loafer—it had come right off her foot.

He pulled over to the curb a block away and watched her. Soon a car came along, from the west, and almost at the same moment somebody came out of the apartment building across the street. The car braked hard, and the driver jumped out and ran over to her, and so did the guy coming out of the building. The two of them leaned over her. The driver put his hand on her neck. Then they both straightened up, and the guy from the apartment building went back there, walking slowly, his hands jerking at the sides of his body like they wanted to be holding on to something. The driver took off his jacket, then, and put it over the top part of her body, covering up her head.

Eddie felt like he was five hundred years old.

He pulled out and moved off up the street, and at Alma Street he turned, and a few blocks later he turned again, and he drove east on Broadway, weeping.

Chapter
Seventeen

"I've come to see my husband's office," said Emma. The young woman behind the desk was leafing briskly through the contents of a file folder she was holding on her lap. She looked up inquiringly. When she recognized Emma, she jerked to her feet and the folder emptied itself upon the floor.

"Hello," said Emma pleasantly.

"Hello, Mrs. O'Brea." The receptionist, clearly flustered, began picking up papers.

Emma moved toward the hall.

"Uh, Mrs. O'Brea," said the receptionist quickly. "I'm really sorry, but I don't think—could you wait till Mr. Carlson's back from lunch?" She was wearing stiletto heels and a skirt that barely covered her thighs, and she looked deservedly ungraceful, scrabbling around on the carpeted floor among the fallen papers.

"No," said Emma, "I'm afraid I can't." She went down the hall to Charlie's office.

His window offered a view of Park Royal.

Her photograph was gone from the top of his desk.

Emma closed the door behind her and leaned on it for a moment. Except for the photograph, everything was as it had been the last time she was here, which had to have been more than a year ago, she thought, calculating, before their fifth anniversary.

There were two large Emily Carr prints on the walls, one above a long, low bookcase, the other near a grouping of two easy chairs, a standing lamp, and a coffee table. The bookcase was still full of books. Emma went near and studied the titles, but all of them had to do with insurance and insurance law. The top of his desk was bare, but then it almost always was— except for Emma's photograph—when he wasn't actually working at it.

She sat in the swivel chair and looked down at the desktop. There were eraser crumbs on it, inexplicable, like the crumbs on the kitchen table.

Emma opened drawers, slowly, one after another. Each was empty. She sat back in the chair and rested her hands on the arms.

There was a light knock on the door, and Peter Carlson came in. Emma noticed that he left the door open.

"Emma. You should have told us you were coming."

"Why?"

"Well, because," he stammered, "because we could have had lunch, or something."

Emma had always thought of him as a kindly man. She had never met his wife. Maybe he didn't have a wife. He wore a gray suit with a white shirt and a brightly patterned tie. He must have a wife, thought Emma. Men don't buy ties like that for themselves.

"Where's Charlie, Peter?"

He looked stricken. "You haven't heard from him?"

Emma shook her head. "Where is he?"

Peter's eyes flickered around the room as he took a step backward, toward the hallway. Then he forced himself to look at Emma straight on. He lifted his hands in a gesture of helplessness. "I don't know."

She stood up and looked out of the window, seeing the exact same things that Charlie had seen every day of his working life these last four years. "I don't understand this."

"I'm sure you'll hear from him, Emma."

"But why? What's he gone and done?" She turned. "Tell me what happened."

"He said he wanted to leave the firm. He said he wanted to

86

do something else; I don't think he'd decided what. That's all I know."

"When did he tell you this?"

"A month ago."

"A month ago," she said wonderingly. "And Friday was his last day here?"

"That's right."

Emma began shaking her head. "Well, something awful has happened. That's for sure. I can't make head or tail out of this situation."

"Do you want some coffee, Emma?"

She picked up her purse from the floor beside the chair. "I don't have time for coffee. I've got to find Charlie."

She drove to Park Royal and left her car in a covered lot across from Eaton's. She had some lunch in a restaurant—an execrable hamburger—and watched other people eat: a small, middle-aged Oriental woman wearing a black dress and a salmon-colored scarf; a young woman with a lot of hair, in a red suit, picking at a shrimp salad while reading *People*; a couple talking animatedly to one another—the woman was blonde, and the man was gray-haired and reminded Emma of the English actor Terence Stamp.

She pushed her half-eaten hamburger away, imagining Charlie doing the same thing, four years ago, and never returning to eat in this place again. He'd probably told the waitress it was an awful hamburger, too. But nicely. Charlie was always very courteous to people. That was one thing she did know about him.

Emma wandered through the mall, which had a lot of sky-lights and greenery, including some trees that were at least twenty feet tall.

On the upper level she came upon a large chessboard painted on the floor. People were moving three-feet high men around on it. Nearby, on a ledge near one of the waterfalls, three normal-size games were underway. Charlie was a fine chess player. Emma wondered if he'd ever played here, while eating his lunch. There was a hot-dog stand nearby, and a place that sold frozen yogurt.

In the drugstore she pretended she was Charlie, inspecting the shelves of shaving products, and men's cologne.

In the bookstore she browsed through the biography section.

In Eaton's she looked at men's clothing.

Finally she sat down on a bench. It was late afternoon now, and the mall was filled with high school students. After a while a woman eating an ice cream cone approached and asked Emma if she could sit next to her.

"I gotta get off my dogs for a minute," she said, plopping down. "Whoof. No break's long enough, you know?"

Emma said she knew. "Where do you work?"

"Over there." She waved the cone toward the entrance to a women's clothing store. "It's not bad, but the hours stink." She took a huge bite of ice cream. She didn't look like the kind of person who ate a lot of ice cream, thought Emma. She was thin as a rake, with extremely round eyes and hair that she'd back-combed into a black halo.

The bench on which they sat was back to back with another. Emma felt it when the people sitting there got up. She felt it a couple of minutes later when somebody new sat down. Looking straight ahead of her at the display window of a children's clothing shop, listening to the chatter of the woman eating ice cream, Emma thought about the person who might have sat down behind her. Finally, she looked back over her shoulder.

A man was there, lying down on the bench. The woman with the cone turned to glance at him too. He was wearing a heavy tweed overcoat and leather boots with laces. He had gray hair and a beard and was apparently asleep.

The woman next to Emma finished her cone. "I've seen him here before." She took a Kleenex from her red plastic purse and wiped her mouth. "There are people like him, you know, they never go home."

"What?"

"I mean, they don't *got* a home, I guess. They live here. Sneak around from place to place in the mall, staying out of the security guys' way. It's easier'n it sounds." She looked at her watch and slapped her knees. "Well. Back to the grindstone.

Seeya around, honey."

"Something must have happened to him," Emma told Staff Sergeant Alberg several hours later. "A person doesn't just disappear."

"Mrs. O'Brea," he said, "I think we have to consider the possibility that he's—gone away."

She stared at him in exasperation. "I don't know what it is with you people. Do you have to stumble over somebody's dead body before you can be convinced there's something wrong? I thought it was your job to prevent bad things from happening, as well as clean them up after they've happened."

He sighed. "There's only so much we can do. Corporal Sanducci put out a bulletin on your husband's vehicle; that's still in effect. We know he hasn't been involved in a motor vehicle accident or been admitted to hospital for any other reason. He left his place of work voluntarily. He's a grown man, no warrants out on him; he's free to come and go as he pleases."

Emma raked her hair away from her temples. "He didn't take his golf clubs. Or his chess set. Or *any* of his things. Don't you see?"

"Mrs. O'Brea," said Alberg gently, "when people decide to disappear, they usually do leave everything behind. Even their most prized possessions."

She lived the moment of his leave-taking again, then. She felt the edge of the door against her hand, the cold wind whiffing at her bare legs; she watched Charlie stride down the walk, carrying his briefcase; she saw him unlock the driver's door and look up to pause, and wave, before climbing into his car. She ran this through her mind several times.

"Yes," she said, thunderstruck. "You're right. He meant to go."

The staff sergeant was watching her sympathetically.

"He took my photograph with him."

Though this might not be true, she thought. All she knew for sure was that he hadn't left it in his office. Maybe he'd disposed of it in some way. Maybe he'd thrown it into the garbage. She imagined him placing it on the floor of an alley somewhere and stomping on it with the heel of his shoe to break the glass and then picking up the pieces and tossing them into a dumpster.

Emma stood up and thanked Alberg for his time. "I'll have to find him myself, I guess."

She saw that this dismayed him.

"Mrs. O'Brea—Emma—why don't you wait for him to contact you, when he's ready?"

She was no longer fearful, or bewildered. That was good.

But what *was* she feeling? she wondered, as she left the police station and went to her car. What *was* she feeling, for Charlie, who had left her?

Alberg put on his jacket and left his office, closing the door behind him. He nodded to the duty officer and left the building through the back door, which led to the parking lot.

Sid Sokolowski was just climbing out of his car.

"Karl. What are you doing here?'

"Oh... well... "

"You're not supposed to back for another week," said the sergeant, locking his car door.

"Yeah, I know." Alberg rested his arms on the top of his Oldsmobile. "But my mother—I think I was more trouble to her than help. So I came home."

"You're not coming back to work yet, though."

"Well, I thought I'd stop by," said Alberg, "see what's happening, see how you're doing.'

"We're doing fine. *I'm* doing fine," said Sokolowski pointedly.

"Hey, I'm not horning in on you, Sid," said Alberg. He pushed himself away from his car and unlocked the driver's door. "I'll stay out of your way. I promise." He tried to smile. "See you next week," he said, and he got into his car and drove home.

Chapter Eighteen

*T*hey proceeded up Broadway in Gardiner's rickety Olds Delta 88. Eddie was finding it hard to get out the words he had to say.

Maybe if he didn't get them out, he thought, maybe if he kept them tight inside him, maybe then the thing wouldn't ever have happened; it wouldn't be real.

But there were a couple of pieces of reality floating around that he absolutely couldn't ignore; he was afraid they were going to screw up his life completely. So somehow he had to find the balls to talk to Gardiner.

They drove into a White Spot restaurant and parked in the back. Gardiner turned on the headlights for car service. Eddie was relieved when the guy came and took their order and Gardiner could turn off the lights and then the motor: it smelled like carbon monoxide in Gardiner's Olds, even with all the windows open. Gardiner kept the radio on, though, and there was country-and-western music rattling out of it, sounding off-key and tinny.

"I'm in some deep shit, Gardiner," Eddie finally blurted.

He told him all about it, while k.d. lang sang from the radio. He was staring out the windshield the whole time he talked, staring at the menu written on the side of the White Spot building, looking at the words for hamburger, and chicken, and milkshake, and not seeing them. At first he heard some muffled squawks from Gardiner—but he ignored them, and went right on talking.

His voice sounded real close up—which of course it was, but he'd never noticed before just how close your voice was to you. It wasn't loud—he was talking very quietly. But it felt real... close up, as if the words weren't moving away from him after he'd said them, as if they were crowding around in the air outside his mouth, all confused, not knowing where to go—making a little crowd of themselves, and then a bigger one, and a real big one. Soon Eddie was afraid that they were going to start forcing their way back inside his mouth, so he clamped his teeth together and only opened his lips a little bit. He finished his speech to Gardiner like that and turned his head when he was done and saw Gardiner leaning toward him, staring at him like he'd gone crazy or something—which maybe he had, Eddie thought to himself, staring mournfully back.

"Say what?" said Gardiner, sounding like he couldn't believe his ears.

"Dead," said Eddie.

"I told you to *scare* her, you stupid weasel, not *kill* the bitch." Gardiner flung himself back in his seat and wiped his mouth with the back of his hand. "First thing you do, you gotta get rid of your car."

Eddie felt grief at this, real grief. "What, sell it? Sell my Camaro?"

"No not sell it. Hide it. You gotta keep it out of sight for a while."

"Where? Where'm I gonna hide it?"

"How the fuck do I know where? Just hide it."

Gloomily, Eddie considered the possibilities.

"Could anybody've seen you? Got the plate number?"

Eddie shook his head. "I thought about that. I put mud all over it before I left home."

"Why?"

"I don't know," said Eddie, surprised.

"You *knew* you were gonna waste her, then!"

"No," Eddie protested. "I told you how it happened. It was an accidental-type thing."

92

"Then why the shit did you put mud all over your plate?"

"I don't know," said Eddie, getting angry. "I saw it on TV."

The guy came with the food, and they paid him. Gardiner vigorously sprinkled vinegar over his chips. Eddie sat very still for a minute, concentrating on his stomach, until he was sure that the combined odors of vinegar and carbon monoxide weren't going to make him puke. Then he emptied two packets of mustard onto his hot dog and started to eat.

"Looks like you're gonna be in the clear, then," said Gardiner, picking up his hamburger. He took a big bite and said, chewing, "You're a lucky sonofabitch, Ed. She coulda sued your ass for aiming your fucking Camaro at her." He broke into laughter, spewing food. "Whoops," he said. "Fuck." He brushed ineffectually at his shirtfront.

"That's not all, though," said Eddie reluctantly.

"You wasted somebody else too?" said Gardiner incredulously.

"No no no," said Eddie. "I mean, I'm not in the clear. I think I'm not anyway." And he told Gardiner the rest of it.

He'd made it his business to find out some things about her. This wasn't hard to do. It was a big city, yeah, but a small neighborhood. You could follow a person, you could ask questions, if you were friendly and casual-like, and you could find out things. Like where she worked, part-time. And what days. And what hours, usually.

And he was thinking about the stuff he'd found out, and mulling over Gardiner's idea for scaring the piss out of her, and still hoping a little bit that she'd do the right thing and answer his letter, or phone him—because, really, he didn't want to scare the piss out of her. And the next thing that happened was seeing her on the street.

She was with some other girl, maybe her roommate, who knows. He saw them from quite a way away, and they were walking straight toward him. He thought about stopping her to ask her if she'd got his letter but then he decided no way, she was the one who should stop him... she'd stop, and put her hand on his shoulder, and, thank you for your letter, she'd say, let's let bygones be bygones, she'd say, something civil like that... but he'd forgotten one important thing.

It was rush hour and there were throngs of people on Broadway, and at first she didn't see him. Eddie moved over as he walked along so that she'd bump right into him if she continued not to see him—and then there it was: her eyes caught on his face, and he saw that she'd recognized him. They were about ten yards apart by now. She turned her head to one side and gently nudged her friend over to the edge of the sidewalk, and they passed him like that, way over on the edge of the sidewalk so the sleeve of her yellow dress wouldn't touch him by accident, the side of her face looking at him, smooth and blind and silent.

The important thing he'd forgotten, of course, was that she wasn't a naturally polite person, despite her airs and graces, despite her bright hair and the softness of her skin.

So Eddie went home and wrote her another note. He didn't have to do it over because he got it right the very first time. "Bitch," was how he started it. "You are not important," was what he said next. "You are going to roast in hell." And then he signed it, like he had the first one.

"You *signed* it?" said Gardiner. He slapped his hands over his ears. "You got no more brains than a piece of snot! Who the fuck taught you what you know, anyhow?"

Eddie sat there meek and unhappy, waiting for Gardiner to stop raging at him and start giving him some good, practical advice.

Chapter Nineteen

*E*mma had grown up feeling her mother's presence constantly behind her, feeling her mother's breath on the back of her neck, feeling her mother's hands pushing her forward, gently but firmly. It was inexorable and terrifying, this sensation. She protested a lot, but felt helpless in the grip of her mother's determination that she learn to ride a bike, ice skate, do gymnastics, handle a horse, and excel at mathematics, and history, and English, and science…

No wonder Emma was worn out by the time she was seventeen.

"I want you to be confident," her mother had told her, a million times if she'd said it once. "Physically, mentally—in every way."

This ambition for her daughter was probably much to be admired. But Emma thought people ought to be left to develop their own ambitions. Unfortunately, whatever interest she might once have had in doing so had been thoroughly extinguished by her upbringing.

Emma looked around, exhausted, at the end of Grade Twelve and decided, enough's enough. She longed for the peace and comfort of a vicarious life.

Now, rummaging through a drawer full of Charlie's underwear, Emma heard her mother's voice saying:

"You're a throwback, that's what you are." She'd been a brittle, pretty woman, relentlessly well-groomed, who sold real estate: her name was Rosie Quinn. "A throwback. I can't believe it. I wish I'd had a son."

This hadn't bothered Emma, who had heard it before. She and her mother had never had much in common. She wondered if she would have had things in common with her father, had he lived, and if so, what these things would have been.

"I just don't see what's so wrong about it," she had said reasonably. Her mother didn't like the idea that Emma was at university to find a husband.

Rosie's eyebrows sprang toward her forehead, and she planted her fists on her hips. "It's dishonest, dishonorable, and lazy; that's what's wrong with it."

"It certainly isn't dishonest," said Emma indignantly. "I've always been very straightforward about my goals. Quite frankly, Mother, it seems to me you ought to admire me for that. I could be pretending I'm all mad keen on some kind of a career, but I'm not."

"Admire you," said Rosie, aghast. She looked closely at her daughter. "Emma, where did you come from?"

"As for dishonorable," Emma went on, "I cannot see that it's dishonorable for a person to assess her strengths and figure out how to make the best possible use of them."

"And what are these poor strengths," said Rosie furiously, "that you can make best use of them by putting yourself in servitude to some damn man?"

"And finally," said Emma, raising her voice a little, "I'm working hard, I'm getting good marks, how can you accuse me of being lazy?"

"You're being lazy about your life—your *life*, Emma!" Rosie's face crinkled, deepening the lines upon it; she was genuinely worried, then, thought Emma, knowing that her mother struggled hard for smoothness of skin.

Rosie sat down on the sofa next to Emma. She looked at her daughter with an expression half curious and half compassionate that made Emma feel impatient. "You mustn't look to a man for money, Emma. You really mustn't," she pleaded.

"Oh Mother," said Emma, moving slightly away from her,

"I'm not. You're putting entirely the wrong emphasis on this."

"Don't depend on a man for shelter, or security, or protection, either," said her mother, with a hand on Emma's upper arm.

Emma looked down at Rosie's hand, and touched it with carefully manicured fingers. She smelled perfume, and wondered whether it was Rosie's, or her own.

"Emma," said her mother urgently. "You must be equipped to pay your own way."

"I have every intention of paying my own way," Emma said staunchly. "I'm going to be the best wife there ever was."

"You're so bright," said her mother with sincerity, trying another tack. "You've got brains, and taste, and you know how to work hard—you can be anything you want to be. Why settle for being somebody's wife? Why not be a—I don't know, an interior designer, or something?"

"My mind's made up," Emma had said. Wifehood was the ideal choice, she'd convinced herself of it; her career would be her husband and *his* career. Perhaps he would be a politician. Or a diplomat. She imagined herself standing beside him, at his right, and both of them were extremely well dressed. She would be his friend, his confidante, his supporter; she'd tend to his needs, nurture him, comfort him, nourish him. And in return, he would expect nothing more of her than this.

Her husband-to-be had no face. He was tall and slim, but faceless. He didn't acquire a face until she met Charlie.

She hadn't expected to pick someone twelve years older than she was. And although he was tall and reasonably slim, there wasn't much likelihood that Charlie would move into the realm of politics. Or diplomacy. Charlie had very little ambition of any kind.

But he was a man who, having been through what he'd been through, knew exactly what he wanted.

Or so they had both believed.

Emma shut the drawer and sat down on the chair in the corner of the bedroom. Those brave words she'd said to her mother echoed around her: "I'm going to be the best wife there ever was." She'd met Charlie by then. But her mother didn't know about him yet. And Charlie didn't know yet that he and

Emma were going to get married. A smile nudged at her mouth, but Emma sent it away.

She got up and started going through the bottom drawer in Charlie's bureau. Scarves, gloves, never-used handkerchiefs, and a small box that contained his U.B.C. ring. Emma had given it to him when he got his master's degree. But Charlie didn't wear jewelry.

Her mother, when she met him, hadn't liked Charlie much.

"Just look at the man," she'd cried, exasperated. "Already divorced once. Already a failure at marriage. He'll never amount to a hill of beans." Which just showed how little Rosie Quinn knew.

Besides, she wouldn't have liked anybody Emma decided to marry. She was against marriage on principle; exactly what principle, Emma couldn't guess.

She tossed the ring box back into the drawer and sat on the floor, leaning against the end of the bed. It was strangely comforting, living side by side with Charlie's belongings. Maybe that's why he'd left them behind. She inhaled the smell of him when she brushed against his bathrobe, which hung from a hook on the back of the bathroom door. Sometimes she took out the bottle of after-shave lotion from the medicine cabinet and sniffed it: nothing summoned memory as potently as the sense of smell.

She closed her eyes. Where to look next? There was his closet, and his bedside table, and boxes and trunks in the basement, and there was lots of stuff in the garage, too. And they used the upstairs bedroom as a kind of office, so there were filing cabinets and things to go through.

Emma felt battered and bewildered, drained by the effort it took to resist succumbing to grief. She saw grief as a mountain ledge from which she would plummet into pain, and did not distinguish between this pain and death. Maybe if he'd died, maybe if he'd been lost to everyone, to the whole world, maybe then she would be prepared to grieve.

She wished she weren't an orphan.

She opened her eyes and got to her feet. He was a clever man, Charlie. But Emma was clever, too.

I must keep my mind completely open, she thought, standing in the bedroom, turning slowly around, her hands out-stretched, palms down. I must not be looking for anything, at least not at first. I must be able to see everything and resist drawing conclusions, at least at first.

She moved to Charlie's side of the bed and opened the drawer in the night table.

It was empty.

Except for the gun.

Emma felt an unpleasant prickling upon the skin of her back. She sat on the edge of the bed. Cautiously, she pulled the drawer fully open. There was nothing else there, only the gun. She thought about the things that were usually kept in that drawer: a notepad and a pen. Whatever paperback book he was currently reading. Before he quit smoking, he'd have had cigarettes in there, and a throwaway lighter.

But never, never the gun. Never.

Chapter Twenty

*A*lberg sat in his car as the ferry approached Langdale. Usually he liked to stand near the prow as the ship approached land, watching the delicacy with which it was maneuvered up to the dock. But today he stayed in his car, thinking about nothing at all, as if his mind were in park, like his automobile.

The docking procedure completed, car engines were coming to life, and the two outermost rows of vehicles started to exit, directed by crew members wearing orange vests with luminescent yellow crosses. Alberg wasn't impatient to get off, as he usually was. He remembered, from some faraway, pre-automobile time in his life, getting on buses and riding to the end of the line and staying on while the driver got off to have a smoke and maybe a coffee, then riding all the way back to where he'd come from.

He'd have liked to do that now, stay on the ferry and go back and forth all day long between Horseshoe Bay and Langdale. He didn't, though. Not that he could have—his car would have been facing the wrong way for the trip back to Horseshoe Bay; the ferry was a "push-me-pull-you" vehicle.

Alberg followed the traffic off the ship and down the ramp and up the long driveway that led to the road. He took the hairpin hill that bypassed the town of Gibsons, and then he was on the highway to Sechelt.

It was a warm, sunny day, so he drove along with his elbow resting on the open window...and this reminded him of summer vacations in his childhood; driving, always driving somewhere; long trips to see relatives in Winnipeg; and at the end of the day his father's left arm was bronzed by the sun, but the right arm wasn't.

His parents hadn't visited him since he moved to the Sunshine Coast. His mother might come this summer, but now his father would never see the place, never see the little house in Gibsons that Alberg lived in and had bought last year, never meet Cassandra or Sid Sokolowski....

Why the hell was he heading for Sechelt?

He kept on driving while he thought about it. Probably he hadn't had Sechelt in mind at all. He was just driving because he felt like it. He'd spent half a day at headquarters, after all. His head needed clearing. Maybe he'd go all the way up to Earl's Cove and take the ferry across Jervis Inlet to Saltery Bay, near Powell River, and from there take another one across Georgia Strait to Nanaimo, on Vancouver Island; and then he could drive down to Victoria and take a third ferry over to Tsawwassen and drive into Vancouver and through the city and up to Horseshoe Bay and finally a fourth ferry back across Howe Sound to Langdale.... He couldn't do that all in one day, though.

He drove slowly past the library and saw Cassandra inside, talking to somebody at the checkout counter.

He ended up in the parking lot behind the detachment, so he cut the motor and got out and went inside.

"What're you doing here?" said Isabella, the detachment's secretary-receptionist, flashing her golden eyes at him.

"I don't know," said Alberg.

She studied him busily for a moment. "Come on over here and sit down at the sergeant's table," she said. She pulled out a chair and shooed him into it. "Since you're here, you might as well have a cup of coffee."

She poured some into his usual mug. It was a plain white mug with no words on it and no pictures, either. Isabella had urged him many times to get himself a more interesting coffee mug, but Alberg had ignored her. Now he was thinking maybe she'd been right; it looked singularly boring among all the others. Norah Gibbons, who'd recently joined the detachment from Williams Lake, had a huge mug with a drawing of a fiendishly grinning woman on it; the woman was saying, "Men who call women 'sweetheart,' 'baby,' or 'honey'...should have their little tiny peckers cut off." Maybe he'd get himself a male-chauvinist-pig mug. If there was such a thing.

Isabella slapped down on the table in front of him a paper napkin and a paper plate on which were displayed a chocolate doughnut and a sugar doughnut.

"What's this?" said Alberg, stunned.

"Enjoy," said Isabella, and she went back to work.

He'd finished the chocolate doughnut and had just started the other one when Sokolowski came out of the hall that led to Alberg's office. Alberg felt guilty, sitting at Sokolowski's desk when he wasn't even supposed to be in the damn building, and he could see from the look on Sid's face that the sergeant felt guilty too, probably because he was enjoying himself, in Alberg's absence.

"How're things at the Puzzle Palace?" said the sergeant.

"As puzzling as ever," said Alberg. "I got us another constable, though, so it wasn't a total waste of time."

"Good," said Sokolowski.

There was an awkward silence as Alberg put down the doughnut and brushed sugar from his hand. "Boy," he said, making a show of looking at his watch, "I've gotta get going. Just dropped in for a minute. Had no idea it was getting so late."

"Karl, who're you kidding," said Sokolowski patiently.

"Not me," said Isabella, not looking up from her computer screen.

"But listen, I'm glad you're here. I got an idea for you." The sergeant beckoned Alberg down the hall and into the staff sergeant's own office, which he was occupying in Alberg's absence. "Here, sit down," he said, pushing Alberg into the chair behind his desk. Sokolowski took the black leather chair in front. "I got a project for you."

"Sid, please," said Alberg, "I don't need a project. In the

first place, I'll be back at work pretty soon. In the second place, I've got projects coming out of my ears. I have to clean out the garage and fix the screen around the sun porch and find somebody to build me a new fence... "

"But this is important, Karl." The sergeant leaned forward. "I heard about Charlie O'Brea. I heard Emma's—well, she's devastated, I guess you'd say."

"Yeah," said Alberg.

"Charlie—" Sokolowski shook his head. "Well, what can you say about a man like that? I thought I knew the guy," he said bitterly.

"Uh huh," said Alberg.

"What you've got on your hands, here," said the sergeant with conviction, "is a disturbed individual. To do such a thing."

"Uh huh," said Alberg, noncommittally.

"So I was thinking, Karl, you put your detective hat on, you use your compassionate leave to—well, you use it in a compassionate cause." Sokolowski looked mildly surprised. "A compassionate cause," he said again, pleased with himself.

"I'm not following you, here," said Alberg.

"You find Charlie," said Sokolowski.

Alberg looked at him intently. "I do what?"

"You find Charlie O'Brea."

"Oh, for god's sake."

"No, I'm serious," said Sokolowski, ponderously earnest. "Think about it."

"I told her and I'm telling you, it isn't a police matter."

"No, it isn't—but Karl, you could do it. You could find him for her. While you're waiting for your leave to run out."

Alberg lifted his hands, exasperated. "I don't think he wants to be found, Sid." The first thing you'd do, he thought, was flag the guy's bank accounts.

"Well, I think you're right about that, sure," said Sid. "But I also think he owes his wife an explanation, first, before he buggers off on her."

"We don't have the right, and we certainly don't have the power, to demand that he explain himself to his wife."

And the Lower Mainland airports and railway and bus stations too. And he'd do a media fan-out. She must have photos of him.

"No," said Sokolowski reluctantly.

Alberg and the sergeant looked at each other.

"I could certainly—suggest it, though," said Alberg. "If I found him."

Chapter
Twenty-One

ernie Peters worked for Alberg on Wednesday afternoons, one o'clock through until five. At first he'd left her notes, telling her what he wanted done. But she paid no attention to his notes. Every Wednesday she dusted his small house, vacuumed, tidied, and cleaned the kitchen and the bathroom. Then she did his ironing. And every week she had time for something extra that she decided needed doing, like polishing the furniture or washing some walls or cleaning out the kitchen cupboards. And before she left, she made a start on his dinner, too. She often went out and bought food, apparently dissatisfied with what she found in the house.

Every Wednesday, Alberg's thoughts wandered home frequently throughout the day. Maybe today Bernie would finally get to the fridge. Or clean the windows. Or the oven. Maybe today she'd make something cold for dinner, instead of corned beef and cabbage, or stew, or chili.

When he left the detachment on this April Wednesday, Alberg went straight home. He found Bernie in the middle of the backyard. She was wearing one of her white dresses and a pair of sturdy white shoes. The stitches in the seam of the left shoe had been opened to allow a bunion to poke through. Alberg watched her for a moment from the sunporch. Her left forearm was pressed across her stomach, and her left hand cradled her right elbow. She was puffing on a cigarette, her toe tapping the grass impatiently, as though smoking were a duty she discharged with reluctance, part of the regrettable baggage of being herself.

"Bernie," said Alberg from the sun porch, and she whirled around. "What are you doing out here?"

"Smoking," said Bernie. "You've quit the filthy habit, and so I don't poison your air." She took another puff. Many little lines fanned out from around her lips. "I heard about your father," she said formally, "and I'm truly sorry for your trouble."

"Thanks, Bernie. Do you want some coffee?" said Alberg.

Bernie pinched the end of her cigarette between her thumb and first finger, dropped the coal into the dirt of a flowerbed, scrubbed it out with her foot. She put what was left of the cigarette into the pocket of her dress. "You don't pay me for sitting around drinking coffee," she said.

"Come on, Bernie. It's after five, anyway. And I want to talk to you." He held the screen door open and waited while she climbed the three steps from the lawn to the sun porch and preceded him into the house.

In the kitchen, Bernie squirted detergent into the sink and turned on the hot water tap. "What about?" she said, starting in on Alberg's breakfast dishes, which, for some reason unfathomable to him, she always left until the end of the day.

"I think you know Emma and Charlie O'Brea, don't you?" said Alberg. He picked up a tea towel and began drying a juice glass.

Bernie snorted. "I know them."

"I guess you know that he's disappeared."

"I know it. Run off on her, he has."

"Sid Sokolowski suggested that I use my leave to try to find him."

Bernie sighed and shook her head. She rinsed a plate, a knife, and a coffee mug and set them in the drainer.

"What can you tell me about them?"

She gave him a suspicious glance.

"I'm trying to figure out what kind of a situation I'm getting myself into." He dried the mug and put it away in the cupboard.

"He didn't appreciate her," said Bernie flatly, unplugging the sink to let the water drain away. "She did everything for him. Looked after him like he was King Tut. But he didn't appreciate her."

"How do you know?" said Alberg, leaning against the counter, the tea towel draped over his shoulder.

She turned to look at him indignantly. Her red-brown curls, unnaturally bright, were squished beneath a hairnet. Her brown face was corrugated with wrinkles. "Well he ran out on her, didn't he?"

"Yeah, but did you know before he left that he didn't appreciate her?"

"Okay, I'm gonna give this some serious thought." She put down the dishcloth, sat down at the table, and stared intently out the window. "He didn't beat on her," she said with conviction. "That I'm sure of."

"Uh huh," said Alberg, sitting down opposite her.

"I would have said they were happy," she said finally. Reluctantly. "At least, I would have said *she* was happy. I don't know about him. He couldn't have been happy, could he? Or he wouldn't have taken off like he did."

"But it came as a surprise to you, did it? That he was gone?"

She nodded vigorously. "You know, she tells me he didn't take a thing with him. Not a single thing. Don't that beat all, now."

"How is she? Is she okay? Angry? What?"

Bernie hesitated. "I don't know how she is. She acts a little peculiar from time to time. She's not an ordinary person," she said seriously, squinting across the table at Alberg.

"How do you mean?"

"Just that," said Bernie, shrugging. "She's not—ordinary." She sighed. "Between you and me and the gatepost, I think she's well shot of him. But of course you can't convince her of that. So I'm glad you're gonna find him for her. Ease her spirits. What happens then—" She shook her head. "It's in the good Lord's hands, I guess."

"I'm going to *try* to find him, Bernie. But he won't want to be found. And I only have a few days."

"You'll do it," said Bernie. She looked at him searchingly, her beady brown eyes fixed on him. "It must be hard, being a policeman. I guess there's lots of things you see that you can't rectify."

"Yeah," said Alberg. "You're right."

She slapped the tabletop and stood up. She swished clean water around in the sink, wrung out the dishcloth, dried the sink with a paper towel, and threw the towel in the trash. "That's it, then," she said, surveying the kitchen. She gestured with her thumb to a pot on top of the stove. "There's some nice lamb stew in there," she said, reaching for her black plastic handbag, which sat upon the counter. "Eat hearty."

Chapter
Twenty-Two

E mma was becoming very familiar with the shopping mall in West Vancouver that was known as Park Royal. Every time she went there she parked in a different lot. Each time she used a different entrance and focused her attention on different stores. By now she knew the whole place well.

There were actually two parts to Park Royal—one on the south side of Marine Drive and one on the north—but Charlie's office had been in a building on the south side, so that's where Emma had decided he spent his time. Besides, it was in the south mall that people played chess, and she knew—she just knew—that Charlie would have played chess.

This Thursday morning, the last day of April, she had brought along a photograph of him. She'd been dismayed when looking through her albums at how few pictures of Charlie she had. But, then, he was the one who was good with a camera... .

His camera. Another thing he'd left behind: another prized possession abandoned. He could always buy himself another one, of course. But maybe he'd decided that he didn't like taking pictures after all. He'd certainly made an awful lot of decisions, Charlie had, all at once, in one fell swoop; reshaping his existence. She felt a stab of envy. Here she was, smothering to death in the detritus of Charlie's discarded life, while he was busy starting all over again. Had he secretly taken courses, while he planned his getaway? Had he learned some other line of work? Even another language, perhaps?

The photograph in her purse showed Charlie about to get into his car, the very same car he'd driven away in last Saturday morning, five days ago. She'd taken the picture last summer, on the first day of their two-week holiday, which they'd spent at a lakeside resort in the Okanagan Valley. It was a little dim, because it had been taken on the car deck of the ferry, but it was a good likeness of Charlie. He'd unlocked the driver's door and was about to open it when Emma called his name, and snapped the picture. She couldn't read his expression, but his features were clear.

She stood outside the bookstore with the photograph in her hand. Finally, she went in.

Nobody in the bookstore recognized Charlie.

Emma trudged from store to store. It was odd, she thought, that nobody asked why she was looking for him. Maybe they were too polite. Or else they didn't want to know. She saw curiosity on their faces, and sometimes their replies were wary or hesitant. Yet she didn't doubt, when they said they didn't recognize him, that they were telling her the truth.

On the lower level of the mall, near the entrance to Eaton's, there was a shop that sold handbags and briefcases and luggage. As she walked through the door the smell of leather was sudden and strong, and it created in Emma a flood of nostalgia so powerful she was made breathless. Somewhere in her head there must be a memory to explain this. What use were one's senses, she thought resentfully, if they were so undisciplined as to create pain without providing an explanation? Quickly she blinked away tears, hoping they hadn't dislodged any mascara, and looked around for a salesperson.

She couldn't see one at first, but she heard somebody humming. She'd never heard a hum with such a robust vibrato. It was issuing from a woman who was energetically cleaning a glass countertop in the corner of the store.

"Excuse me," said Emma, and the woman looked up and smiled.

"I use vinegar and water," she said, "in my own house, but

it's the smell, which doesn't bother me, you understand, except in here it just doesn't seem right, because of the leather; it's the smell of the leather that sells things in this store, and to have the place stinking of vinegar just doesn't make sense." She reached down to stow the bottle of Windex under the counter, and threw the paper towel she'd been using into a wastebasket. "So. What can I do for you, dear?"

Emma held up the photograph of Charlie. "Do you recognize this man?"

She saw in the woman's eyes that she did.

"What's your name?" said Emma.

"Rita Hemming," said the woman, who was about fifty years old and had short gray hair. She was Emma's height, but considerably heavier, and wore a gray skirt and a bright red short-sleeved sweater. Emma noted that her lipstick matched the sweater exactly, and that she used mascara and blusher but no eyeliner or eyeshadow. "Who is he?"

Emma averted her eyes and looked sadly at the floor. "He's my husband."

Rita Hemming looked from the picture to Emma and back again. "Why are you looking for him?"

Emma sighed. "I'm not looking for him. I know where he is. He's in the hospital." She curled her tongue around the delicious phrase and delicately eased it from her mouth: "Suffering from amnesia."

Rita looked at her in awe. "Really," she breathed.

"He was in a car wreck," said Emma. "When he came to, in the hospital, he couldn't remember a thing."

Rita shook her head in wonderment.

"He had identification, of course," Emma went on, "and so the police called me, and I rushed straight to his side."

"And he didn't know you? His own wife?"

Emma, surprised and gratified, realized that there were tears in her eyes. She reached into her purse for a tissue. "Physically, he's fine. But it's very hard on him—psychologically."

"And on you too," said Rita, exclaiming her indignation.

"The doctors feel that if I can recreate the days before the accident for him," Emma said, marveling at her ingenuity, "and fill in as many gaps as possible, it might help his memory to come back."

"Well, I can tell you right now that I do recognize him, I do indeed."

"Oh, I'm so glad," said Emma in a tremulous whisper.

And she heard a voice in her head, as clear as a bell, and it was saying: *I'm going to get you. I'm going to get you, you bastard.*

Chapter
Twenty-Three

*E*ddie stood indecisively on the corner of Fourth and Macdonald and let the stream of pedestrians break against him and flow around him. The weather had turned cold and blustery again, even though it would be May tomorrow, so he was wearing his beige jacket with the zipper in the front. There was a splotch of grease on the right-hand pocket, which held a retractable ballpoint pen and a small notebook, three inches by five inches, with a coil at the top and a picture of a cat on the cover: he'd bought them at the drugstore.

He was oblivious to the irritated glances thrown by the people swirling against and around him.

He had on brown cotton pants that had become baggy in the knees and high-top running shoes. His shirt was dark blue, and under it he wore a gray T-shirt.

He was full of anxiety, standing there. There were three things he had to do today, and for the moment he was helpless in the thrall of this; he had to go to work, and he had to go to the gym, and he had to go to that house.

He didn't have to be at work until two o'clock, and it was only nine in the morning now. So he had lots of time.

He just couldn't figure out whether to work out first or do the house first. They were both extremely important things.

Was one more important than the other one? That was what he was trying to decide.

Eddie recalled that both the house and the gym were south and west of where he stood, so he began walking. He didn't think to look before he stepped off the curb, and he collided with a woman crossing the sidewalk in front of him. Flustered, he tried to apologize, but she was rushing to catch the light. He blundered on, into the intersection. A car served to miss him, and the driver hit the horn and let it blare and blare while Eddie, scrambling back onto the sidewalk, felt his face get beet red with embarrassment. The WALK light came on, and he made his way across the street. He stopped to dig his cigarettes and lighter out of his inside jacket pocket. His hands shook as he lit up. That kind of thing was always happening to him. It made him so damn mad.

After a while he'd calmed down some, so he tossed the cigarette butt away and started walking again, west on Fourth Avenue.

It was a gray, miserable day. He didn't feel much like working out; but he had to keep his strength up. Eddie was very strong. He didn't look like the other guys who used the gym, though, which sometimes made him depressed, because although strength was what he went there for, what he worked so hard there for, it would have been good if he'd *looked* strong, too. He couldn't figure out why his pecs were flabby, and his gut was soft, and his waist had a roll of fat around it. Someday pretty soon now he was going to complain about this to the guy who ran the gym.

He trudged on, hunched against the cold. He missed his car a lot. He looked forward to the day when it would be safe to drive it again. He daydreamed about that: he'd go out to Abbotsford on the Greyhound bus, and he'd walk up Delair Road to Rollie's place and head out to his barn and open the door—and there it'd be, the Camaro, all ready and waiting for him, shiny and purring, just like he'd left it. He'd had the broken light fixed, so it was perfect again. Pristine. (This was a word Eddie had recently looked up in the dictionary. "Extremely pure." He thought it was the perfect word for the Camaro.)

While it was away, though, he didn't mind using the city buses to get places. And often he got rides with Gardiner. And sometimes he walked. Walking wasn't so bad. Except on a day like this, that felt more like winter than goddamn spring. I should have worn my gloves, he thought—but then he remembered that he had a reason for not wearing them; you can't write when you're wearing gloves. Eddie fumbled quickly at his pocket to make sure the pad and the pen were there ...and that decided him, feeling the pen there and the little notepad, that made up his mind.

He felt a huge wave of relief. He hated not being able to make up his mind about something. There was nothing, nothing, he hated so much. And no matter how often he reminded himself that his mind would make *itself* up when it was ready, because after all it always had, Eddie was afraid that this time it wouldn't, and he'd be dangling there helpless hour after hour, not being able to do anything, not *one single thing*, because he couldn't make up his goddamn mind which thing to do next.

He strode confidently down Fourth Avenue and passed the gym without giving it a glance, and eventually he turned right and then left.

Eddie was now on a narrow, treelined street of two- and three-story houses. He was in the general neighborhood that Sylvia lived in, except she lived on a street that wasn't nearly as nice as this one. Whistling under his breath, Eddie eventually stopped across the street from a house that was partially obscured by a tall hedge.

He hunkered down against the trunk of a tree and pulled out his notebook and his pen. He noted the time and entered it at the top of the first page. He hesitated because he'd never done this kind of thing before and wasn't sure how to go about it. Then he wrote: "No sign of life."

Though of course there *was* life inside the house. That was the problem. One of the problems.

"*Roommate*???" It had come out of Gardiner's face like a yelp. "She had a *roommate*???" He'd slapped his knee and near to killed himself laughing.

117

Well, Eddie didn't need that. He already knew he was in trouble. "So you see what I mean," he'd said doggedly, ignoring Gardiner's high-pitched cackle. "She must have talked to her about me. And now she'll tell. The cops. Or Harold. Somebody. She'll tell. I know she will, because you can't shut up a woman; they all talk, yak-yak-yak, can't keep their dumb mouths shut for a minute, none of them."

"You don't need to worry about that," said Gardiner, wiping his eyes with his hand and then wiping his hand on his jeans. He leaned against the fender of his beat-up Olds, which was parked outside the liquor store at the corner of Broadway and Cypress. Eddie hated the way Gardiner treated that Olds. It caused him real pain to see a good car go unappreciated, uncared for. Gardiner was grinning at him. "At least," he said, "you don't need to worry about her telling the cops. That's hearsay, and it don't count for a rat's ass."

Eddie felt a great deal better. He was sometimes skeptical about things Gardiner told him, but not when they were things having to do with the law and crime. Gardiner was something of an expert when it came to law and crime. And although most of the time Eddie disapproved of this—Gardiner's life was haphazard and uncertain, and he'd already been sent twice to the slammer—it did come in handy, now and then, to know somebody in the crime field, even if he was kind of a low-ranking criminal.

His relief didn't last long, though.

"It's the fucking notes you gotta worry about," Gardiner said, unlocking the trunk and pushing up the lid. "Especially the second one. Jesus," he said, shaking his head, "you can be so stupid, Ed." He threw his cigarette onto the street and leaned into the trunk, where several cases of empty beer cans sprawled on top of a box of tools, an old piece of orange tarpaulin, a big-eyed teddy bear with one ear missing, and— Eddie could hardly believe this—a shotgun, a Winchester Defender, for god's sake, with a pistol grip, clumsily wrapped in a sheet that had come unwound.

"What're you doing with that thing?" he said, momentarily distracted.

"A guy owed me," said Gardiner vaguely. "Come on,

gimme a hand, here, willya?" he said, hauling out the beer cans and dropping them on the pavement next to the car: he was going to cash them in at the liquor store.

Eddie reached into the trunk and plucked out two cases of cans.

"You know what you gotta do, don't you?" said Gardiner.

"No. What?" Eddie heard the whine in his voice and was disgusted with himself.

Gardiner looked up at him, exasperated. "Get the fucking things back," he'd said.

So that was why Eddie had parked himself, shivering, on his hams in front of that damn house. He was studying the place and brooding about how to get inside it. He already knew that he'd forgotten something important: he hadn't thought to bring anything to eat. And when he was concentrating or worrying or fretting about something, he absolutely needed to eat. It was a stomach condition he had—too much acid, or not enough, or some damn thing. He stared at the gap in the laurel hedge, and wished he had a milkshake, or a bag of chocolate chip cookies.

Time passed, and his rear end got cold, and his stomach started acting up, like he'd known it would. He wondered how long he ought to stay. This kind of work—surveillance—it was a strain on a person. And after a certain amount of time he'd be bound to attract somebody's attention, which would be bad. He thought about it for a while, and decided he'd do two hours at a stretch.

No, an hour and a half.

He'd been sitting there for thirty-five minutes when he got a glimpse of the front door of the place opening. Somebody ran down the steps and came out through the hedge: a girl with red hair. Eddie wrote her description in his notebook, as she bustled off down the street.

Eddie was extremely pleased with himself.

He checked his watch. Another half hour to go.

But after a while it occurred to him that the place was empty now. He sat up straighter. His stomach started to churn. He could pretend he was a repairman, maybe. Bang on the door, and when nobody answered—what?

Break the window. He could get in that way.

Or maybe she'd left the back door unlocked.

He put the notepad and the pen in his pocket and stood up. His butt ached from sitting on the cold ground. He wiped the palms of his hands on his cotton pants and got ready to cross the street—and all of a sudden a second girl came out the door. Eddie watched, half-hidden behind the tree, as she emerged from the gap in the hedge and headed for a gray Plymouth Reliant parked in front of the house. This one had dark hair that was short on one side and long on the other, like some-body had made a big mistake. Eddie scrunched his head down into his shoulders and wrote her license plate number in his notebook. *Two* roommates she'd had.

Okay. So *now* the place was empty. Eddie started across the street, putting himself in the frame of mind of somebody who was a repairman, trying to decide if he was going to be an elec-trical-type repairman, or a jack-of-all trades, or what.

He was halfway to the opposite sidewalk when the front door opened *again*, and *another* damn girl came out. Eddie's heart lurched, and began to pound. He swerved to the right, walked to the corner and around it, and went into the first café he saw.

He sat down and ordered a milkshake, and hid his shaking hands under the table while he waited for it.

Next time he'd take along a toolbox, he decided. This would make him look like a repairman, and would also pro-vide him with break-in tools.

But before he barged in there, he had to find out just how the hell many girls lived there, anyway.

Chapter
Twenty-Four

*L*ater that same day, Alberg went through the gate in the picket fence that marched past the front of Emma O'Brea's house. It was a very ordinary looking house— a lot more ordinary than the Sokolowskis' next door, which was painted a deep sunny yellow. The house that Emma lived in was white. It looked tranquil, almost sleepy; the windows were covered with glass curtains that revealed nothing of the inside—like Charlie's eyes, thought Alberg, remembering. There was a small lawn, bisected by a sidewalk that led straight to the porch and then broke off to either side in the shape of Y. Some bushes grew close to the house and Alberg, climbing the four steps to the front door, saw narrow basement windows half-hidden behind them.

He knocked on the door, and through its small window he saw Bernie emerge into the hall and hurry to open the door. She was holding an oily dusting cloth, wearing her white dress that buttoned up the front and her white nurse's shoes with the hole cut out of the left one. Her brassy auburn hair was covered with a hairnet, as usual. Alberg smiled at the sight of her and wondered what his mother would make of Bernie Peters.

"Hi, Bernie," he said when she opened the door.

"I'll go get her," said Bernie, stepping back and gesturing Alberg inside. A package of cigarettes and a disposable lighter were tucked into the pocket of her dress. She smoked the same brand that Alberg's father had smoked. Alberg watched her walking away from him, sturdy and brisk, her legs slightly bowed. He wondered how much cigarettes he had to do with his father's death. People blamed everything on smoking now. Smoking, or eating the wrong kind of fat.

He waited in the hall, looking around. Doors on the left and right led into the living room and the dining room. The hall appeared to divide the lower floor in two; he could see another door at the end, which must lead into the backyard. He figured that the kitchen would be behind the dining room and a large bedroom across the hall from it.

Soon Bernie reappeared, with Emma in tow.

"I've got some time off," said Alberg, "and Sid Sokolowski suggested I volunteer to look for your husband. Unofficially," he added quickly.

"You take him up on it," said Bernie to Emma, poking her in the shoulder. "I'll get coffee," she said, and hurried away.

Emma stood in the middle of the hallway, looking at him, her eyes searching; Alberg felt them moving over his face like the searching fingertips of a blind person. He felt his skin begin to itch.

"That would be very good of you," said Emma finally. "Oh, that would be wonderful. Thank you."

"I can't promise anything. I mean, I might get nowhere at all." She nodded solemnly, her eyes continuing to explore him. Then he felt the mask settle down upon his face, and he relaxed and smiled at her, through his mask, safe, now. "Let's sit down somewhere, okay?"

"Oh, yes, of course, I'm sorry," said Emma, and led him into the living room. "I've been looking for him on my own. It'll be such a relief to have somebody helping me. But I've made progress," she said eagerly. "A little bit, anyway. Just a minute." She hurried away and returned almost immediately. "You'll need this," she said, handing Alberg a snapshot of her husband. "I found somebody who recognized him," she said, and told Alberg about the woman in the leather store. Then she hesitated, embarrassment on her face. "For some reason I thought he might be living there. In Park Royal. Up in the rafters or in the washrooms or somewhere. I don't know what put such an idea in my head, but there it was. Until I found out that he'd bought a set of luggage."

Alberg sat in the middle of the sofa, holding the snapshot. "Mrs. O'Brea—are you sure you want to find him?" She accepted this calmly; he watched her consider it. She looked away from him, around the room, her gaze touching on the furnishings, the carpet, the curtains at the window, and through the doorway into the hall.

"Am I sure that I want to find him." She gave a sigh and folded her hands in her lap. She was wearing jeans and a gray sweatshirt. Her hair gleamed and her face was bare of makeup. She looked directly at Alberg again. He thought she probably believed herself to be a perfectly honest and straightforward person with nothing whatsoever to hide. "No, I'm not sure I want to find him. But I have to do it anyway."

"Why?"

"Because—I don't know. To ask him why he left, I guess. To see if he really means it, maybe."

Bernie entered the room bearing a tray on which she'd placed two cups of coffee, cream and sugar, and a plate of what Alberg recognized as her own homemade oatmeal cookies. Bernie held out the plate to Emma, who shook her head.

But Bernie said, "You don't need to tell me you had no breakfast, and I got no guarantee you'll eat the supper I'll make for you, so at least let me see you eat one of these cookies."

Emma took one and began to nibble at it.

Bernie left, and they heard her lugging something upstairs, and then the vacuum cleaner went on up there.

Alberg took out his notebook. "Okay. Let's get started." And Emma went through it again: the morning of Charlie's departure, calling his office on Monday, checking the bank accounts. When she'd finished, she sank back in her chair, and Alberg saw her exhaustion.

"What do you think's happened here, Emma?" he said quietly.

Emma got up, slowly, and moved across the room to the white upright piano that stood in the corner. She played a few notes with her right hand. "Charlie bought me this piano. I was just about to start taking lessons." She sat on the stool, her back to the piano. "He's left me," she said, almost matter-of-fact. "That's what's happened."

"But why?"

"I don't know." Tears flooded her eyes, and spilled down her cheeks. She pulled a tissue from the pocket of her jeans and wiped them away.

"Are you angry with him?"

"Well, what on earth do you think?" She ducked her head. "I don't think that's pertinent," she said, brushing nonexistent crumbs from her thigh.

Alberg looked curiously around the living room, which felt like a department store display. This was partly due to its spectacular cleanliness, for which he could blame Bernie; but due, also, to the peculiar feeling of emptiness that pervaded it. He imagined Charlie making his escape from here, slipping from this room into his own private future—the room would never miss him.

"Exactly what is it that you'll be doing?" said Emma.

"First, I'll need a letter from you, authorizing me to make inquiries," he said. "Then I'll want information about your bank accounts. I've got the details on his car. I need names of friends and relatives. His business address, his partner's name. Also who's his doctor, his dentist, his lawyer, his mechanic, etcetera. And a list of every place you know of that he's ever been."

"I can give you all that."

"Plus I want to look through everything he left behind. Clothes, desk drawers, filing cabinets—everything."

"Of course," said Emma, nodding.

"Finally, I need you to tell me every single thing you know about him. Hobbies. Educational background. His medical and family history. Sexual habits."

Emma placed her feet close together, side by side, and examined her sneakers. They were dark gray, with shiny gray patterns shaped like flames, and heels and toes that were dark pink.

Alberg said, "I'll also be checking airports, airlines, buses, trains—okay?" He was smiling to her, trying to be reassuring.

Emma looked up at him. "You won't lie to me, will you?"

"What do you mean?"

"I mean, if you find out that—that he's ..."

"If I find out that something's happened to him?" He shook his head. "No. Of course I won't lie to you. I think that's unlikely, though. I think, if anything had happened to him, you would have been notified by now."

She nodded, wearily. "I know. I think so too."

"Emma—are you sure you can't tell me something that might explain why he'd want to leave?"

She shook her head, and knew immediately that she'd done it too quickly. She tried to look thoughtful. It was hard not to tell him about that business with the gun. The only reason she didn't was so as not to confuse him. It would sound positively melodramatic, and he'd never be able to get it out of his mind, and probably he'd decide, privately, that she was better off without Charlie, and he wouldn't look for him at all, he'd just pretend to look for him, and then eventually he'd come back to the house and report his failure.

"I honestly can't. No." She moved away from the piano and sat down in the easy chair again, reaching for her coffee cup. "I know this is a cliché, but I thought we had a very good marriage. I really did. And I deserve to know if I was wrong."

"Sometimes there just aren't any good answers," said Alberg, "no matter how important the questions are."

"People should be required to provide some, though," Emma said sharply, "as unsatisfactory as they may be."

"You're right," he said, flipping open his notebook. "Okay. Let's get started. Tell me about Charlie. Don't leave anything out," he said—but he knew she would.

125

Chapter
Twenty-Five

"Sometimes I talk to myself," Eddie confided to Sylvia.
"Me too."

He looked at her in surprise. "Really?" Then he saw her grinning at him, and understood that she was making a joke. Of course she didn't talk to herself. A person living with those kids would never get a chance to talk to herself.

"You should have another pet, maybe," said Sylvia, glancing up at him from her supper. He'd cooked pasta, and a sauce made from tomatoes, zucchini, bacon, and onion. Usually he just ate easy stuff, but whenever Sylvia came over, he did up something special. "You could get one free, from the S.P.C.A."

"That's a dumb idea," Eddie scoffed. "I got my job. I got the gym. I got my project." He slathered margarine over one of the rolls he'd picked up from the Safeway on his way home. "I got no time for pets." He'd had gerbils once. Woke up one morning and instead of two of them, he had fourteen. This had rattled Eddie, and he hadn't wanted a pet since.

"What is this project, anyway?"

He made his eyes very narrow, and peeked at her. Sylvia was wearing jeans and a yellow sweater, and she'd let her long brown hair fall loose. He wished he could confide in her about the notes, about having to do surveillance on that house full of girls. But he'd gone past that point, now, the point where Sylvia could help him. Melanie dying like that—he knew

Sylvia wouldn't stand for it.

"Oh, you know," he said vaguely. He blotted up the last of the pasta sauce on his plate with a chunk of roll and stuffed the roll into his mouth. "A project. Nothing."

He knew how much he owed Sylvia. He trusted her more than anybody else in the world.

"It must be pretty important, you need a new envelope for it," she said. "Why can't you just take from MISCELLA-NEOUS?"

But he didn't trust her completely. That would be too much responsibility for anybody, Eddie thought, to be trusted completely.

He grunted, instead of answering her, and stood up to clear the table. "I got ice cream for dessert. And a nice cantaloupe."

"So did you do it?" she asked him, casually, over dessert. "Apologize?"

He'd been expecting this, of course, so he was ready for it. "She came into the drugstore one day," he said, digging into his cantaloupe. "And I spoke to her. Yeah."

Sylvia was looking at him fondly, with a little smile. "There. You see?"

And he hadn't lied, either.

When Sylvia had left, Eddie washed the dishes and put them away, and wiped off the cracked linoleum that covered the kitchen countertop, and he even cleaned the tiny window above the sink, the one that looked into the bottom of a hydrangea bush.

Then he sat at the kitchen table with his shoe box of envelopes and went through them carefully, one by one. They were full of money. He'd cashed his paycheck today—that was why Sylvia had come over for supper. She came once a month to help him organize his finances, and in real life—that is to say, when things were normal, not all jerked around, like now—these were Eddie's favorite days. He felt very wealthy, peering into his envelopes, as though he could afford anything in the world.

He also had a bank account. He used to have two of them, one for paying for stuff and one for saving, but that got too confusing, so Sylvia said he could make do with just one, the one for saving. A little book came with it, in which it got written down how much money was in there. Which wasn't much. But Sylvia said it was important to put in a little bit every time he got paid. She said that gradually it would pile up on itself, and one day he'd look in the little book and be flabbergasted at how much was there. "Flabbergasted." That was the word she'd said. He'd be "just flabbergasted" to find out how much money he had, all of a sudden. This made Eddie laugh and shake his head. But he did it. Every two weeks. He took his paycheck into the bank and cashed it and then put a little bit into his savings account. And when Sylvia came, he showed her the book. The pile of money did get bigger too; he had to admit it. But so far he wasn't flabbergasted.

The envelopes in the shoe box were four inches high and nine and a half inches long. They had to be that size so the bills inside didn't get all squeezed. Each one had a word printed on it, and a number: for example, one said RENT, $450. There were envelopes that said "FOOD," "TELEPHONE," "CIGA-RETTES," "MOVIES"—all spelled right, all with figures on them worked out by Eddie and Sylvia together. And if one of the envelopes came up empty before he got another paycheck, well then—like Sylvia said, putting on a deep voice, pretending to be Dad, "that's how the cookie crumbles, my man, that's how she crumbles."

Eddie often thought about how different things might be— things like his life and the way he lived it—if his dad hadn't died.

Eddie didn't have to worry about stuff like heat and electricity, because they were included in his rent. He didn't have to worry about remembering to pay the rent, because the man who lived upstairs (or sometimes it was the woman) came down on the first day of the month and knocked on his door, and Eddie went to the shoe box and got the envelope marked "RENT"—which he never touched except for then—and took the money out of it and handed it to the landlord, and that would be that.

He might even still be living at home if his dad hadn't died. This had happened a long long time ago. Eddie had trouble remembering his dad, which was why Sylvia, who was older, did his voice from time to time. She *could* remember him, and she tried to bring him back a little bit for Eddie.

He didn't have to worry about his medical insurance, either, because the drugstore looked after that for him. Same with his taxes.

He'd been worried when he first learned about all the stuff you had to do, living on your own. But Sylvia had gotten him so well organized he hardly worried about anything anymore. He considered himself to be a very happy person. And so it was no damn wonder ...

His mom hadn't died, but he hadn't seen her for years. She'd run off with some guy. Well, she'd run off with several guys. But the last time, when Eddie was fourteen and Sylvia was twenty, she hadn't bothered to come back.

The PROJECTS envelope had fifty dollars in it. He didn't know whether this would be enough or not.

Hell, he could always use some of the money in his bank account if he had to. Sylvia wouldn't like that. But it was his money, after all.

He used to have a car payment to look after, too, but he never had an envelope for that. And now the Camaro was all his, thought Eddie, and he felt a great whuff of pride in his chest, even though he couldn't drive his car right now. It was lucky Sylvia hadn't asked him about his Camaro. But then why would she? Sylvia wasn't much interested in cars, which always surprised Eddie, because of her job.

He'd had to get a loan to buy the Camaro—a bronze '81 Z-28 with a hatch roof, which was two removable glass panels. Sylvia went to the bank with him. He hadn't gotten things quite straight in his mind, though, not right away. He hadn't understood that he was supposed to put all this extra money in his bank account so that the bank could take it out to pay for his loan. And so when the bank poked around in his bank account looking for its money, it wasn't there. He got into trouble about that.

It started eating away at him, that damn loan. He hated the idea that he was driving around in this car that really wasn't his at all, but the damn bank's.

It happened there was a big snowstorm right about then,

and Eddie hired himself out as a snow shoveler. He worked hard at that, and he put in extra time at work, as much as they'd give him, and when the snow melted, he looked in the paper and got other kinds of work. He didn't do anything for months except work. All he had in his mind was paying the bank as fast as he could. And finally one day the loan was gone and the Camaro was his.

It wasn't just not really owning the car that had bothered him. It was also the fact that the bank could go snuffling around in his private account like they had. He was outraged to find this out. It was very very wrong. It was just as wrong as if his landlord had come downstairs and unlocked Eddie's door and snuffled around in Eddie's private stuff just because the landlord owned the house Eddie was living in.

He said this over and over to Sylvia, and finally she agreed that he was right. But she told him being right wasn't going to change anything: the bank was still going to poke around in his accounts if he owed them money.

So he decided to make damn sure never to owe them money again. From now on, he told Sylvia grimly, he'd save up his damn money until he had what he needed to buy stuff with.

"Even a house?" Sylvia had said with a grin.

But Eddie just looked disgusted at her, because what would he want with a house?

Sitting outside the girls' house with his notebook and pen, he'd thought it again: what would he ever want with a house? Too damn big. Too damn scary. Who the hell would ever want a whole house folded around them?

Eddie looked into the envelope marked "CIGARETTES." Now, here was a depressing state of affairs. He could only afford one package of cigarettes a week. That worked out to three smokes a day every day but Sunday, when he only got to have two. Which made him pretty damn mad.

This was partly what the fifty dollars in his PROJECTS envelope was for. Extra cigarettes. You couldn't stand watch for hours on end without having a few extra smokes to pass the time.

The MOVIES envelope contained forty-five dollars. That

was enough for three movies, including a small bag of popcorn and a diet Sprite every time. If he got real busy with the surveillance project, he might not be able to go to three movies, and then he could use some of that money for more smokes.

He put the lid on the shoe box and pushed it into the middle of the table. He held on to the edge of the tabletop and tilted his chair back so that it was resting on only its back legs. The shoe box was a symbol of peace and good order. He looked around the kitchen with a little sigh.

After a while he stood up and got a beer from the fridge. He went over to the TV set and turned it on, then went to the hook on the wall by the door and got the notebook and pen out of his jacket pocket. He sat down in a big stuffed chair that was covered with a plaid blanket. He put the beer on the coffee table and put his feet up next to it and opened the notebook.

There were just the three of them, no more. That much he'd found out.

Now he had to keep on watching the house until he'd figured out when they were all likely to be away at the same time. And then he'd go up to the door, carrying his repairman's toolbox, and get inside, one way or another, forcing the lock or breaking the window or something...

Commotion began occurring in Eddie's stomach. He closed the notebook, focused on the TV, and drank from his can of beer with one hand, while gently rubbing his gut with the other.

Chapter
Twenty-Six

*E*mma was asleep, dreaming. In her dream she became aware of place—bedroom—and of self—Emma in the bedroom, in the bed, covered up by the quilt, sleeping...

Gradually she drifted, in her dream, out of sleep and into wakefulness. She began hearing sounds—someone, somewhere, was crying. At first she thought it was a baby, then in her dream reminded herself that they didn't have any babies yet. And then she thought maybe it was an animal, and reminded herself that animals don't weep. Maybe it's me, then, she thought; maybe it's me weeping. But she was aware in her dream that her closed eyes were empty of tears.

The sound had been faraway. Now it got closer ... and a terrible cold thrill swept over Emma in her dream as she realized that it wasn't weeping at all she was hearing, but laughter. The laughter was becoming louder, moving nearer and nearer to her bed. Emma tried to open her eyes but couldn't: it was as though they'd been stuck shut with glue. She struggled to see through her forehead, or through the upper part of her cheeks, but couldn't. She began clawing at her face—trying to claw her eyes open—and the laughter was very close now, almost on top of her—

Emma's eyes flew open and she stared with them, seeing and not seeing, her heart beating fast and her hands all sweaty, clutched together between her breasts.

She was lying on her side, looking at the bedside table, seeing that the clock read 6:19.

She threw back the quilt and got up and went into the bathroom.

When she came out, she put on a robe and got a glass of orange juice from the kitchen, then climbed back into bed and sat there, leaning against two pillows, watching the light filter through the curtains that covered the French doors and the window.

She'd never had that dream before. Emma seldom dreamed at all—or at least she seldom remembered her dreams. She knew she must dream because everybody did; it was necessary for healthy sleep, necessary to have the kind of dreams that made your eyeballs move back and forth behind your closed lids. So she supposed she did it, all right, but just never remembered that she dreamed. Well, seldom. She knew she'd never dreamed that dream before.

It was no mystery to her, though, this nightmare she'd had. It was obviously a dream about when Charlie thought he'd wanted to shoot her. But it was upsetting to have that unfortunate event come slipping evilly back into her life. As if it weren't terrible enough that the man had disappeared, now bad memories of him had to start popping up her in her dreams. Emma felt she'd been ambushed, bushwhacked by a nightmare.

She noticed that her hands trembled a little, holding the glass of orange juice. She was aware of the silence in the bedroom. She began taking small, jerky glances around the room. What's going on? she thought, worried.

Of course I'm nervous, she told herself, and of course I understand why: I just had a damn nightmare, and it's taking me a while to readjust to the real world, that's all.

There was nothing on Charlie's night table but dust.

Nothing in the drawer but the gun. When had he moved it there? Before he left?

Of course before he left, she thought impatiently.

His closet was still stuffed with his clothes. At least it was as far as Emma knew; they'd all been there the last time she looked, all of his clothes except, of course, the ones he was wearing when he left.

But staring at the closet door, she became uncertain about this and visualized a lot of empty hangers.

Oh, shit, she thought angrily. She got out of bed, crossed the room, slid open the mirrored door to Charlie's closet, and, yes, his clothes were still there.

Of course they're still there, thought Emma. Did she think he'd sneaked back in the night to collect them?

She wondered: What are his plans for me?

She pushed the closet door closed and went back to bed.

He had worked everything out with the utmost care. Including her money supply. She hadn't thought about money at first. She'd had plenty of cash in her wallet and was, of course, preoccupied with Charlie, with worry and anguish...

It wasn't until she had to write a check, maybe it was for Bernie, or maybe for the phone bill—anyway, this focused her thinking upon money, and she was suddenly alarmed: what if he'd taken it all? So she hurried to the bank machine.

She inserted her card, and the machine blinked WELCOME and BIENVENUE and asked which language she preferred. Emma chose English and requested a balance, and then another balance. In the checking account there was $2,372.87. In the savings account there was $13,944.16. Emma looked after the household finances. She knew there was nothing missing from either account.

At first this had consoled her. She'd told herself that nobody goes off to start a new life without money. Charlie hadn't taken any money; ergo, he hadn't gone off to start a new life. He'd probably killed himself, she'd thought, feeling reckless with Charlie's life, feeling impatient about Charlie's life, wanting to put him somewhere in her mind—in her past, in her memories?—wanting to get him out of the way.

He wasn't dead, though, she thought now, drinking orange juice in tiny sips, holding the glass in both hands, with the quilt drawn up almost to her chin. She knew that because of her dream.

They'd had a crisis that night; there was no question about it. But everything had turned out fine. Better than fine. Well. In fact, very well indeed. They'd talked, and she'd comforted him, and he'd apologized, and she'd admitted her faults too and resolved to be an even better wife. And then they'd gotten on with things, with life, with their marriage. She'd tried to persuade Charlie to get some therapy, but he'd resisted—gently, and lovingly, but firmly. And Emma had to admit that as it turned out, he hadn't needed it.

She remembered the feel of his head pressed against her, the heat generated by his body; she felt it on her hands, and on her breasts, and the shudder, and the tears.

And before that ...

Emma set the glass down hard and got out of bed. She whipped jeans and a sweater from her closet, socks and underwear from a drawer, and took her clothes into the bathroom and turned on the shower. She pulled off her nightgown and stepped out of her panties.

And then, suddenly, she had no energy. There was no strength in her muscles; her bones had turned to rubber. Emma let herself sit down on the edge of the tub...

She saw the gun barrel clearly, moving spasmodically through the air, as if Charlie's arm were twitching. What if he misses? she'd thought. What'll he do if he misses? What if it doesn't kill me? What if it kills part of my brain and leaves part of it alive? It won't hurt if it hits my brain, she'd thought, because the brain doesn't feel pain...

All these thoughts she'd had. It amazed her, remembering, that, paralyzed with terror, she'd had any thoughts at all.

"Charlie," she'd said to him. "Charlie." Soft and gentle. Saying his name. Saying—what? "Don't?" "Good-bye?" "I love you?" Anyway. Saying his name.

And he'd lowered the gun.

And then she realized she was lying in a puddle of her own urine.

Emma stood up and went over to the bathroom door and locked it. Today, she decided, she would have every single lock in the house changed.

Chapter Twenty-Seven

assandra Mitchell drove to work on Friday, the first of
May, through a brilliant morning, breezy and fragrant.
The window was open, and her hair was blowing around
her face. She felt recklessly happy, for no reason at all except
that it was spring. And because she was happy, she felt slim
and supple and full of grace. Maybe even attractive. Oh, hell,
she thought modestly, let's face it, I *am* attractive.

She slowed and stopped to let a pair of elderly women
cross the street; they waved a greeting, and she smiled, waving
back, feeling good, like a useful and even important part of the
community. She'd miss that if she left. But she'd find it again,
she told herself, in another small town, or in a big-city neighborhood.

She drove past a young man who was painting the exterior
of a shop that professed to sell antiques. He wore cutoffs and
sneakers and a bright orange eyeshade. His bare back was
smooth and already becoming tanned. She admired his broad
shoulders, and observed the slimness of his hips. One leg sup-
ported all his weight; the other was bent, resting. Under his
arms she saw tufts of dark hair. It would be a simple, natural
thing for anybody, Cassandra thought, of either sex, to fall in
love with such a body. She wheeled around the corner,
indulging herself for a moment in a delicious sexual fantasy

having to do with beautiful male bodies and seawater the color of emeralds and a hot deserted beach with a big swing suspended from the branch of an arbutus tree. She wondered about Karl's sexual fantasies. If he had any, he sure didn't share them with her.

She parked the car, let herself into the library and locked the door behind her. She had some paperwork to do in the two hours remaining before the library opened.

The place had a lot of windows—one whole wall was made of glass—and Cassandra felt furtive in there with the CLOSED sign on the door. She tiptoed around like an intruder, watering the fig trees and the ferns, wishing she couldn't be seen by people passing by.

Suddenly there was a loud banging on the window. Cassandra whirled around to see a face crushed hard against the glass. His features were deformed by the pressure but she recognized the spiky hair and the red-and-black-checked jacket. "No!" she said sternly, waving her hand in energetic dismissal. "Go away."

He pushed harder on the glass. His upper lip flattened to reveal his gums, his nose squashed itself almost flat.

"Peter," said Cassandra loudly. "The library's not open yet. Go away."

He beat his fists against the glass. She heard him weeping.

"You can't come in until ten o'clock," she said sternly.

He began to moan, and turned around, leaning against the window, and banged the back of his head, slowly, again and again, on the glass.

"Peter, I'm going to call the police again," she yelled at him. "Go away. Beat it. I don't want you here."

Suddenly he slumped; his entire body sagged, she thought he might collapse in a boneless heap on the sidewalk. But he didn't. He drooped off down the street without a backward glance.

Cassandra took refuge in the windowless office behind the counter and put on a pot of coffee.

She was used to people using the library as shelter, people who lived alone—maybe some of them didn't live anywhere at all, although she didn't like to consider that possibility. She told herself it was very unlikely there were homeless people in Sechelt. But there certainly were people who, for whatever reason, sought out the library more for its warmth, sociability, and comfortable chairs than for the reading material it offered. Cassandra didn't mind this. She considered it one of the services the library provided, no less useful because it was inadvertent.

Peter had started out as one of these people. A middle-aged man on welfare whose brain didn't work like other people's, who had nothing to do with his days. He was lonely and wistful, and Cassandra had welcomed him at first—not making too much of it, asking him what he liked to read and helping him find easy things he could manage, pleased to see him become absorbed.

But then she'd noticed him watching her. He held an open book in two hands, but his eyes weren't on the book, they were following Cassandra; he wasn't even bothering to turn the page now and then, just for show.

She began to pay him less attention.

One day he came in holding a piece of cardboard and held it up for her to read the message printed there: "I love you." And things had gone from bad to worse.

She did call the police, from time to time, when his attentions became insistent, but there wasn't much they could do. They escorted him home, but he often just came back again and took up residence on the sidewalk across the street for a while, in front of the real estate office, squatting there with his legs splayed apart, elbows on his knees, fists supporting his chin, staring over at the library until the manager of the real estate office came out and sent him packing.

Cassandra sat at her desk and picked up a stack of file folders. She looked at the wall and held the files close to her chest. She felt as though something ominous had occurred and wondered if she was having a premonition—even though she didn't believe in premonitions. At least she thought she didn't. She lamented all her laziness, all the thoughtful things she'd left undone: the grit of insufficiency, she thought, is clogging up my motor. It was living in a small town that was doing it. Living in a city would be a lot better for her. Less is required of one's neighbor in a big city, and anonymity is easily achieved.

Peter hadn't come back, when she opened the library. If she was lucky, he'd forget about her for the rest of the day.

Phyllis Dempter bustled in with an armful of books just before noon. By that time the volunteer had arrived, and Cassandra allowed herself to be dragged off for lunch at Earl's Café. Afterward she and Phyllis walked along the beach for a while, and Phyllis tried to get Cassandra to talk about Alberg.

"It's because of me that you met him, after all," she argued. "Therefore you owe me periodic updates." Cassandra and Alberg had met through the "Companions" section of *The Vancouver Sun*, where Cassandra, at Phyllis's urging, had placed an ad. "So? How're things going? Are you two going to get married, or what?"

Cassandra sat down on a log and scooped up a handful of sand and let it trickle through her fingers. "Believe me, Phyllis, there is nothing to tell. Nothing."

She looked up at her friend, shading her eyes with her hand. Phyllis had let her blonde hair grow and was wearing it in a chignon. She looked elegant and dissatisfied. Cassandra knew she was feeling even more restless than usual these days, since her youngest child had left home.

"What makes you think I'd even want to get married?"

Phyllis sat down next to her. "I don't, particularly. But usually, when you're seeing a guy for as long as you've been seeing Karl, usually something happens, something develops. You don't just, you know, tread water, year after year."

Cassandra gazed out across Trail Bay. "You're right," she said after a while. "Treading water. That's what it is, all right." Regret raced swiftly across her heart, catching her by surprise. She got up, wrapping her sunglasses across her eyes to hide her tears. "I think I have to take some action, Phyllis. Oh, dear." She bowed her head, and Phyllis put her arms around her.

"Oh, Cassandra, I didn't mean to upset you. Don't. Stop crying. Please. Oh, now look, I'm doing it too... "

Chapter
Twenty-Eight

O ne day when she and Charlie had been married for almost two years, Emma was loading the washing machine when she became aware of perfume. Startled, she turned swiftly around to see who had come into the laundry room so silently: but there was no one.

Emma lifted Charlie's white shirt to her face and sniffed.

She was looking out the window in the top of the laundry room door, and she saw that there were flakes of snow in the air, drifting lazily down. If the snow started falling thickly, she thought, Charlie would call to say he wouldn't be coming home, that he'd stay in a hotel somewhere. She watched the snowflakes, the white shirt pressed to her face, and as she watched, they stopped falling.

"Emma? I'm home."

Emma waited for him in the kitchen. She heard the hall closet open and close. She heard him move down the hall and into the bedroom, then the living room. A few minutes later he appeared with a glass of scotch, looking for ice.

"Hi," he said, smiling at her.

"Charlie, are you having an affair?"

He looked at her quickly, and Emma fancied she saw guilt oozing from his pores, along with a considerable amount of self-satisfaction. She waited for his denial. She imagined it would be forceful and in some way accusatory: she was prepared to deal with that.

"How did you find out?" said Charlie.

Emma blinked through her shock. "Who is it?"

"Nobody you know."

"But who is it?"

"It doesn't matter."

Emma, unsteady, wanted to sit down, but instead she pressed her left hand against the refrigerator for support. "Doesn't matter?" She was incredulous. "Doesn't matter?" She gazed into Charlie's face. He was physically very close to her, yet the distance between them seemed vast. Emma struggled for words. "Of course it matters. It's extremely important, in fact. It—who she is, that—that defines my problem."

"No," said Charlie. "No, it doesn't, Emma." He was looking at her gently now, and politely, suffering patiently through her pain.

"Do you love her?" said Emma, her voice sounding comically strangled.

"Love her?" said Charlie. "No."

"Why do you sound surprised?"

"I'm not—I don't know. Did I sound surprised?"

Emma couldn't stand to look at him anymore. "I'm going out," she said abruptly. She thought he might try to prevent her, but he didn't.

She drove aimlessly along the highway, and when she got to Gibsons, she went into a café and sat there drinking coffee and measuring the length and breadth of her humiliation. She considered catching the last ferry from Langdale and spending the night with Lorraine, who could be counted on for sympathy and support because she'd never liked Charlie. But Emma didn't want Lorraine to know about Charlie's faithlessness.

She drove home slowly, through the snow that had begun falling again, thinking about what to do, how to handle the situation. When she got there, Charlie was in bed, asleep. Pretending to be asleep, probably. Emma had a long, hot bath. By the time she climbed into bed, Charlie's slumber was real.

Before she and Charlie got married, Emma had bought and

read just about every book there was about being a spouse. She was studying, preparing for her new life. Now she hauled the books out again and pored over them with grim concentration. She was particularly concerned with the sections that dealt with infidelity. Two years ago she had skimmed these chapters, so certain had she been of Charlie. Her simplemindedness took her breath away.

As Emma interpreted what she read, adultery was something for which she ought definitely to have been prepared. She concluded—not pleased to do so—that if she'd been properly alert to Charlie's unconscious signaling, she could have prevented this awful thing from happening.

But despite her stupidity, her marriage was apparently by no means a lost cause. There were, she read, things she could do that would effectively put the whole shabby enterprise behind her.

She would throw herself more devotedly than ever into being Charlie's wife, and would say no more about his affair.

And that's exactly what she'd done. She'd ignored it. Wiped it from her mind. Soldiered on as though adultery had never occurred. Never mentioned it again.

"Charlie got the wrong idea about you," said Lorraine on Sunday.

Emma hadn't discussed Charlie's infidelity with Lorraine, but now, four years later, she could hardly conceal his disappearance.

"Because of that damn play you were in," said Lorraine.

Emma had done all sorts of extracurricular things at college. Not in a helter-skelter fashion, but calculatedly. It was important, she'd decided, not to become involved in anything she'd have to merely pretend to enjoy. She could be trapped into doing it all her life, if it happened to be the thing that brought her together with her future husband. She avoided athletics, therefore. And the chess club. And the various activities having to do with computers.

She ended up being stuck, almost by default, with the arts. She found it pleasant, though, to sit in the music department's recital hall listening to people sing or play instruments. It was diverting to attend exhibits of work done by art students. And she liked going to plays. When one day she saw a poster in the Student Union Building inviting people to audition for parts in the Players' Club production of something called *Crimes of the Heart*, she thought, Why not? And was astonished when she ended up playing one of the three leading roles.

"Why did he get the wrong idea about me?" she asked Lorraine. "Because I shot my husband in the stomach?"

Lorraine shook her head and stubbed out her cigarette. "Because you talked in that fake Southern accent and looked pretty and helpless."

Emma frowned. "I *was* pretty. And helpless."

Lorraine hooted. "Also," she went on, linking her hands behind her head, "it was a big part, and he probably thought you were a serious actress."

"I wasn't very good, though."

"No, but you could have been serious without being good yet, couldn't you? So maybe Charlie thought he was marrying an artist."

Emma was becoming depressed. "You mean, and then when he knew better, he was disappointed."

"Yeah. Maybe."

Emma stood up and went to the window. Lorraine lived not far from the university, where she went to summer school every year to upgrade her teaching certificate. Emma liked Dunbar Street. It was a busy street, full of little shops and restaurants and gas stations and low-rise apartment buildings and every so often a supermarket. Emma rested her forehead against the glass and looked out at the bright spring evening.

"I hardly miss him, you know. His things are there; it's easy to pretend he's at work, or out doing something, and any minute he'll be home. Even in bed . . . "

Lorraine laughed softly, from her Swedish lounging chair.

A young woman came out of the fitness place across the street, wearing shorts and a sleeveless T-shirt, a gym bag slung across her shoulders. She unlocked her bicycle, put on her helmet, swung onto the seat, and rode off, merging smoothly with the traffic. Emma marveled at her confidence, the way she acted as if she and her bicycle belonged on the street with all those cars and trucks, and she admired the tautness of the young girl's calves and thighs, and the speed and purposeful-ness with which she pedaled out of sight.

Emma turned from the window. "Maybe I'll move back to the city."

"Think again." Lorraine reached for her cigarettes and lighter. "This used to be a nice quiet part of town. There've been four burglaries and two places set on fire—all in the last six months." She lit a cigarette and emptied her glass, which had contained scotch and water. "Besides. You want Charlie to know where to find you, don't you?"

Emma sat down on the edge of a loveseat and smoothed her dress over her thighs. It was badly creased, because it was linen. Why did people wear linen, anyway? Why was she stu-pid enough to keep on buying things made of linen when she knew very well that they would always look as if she'd slept in them.

"Do you really think he's likely to come back?" Emma was surprised at how angry she sounded.

Lorraine shrugged.

"Do you think one day I'll pick up the phone," Emma went on, "and it'll be him? Or answer the doorbell—he'd have to ring the bell, even if he kept his keys, because I've had the locks changed." At least if he did come back, she thought, he wouldn't be bringing that damn gun to point at her head again. She had the gun now.

"I don't know, Emma. Personally, I don't know why you'd want him back."

Emma looked at her, thinking. Lorraine was tall, lanky, and untidy, with a generous amount of thick brown hair, almond-shaped brown eyes, and in summer a sprinkling of freckles across her cheekbones. Today she was wearing pull-on khaki-colored shorts and a gray T-shirt that said "Vancouver" in elec-tric blue letters. A couple of her fingers were stained with ciga-rette smoke. She was barefoot.

"*Do* you want him back?"

"He probably threw his house keys away," said Emma. "Into the dumpster, with my picture."

"What dumpster?" Lorraine sounded exasperated now.

"What picture?"

"There's a man trying to find Charlie for me. A policeman. But he's only doing it as a favor. Will you talk to him?"

"What do you mean, he's doing it as a favor?"

"I guess I'll have to pay him. He's not doing it as his job, that's what I mean. If a person goes away because he wants to, you can't get the police to go after him."

"Jesus, Emma. What a dork he is, that Charlie." She looked into Emma's face. "Are you in a lot of pain?"

Emma thought there ought to be more to friendship than whatever existed between her and Lorraine. They had met at university, in an English class, and Lorraine had introduced Emma to Charlie, whom she'd known for most of her life. This had been enough to forge something between them, but it was an odd relationship. Emma thought Lorraine continued it at least partly out of guilt for having gotten her and Charlie together, even though that's what Emma had wanted.

"Of course I'm in pain."

She needed Lorraine, Emma realized. She was practically the only friend she had.

My god, she thought, gazing at Lorraine—who had friends and colleagues and parents and brothers and sisters-in-law and two nephews and a niece—how did this happen? How did I get to be so alone?

She left Lorraine's apartment in the early evening and drove to a small apartment house, a four-plex, on West Seventh Avenue. She looked at the name of the letter box for apartment 1 and saw that it had changed.

But she had to be absolutely sure.

Emma rang the bell for the caretaker and made her inquiry.

"Oh, Helena moved out months ago," said the caretaker, a large woman with tightly permed gray hair. "In the summer."

"Did she leave a forwarding address?"

"Yeah, sure, but I can't remember what the hell it was now, at this late date."

"But—it was somewhere else in the city, was it?"

"Hell, no. She went home to her folks. Someplace in Saskatchewan."

A nagging weight lifted from Emma's heart. "Thank you," she said with a luminous smile.

Chapter
Twenty-Nine

Ray Knudson leaned across the counter of the restaurant he owned with his wife, Frieda. "What an awful thing," he said, almost in a whisper so as not to be overheard by the red-haired man in the beige jacket who was reading a newspaper three stools away.

Kathy nodded.

"I still can't believe it," said Ray, who was tall and bony, with very wide shoulders and no hips. "I feel like it was my fault, you know?" He was wearing an apron with a bib. "I mean, she wouldn't have been out on the street at that hour, except she was on her way here, you know?" His long brown hair was pulled back sleek and clean and secured with an elastic band.

"It wasn't your fault, Ray," said Kathy.

"I know it. But it *feels* like it was." He reached under the counter for a small cardboard box. "Here's her stuff." She took the box from him and headed toward the door. "We really miss her," he said quietly.

Kathy looked through the restaurant's glass door at the post office across the street. People were hurrying in and out—it looked very busy over there, almost as if it were Christmastime. Kathy counted the months between today and Christmas and wondered if it was enough time in which to get over the death of a friend.

"Yeah. Me too," she said, and went out onto the street.

She walked home, through a neighborhood that during the last three years had become as familiar as the one in which she'd grown up. She liked this. It was good to feel comfortable in a house, a neighborhood, that was unknown to her family. Having one's own neighborhood, she thought, verified one's independence.

She walked down the street, the box casually nestled in the crook of her arm, and gazed upon the establishments she frequented: the dry cleaner, the bakery, the hardware store, the convenience store that sold almost nothing but flowers.

Then the ache was there again, twisting in the back of her throat—the ache of mourning.

And she thought that she probably wouldn't be going to Ray's café anymore. Probably none of them would.

For the first time Kathy acknowledged that she might not continue to live here—in this neighborhood, in that house. Even if the three of them carried on with the original plan for the summer—and that wasn't certain, they were all mulling it over—but even if they did, who was to say whether they'd be back here in the fall?

Kathy walked on to end of the block and then stopped and carefully leaned her body against the corner of the gourmet coffee store. Her day-to-day life seemed to consist of nothing but a series of shocks. Of course, she'd never had anybody die on her before. It was probably totally normal that the world went out of joint for a while when a person you cared about died. But if you weren't prepared for it, you could get pretty shook up. Kathy staggered through each day bewildered and tense, with an arm raised, metaphorically speaking, against the new blows that she knew would fall.

People walked past her, and some of them she recognized, but most of them she didn't. For the most part, they ignored her, which was soothing.

Kathy closed her eyes and rested, her bum and her knapsack and the back of her head pressed against the concrete wall of the coffee store. You'd think the news would have swept everywhere by now, into every little nook and cranny of the neighborhood. The police had investigated—they'd treated it like the serious crime it was. Kathy had thought everyone in the whole city must have known what happened. But the woman in the bakery had asked just two days ago where Melanie was, and the harassed young mother down the street had come over last night, looking for Melanie to babysit, and mail was still coming for her, and phone calls, too. She wasn't erased; she hadn't been expunged; traces of Melanie remained, little bits of her continued to trail through Kathy's days. A little bit of Melanie had gotten woven permanently into Kathy's life; a little bit of her had become part of Kathy herself. And Kathy liked that. But it hurt too.

She opened her eyes. A big man with red hair was standing on the sidewalk across the street, staring at her intensely. Now this was the kind of stuff she meant. I go all weird, she thought, and start falling asleep against buildings, causing people to stop and stare at me. Flustered, she pushed herself away form the wall and adjusted the straps of her knapsack. When she glanced back at him, the man was gone.

Kathy trudged around the corner and headed for home. It was a cloudy day, cool and fragrant, the kind of day against which spring blossoms glow most brightly, in the absence of competition from the sun. Kathy walked home through the quiet afternoon thinking about decisions that had to be made, and as she approached the house she walked more and more slowly.

She stood on the sidewalk in front of the laurel hedge, holding the box, which was so light she'd barely been aware of it, carrying it all this way. She stood with her weight on one foot, looking down at the cracks in the sidewalk. She was wearing jeans, tucked into hiking boots, and a long long sweater, wine colored. She felt as if she were about to set off on a journey.

She pushed her hair away from her face and looked up and down the block. Some of the ornamental plum trees were still blooming, but most of the petals had fallen to the ground. Across the street, Mrs. Garber's huge rhododendron bush was smothered in ivory-colored blooms. Kathy had been staring at it admiringly one day, the first spring she'd lived here, and

Mrs. Garber had come outside and told her what it was, and that it was more than fifty years old. She was the only person on the block who'd lived in her house ever since it was built; most of the houses in this part of town had been renovated and turned into rental accommodations—the house Kathy lived in, for instance, contained three suites, one on each floor. Kathy was fond of Mrs. Garber. She thought about going over there right now and inviting herself in for a cup of coffee.

Instead, she turned and went through the gap in the hedge.

There was a big climbing rose at the front of the house. It grew upon a trellis between the porch and one of the main-floor windows. It was so old that its stem was as thick as the trunk of a small tree. Once a year the owner of the house sent somebody around to cut it back, and the apple tree in the back-yard, as well. Kathy noticed dozens of rosebuds, as she climbed onto the porch and fitted her key in the lock. It was amazing that the thing went on blooming like mad, year after year, when nobody paid it any attention at all.

She went into what had been Melanie's room and put the box from the restaurant on the bed. Then she joined her room-mates in the kitchen, which was at the back of the house, next to the large bedroom Sandy and Caroline shared.

"I think we should go," she told them. "Just like we planned."

"Yeah," said Sandy wearily. "That's what we figure too."

"I mean, lotsa luck finding anything else to do, at this late date," said Caroline.

"Good," said Kathy with relief. "That's settled, then." She poured herself some coffee. "I'm going to finish packing up Melanie's stuff." They had offered to take her things home to her parents.

An hour later Sandy and Caroline left to get some take-out food. Kathy sat, exhausted, on the edge of Melanie's bed and looked at the room's bare walls. Large clean rectangles indicat-ed where her movie posters had hung. Surrounded by boxes filled with Melanie's belongings, Kathy couldn't find Melanie anywhere. Eventually she got a felt pen from the kitchen and printed Melanie's name in big red letters on each of the boxes.

She was putting the cap back on the pen when she heard

the mailman climb the steps and make his deliveries.

Kathy smoothed Melanie's mattress and left the room, closing the door gently behind her.

She went into her bedroom, undressed, and put on a robe. Then she remembered the mail and stepped out on the porch to check the box, but it was empty. She glanced at the other two boxes, both stuffed full, and stood there frowning for a moment, puzzled.

Kathy had a quick bath and put on clean jeans and underwear and the same wine-colored sweater. She was in the kitchen setting out plates and cutlery when her roommates returned with dinner. Caroline put the bag on the counter, and Sandy tossed the mail onto the table.

Kathy stared at it. "Where'd you get this?"

"Would you believe, the mailbox?" said Sandy, leafing through the envelopes. "Shit, another one for Melanie." She dropped it into a box on the counter.

"I looked before," said Kathy. "There wasn't any."

"I guess he hadn't come yet," said Caroline, taking a barrel of chicken out of the bag.

"No, he'd come; I heard him."

"Maybe ours got put in one of the other boxes by mistake," said Caroline, removing a box of French fries and then another.

"No," said Kathy loudly.

Her roommates turned to her. "What's the matter?" said Sandy.

"I heard him. That's what—" Kathy waved a handful of forks in the air. "I *knew* there was something weird. I heard him open the boxes, all of them."

She remembered it vividly: Here's the mailman, she'd thought as she heard the first box being opened...and then she'd chastised herself for having thought mail*man*. Even though she knew that the person who delivered their mail was, in fact, a man, she tried always to use terms that were not gender specific. Mailperson, she'd thought, as the second box was opened. Or maybe we should just call them letter carriers, like the post office does, she'd thought, listening for the third box... and there it was—the metallic sound of the lid being lifted and the shuffling sound of mail being thrust inside.

She told her roommates this.

Sandy, bewildered, asked, "So what are you saying?"

"Jesus," said Caroline, staring at Kathy.

"Yeah," Kathy said, nodding. She looked through the mail and dropped it back on the table. "It doesn't look like it's been tampered with. I think somebody took it out of the box and looked at it and then put it back."

"But why, for god's sake?" said Sandy.

"Maybe they took something. How would we ever know?" said Caroline.

"We wouldn't," said Kathy.

Chapter Thirty

*A*lberg put the phone down after his seventeenth call of the morning and jotted some notes on a legal-size pad of lined yellow paper. He now knew that Charlie O'Brea was in good health; that he had not (at least under his true name) applied to renew his passport, changed his mailing address, booked an airline flight, or bought a train or a bus ticket; nor had he, since his disappearance, dipped into any bank accounts, charged anything on any of his several credit cards, gotten in touch with any of his friends, landed in the hospital, or gotten arrested. They still hadn't found his car.

Alberg put his mug of coffee on the dining room table, tossed the yellow pad next to it, and sat down. He took off his reading glasses, rubbed his eyes, and put the glasses back on. Charlie O'Brea was a thoroughly exasperating guy.

With Emma's help, Alberg had spent several hours going through Charlie's things. But apart from clothes, there was little in the house that was specifically his. Almost everything in the filing cabinet in the upstairs bedroom, for instance, had to do with the operation of the household. In the desk drawers Alberg found plain white stationery and office supplies and a pile of bills that Charlie had paid, but no personal letters, no address book, no old shopping lists or notes to himself or newspaper clippings—none of the fragments people usually strew behind them as they go through their days. Emma had said he'd had his briefcase with him when he left: that was where Alberg would expect him to keep an appointment book, address book, checkbook, business cards, so it wasn't surprising that these things hadn't been in the desk.

He'd also opened cardboard boxes in the basement that turned out to be full of books.

"Charlie was going to build floor-to-ceiling shelves," Emma explained. "In the upstairs bedroom. But he never got around to it."

And there was a trunk too. Emma found the key in a bureau drawer. "This is where he kept things from his childhood," she said, unlocking it, "and from his years at university."

Textbooks. Notebooks. Term papers. Yearbooks. Alberg went through them all.

He was convinced, sitting at his dining room table, drinking lukewarm coffee, that Charlie had been working on this plan for a long time. He'd taken great care to leave absolutely nothing behind that was personal, to remove everything from which any useful inferences might be drawn. And he'd done it slowly and cautiously, over time, so as not to attract Emma's attention.

Alberg consulted the list she'd given him. Today he would cover Charlie's partner and his lawyer, and if there was enough time, he'd try to see the person Emma said had introduced her to Charlie, at university.

Alberg put his reading glasses back in their case. The sun slanted through the wide windows of the sun porch and fell upon the kitchen floor and was inching tentatively into the dining room. Alberg, enjoying the quiet, found himself rubbing the surface of the table with the flat of his hand. He was very fond of this table. He'd spotted it at a used-furniture place in Sechelt shortly after he moved to the Sunshine Coast—a big, round, sturdy, pedestal table that looked like a table he remembered from his childhood. A single thick piece of oak was its top, and there were slats beneath, for additional support. His father would have liked it.

He drank more coffee, pleased with himself because he

hadn't had breakfast but already planning the big lunch he could have as a reward. He looked out the living room window into the sunny morning and knew his grass was growing, stealthily, and so were the hydrangea bushes and the roses, furtive and shifty, getting bigger and taller while he wasn't looking. But it was on his list—on one of his lists—to find somebody else to take care of all that so he could spend his free time sailing.

He'd narrowed down his choice of boats to three.

"Why don't you just go out and do it for pete's sake," Cassandra had said to him. She'd sounded unreasonably exasperated—it wasn't going to be her boat, after all. "I'm so tired of hearing you talk about it," she'd exclaimed. "When did you get so damn cautious?"

Alberg had been mulling that over ever since. He didn't like to think of himself as cautious. He liked to believe he had a wide streak of recklessness in him, and he had to keep a wary eye on it, lest it get him into trouble again.

He stood up and went to the window, taking his coffee along. Then he went outside and stood on the wobbly porch, looking at the fence, virtually collapsed, smothered by the hydrangeas. The air was fresh and fragrant, and after a while he wandered out of his yard and looked down at Gibsons, lying like a toy village at the bottom of the hill. He found this panorama of town, water, and distant mountains soothing to his soul.

He heard the phone ringing, and even as he considered not answering it, he was on his way back into the house.

"Alberg," he said.

"Martin," said his mother.

"What's the matter? Are you all right?"

"Of course I'm all right."

Alberg sat down on the kitchen stool.

"I've had an idea," said his mother, "and I wanted to discuss it with you."

"Okay. Fine. What?"

"I've been thinking of opening up a bed and breakfast place."

"What, in your house?" He was incredulous.

"Of course in the house, Martin, where else?" There was a pause. "You don't like the idea."

"No, I don't like the idea, right, I don't. Why? You aren't going to be short of money, are you?"

"No, I'm fine for money. It's just—I want to be doing something, Martin."

"Well, but what about—I don't know, volunteer work. Listen, we've got a group here, mostly volunteers, who work with victims of crime. There must be something like it in London. I could phone around for you..."

"Martin, for goodness sake. I've been running my own life for a lot of years now. I don't need any help from you."

Alberg sat back, leaning against the kitchen wall. "You're right." Something cool and metallic, like water from melting snow, began trickling through him; he didn't know its source, but he knew it was something not new; it was something returning. "What *do* you need from me, Mother?"

"I need you to know this is what I want to do, and to understand why, and to accept it." She hesitated. "I had a dream, you see."

"Well, then," said Alberg softly, "of course I understand."

A young woman sat at a desk in the middle of the reception area behind a raised counter on which stood a small sign that read NOLA KING.

Alberg, introducing himself, noticed a glass jar half-filled with the gold dollar coins known as Loonies sitting on her desk.

"It's for the Christmas party," said Nola King, smiling. She looked even younger than Alberg's daughters, who were in their mid-twenties. "Last year we collected five hundred dollars in that jar."

"And what about that?" said Alberg, reaching down across the counter to indicate the fishbowl sitting beside her computer screen. "Is that business cards in there?"

She nodded. "I collect them. For my bathroom walls."

He was still marveling at this when Peter Carlson hurried into the reception area and escorted Albert to his office.

"This isn't anything official," Alberg began. "I've got some time on my hands, and I've agreed to try to get a little more information for Mrs. O'Brea."

"It's very embarrassing," said Carlson. "I had no idea he—well, all I knew was that he'd decided to leave the firm. I didn't know he was going to..."

"I know, Mr. Carlson."

"It was—I wish I'd had something to tell Emma."

"Maybe something's occurred to you since she was here?" said Alberg hopefully.

Carlson shook his head. He was wearing a dark blue suit with a white shirt and a red-and-white striped tie and black shoes, highly polished. He looked genuinely distressed. "We weren't close, Charlie and I. But the partnership worked very well. I had no reason to believe he was discontented."

"What did he tell you about why he was leaving?"

"He said—I think he didn't want to hurt my feelings. It dawned on me as he was talking that maybe he'd never been as enthusiastic about the work as I'd thought he was. Because he looked so completely different when he said he was leaving. Very—bright. Happy, I guess you'd say."

"But he didn't tell you what he was going to do?"

"No. I asked him, of course. He said he hadn't decided yet."

"Did you believe that?"

Carlson shook his head. "No. I think he knew, all right."

"He gave you a month's notice, Emma says."

"That's right."

"Not much time to extricate yourself from a partnership."

"No. It put a strain on things. But he was very restless. Like he'd made up his mind suddenly, and now he just wanted to get it done. So I accommodated him." He shrugged. "What else could I do?"

"What did you notice during that last month?" said Alberg. "Was he on the phone a lot? Did he take time off? Get personal mail?"

"No, he worked just like always. Did an exemplary job for us right up to the last day. The only thing was, he told me that he didn't want a going-away party, or a gift, or even an after-work drink with the staff; he made that very plain."

159

"Probably because you would naturally have involved Emma in anything like that."

"I guess so," said Carlson.

"Tell me what you know about his personal life. What did he like to do? What did he talk about, when you weren't discussing work?"

"Let's see." Carlson gazed through his office window, absentmindedly clicking the push button of the ballpoint pen he held in his right hand. "He liked music. He'd often stay in town overnight to go to a concert. Sometimes a play—he liked the theater too. Now, this isn't lately—he hasn't done it that much lately. But up to, I don't know, a few months ago, maybe a year, he'd do this a couple of times a month."

"With his wife?"

"Usually, yes, Emma would meet him here."

"But not in the last year?"

"Right. I think that's right."

"Were there any other changes in the last year?"

Carlson slowly nodded. "Yes. He was a little less talkative. A little less forthcoming. He did as much work as ever, but he took more time off too."

"To do what?"

"I don't know. He never did talk much about his private life. And not at all, lately. We didn't have a close personal relationship, although we liked each other."

Alberg looked down at his notebook, dissatisfied. "What did the guy do, Mr. Carlson, besides work and go to plays? Did he do sports? Did he read? Did he—I don't know, collect things?"

"He played chess." Carlson looked surprised. "I forgot all about that. I think he belonged to a chess club. And sometimes he'd go over to Park Royal at lunchtime and get involved in a game there."

"How come you forgot about it? Was this another thing he'd stopped doing?"

"Yes," said Carlson, nodding.

Alberg sighed. "Okay." He closed his notebook and stood up. "Thanks for your time. I'll see myself out."

In the reception area he stopped and gazed thoughtfully at

the fishbowl. He waited while the receptionist dealt with an incoming call. Then he said, "Tell me again what you do with those business cards, Miss King."

"Well, when the bowl gets full," she said, scribbling on a phone message slip, "I take it home, and I take all the old cards off my bathroom walls, and I put the new ones up." She put the message into a cubbyhole beneath the counter. "It's a very small bathroom, and two whole walls are covered in tile, so it's only two walls, really."

"And where do they come from? Where do you get them?"

"Well, everybody contributes. It's amazing how many people have business cards. And they're always handing them out. So I asked the people in the office if they'd give me the ones they don't want. So they all drop cards in here. Mr. Carlson and Jennie, the secretary, Mr. O'Brea—"

"When did you empty it last?"

"I don't know, let me think. Three, four months ago?"

Alberg looked into the bowl. There had to be a hundred damn cards in there, he thought. "Miss King—would it be all right if I borrowed this fishbowl? Just for a few days?"

Alberg had lunch at a restaurant in Park Royal and made some inquiries around the chessboard on the second level, but nobody was there who remembered Charlie O'Brea.

O'Brea's lawyer had an office on Marine Drive in Dundarave, a few miles west of Park Royal. Alberg saw her at four o'clock.

As soon as he got out of her office, he phoned Emma and arranged to see her when he got back to Sechelt.

She made tea, and they took their cups outside and sat at the picnic table on the patio. Alberg reported what he'd learned from the lawyer: Charlie had removed his wife as beneficiary from his insurance policies and removed her from his will. But he'd left a document with the lawyer that turned over the house, the contents of the house, and the contents of the joint bank accounts to Emma. The lawyer had been instructed to inform Emma of these matters on Friday, May 8: Alberg had persuaded her to release the information, under the circumstances, four days early.

Emma received the news in silence. Her gaze was fixed on the enormous cedar tree that stood in the back corner of the yard. "Pretty soon I'll have to get a job," she said after a while. She glanced at Alberg. "But that won't be a bad thing."

He thought she looked more melancholy than anguished, more thoughtful than outraged. "Peter Carlson says Charlie changed, about a year ago," he said. "Stopped going to plays and things. Had less to say. Started taking some time off. Have you any idea why?"

Emma looked at him for a long time but said nothing.

"What happened a year ago?"

"It was—inconsequential," she said at last.

"You better tell me anyway."

"Charlie became very upset."

Alberg waited, but she apparently had nothing more to say. "Why?"

"He was having—he got to a crisis point, you might say, in his life."

"A crisis point."

"That's right."

"Uh huh. What precipitated this crisis?"

"Well, I don't know, do I? It wasn't my crisis, it was Charlie's."

"How did he behave, what were his—symptoms?"

Emma stood up and brushed energetically at her plaid skirt. She wore a red sweater with it and loafers and navy blue tights. She pushed her hair away from her face. "He got very irritable, extremely irritable, I couldn't do anything right, everything I did was wrong—" She sat down again.

"And?"

"What do you mean, 'and'?"

"You were going to say something else."

"No I wasn't. That's it." She poured herself more tea.

Alberg doodled in his notebook. He drew a tree and made it into something resembling an arbutus and added a rocky beach and the sea.

"And one day we had a big fight," she said. "And then we talked for a long time, and each of us agreed to do certain things and we did them." She raised her hands. "And—and things were fine again. Better than fine. They were very good. Wonderful."

"So wonderful that he's run away from you."

Her face flushed. "Right. That's right. Obviously, something was going on that I wasn't aware of." She was so rigid she was almost trembling.

"Emma—I have to ask you this."

"You want to know if there was somebody else," she said quickly. She shook her head. "No."

"You sound very sure of that."

"I am. Very sure."

She wouldn't keep anything from Alberg, no matter how small, no matter how disgraceful, if it might help him find Charlie. But she certainly had no intention of telling him embarrassing things that couldn't possibly be relevant, no desire whatsoever to wave her dirty laundry around in front of his eyes.

She smiled at him. "More tea, Mr. Alberg?"

Chapter
Thirty-One

*K*arl Alberg got in touch with Emma again, by telephone, late Tuesday afternoon. She had remembered
to tell him about Charlie's retirement savings plan and
the Canada Savings Bonds, and he'd been to see the O'Breas'
bank manager again. Now he told Emma that Charlie had
cashed in the R.S.P., which was worth seventy-five thousand
dollars, and instead of rolling over the bonds, which had
matured in March, Charlie had cashed them, too. For a total of
one hundred and twenty-five thousand dollars.

When Emma got off the phone, she went into the bathroom
and turned on the taps in the tub. She undressed and got out
clean nightclothes. It was only five o'clock, but she was ending
her day.

Half an hour later she lay in her bath, immersed in bubbles,
breathing fragrant steam. Someday she would have a big bathroom, a huge bathroom. There would be a large window made
of glass blocks, and beneath it she'd have a long, narrow, mar-
ble-topped table with several plants on it. There would be a
chaise longue, too. And the tub would be placed diagonally
within an enormous square of porcelain, providing a wide
ledge for Emma's wineglass and whatever book she might be
reading. She would place white pottery candlelabra, each holding three white candles, in two corners of the square, and

maybe another plant or two in another one, beneath a second, smaller, glass-block window.

It would have a separate shower stall, too, and a towel cupboard, and two dressing tables that would take up almost a whole wall.

No, not two dressing tables. One.

Wherever Charlie was, he had one hundred and twenty-five thousand dollars with him. Emma figured he could live for quite a while on that, without having to get a job, without having to lift a finger.

It was a relief, she thought, soaping her arms, to have Karl Alberg looking for Charlie. Emma had to admit that her chances of finding him were not good without the help of somebody who knew something about this kind of thing.

After a while Emma stood up, reached for the folded towel she'd left on the toilet seat, and dried herself while the water slurped away down the drain. Then she tossed the towel aside and studied herself in the mirror behind the sink. She moved this way and that. She struck poses. Finally, she gathered her hair on top of her head with both hands. She acknowledged the loveliness of her uplifted arms, the swell of her breasts, the flatness of her stomach, the sweet surge of her hips. It is not because of my body, she thought, that he left me....

She held out her hands and looked at them. Charlie had always admired her hands. He'd said she had a nurse's fingernails.

She always put a few drops of her favorite perfume in the steam iron, before she pressed her sweaters.

She always made sure to apply lotion to the back of her neck, as well as her face and throat.

She always dried herself carefully, after a bath or a shower, holding the towel by its opposite corners and pulling it back and forth from left shoulder to right buttock, and then switching to the other side, right shoulder to left buttock, and she creamed where her skin was rough, and powdered where it was smooth, and shaved her legs and her underarms regularly, and washed her hair every day, and used the most expensive shampoo and conditioner, and at least twice a week she gave her nurse's fingernails a manicure.

Well, no more. No more.

She got out of the tub and put her robe on, thinking. She spent a lot of time thinking, now. She didn't know what she'd done with her days, before Charlie disappeared and she'd started thinking again. Absorbing herself in speculation. In study, in scrutiny. Investigation. Calculation. Analysis.

This thing that's happened to me—it's not what I know, she thought.

Get to know it, she thought.

Why did I have the locks changed?

What was there between us?

Emma, listening for a reply, heard only white sound.

In the kitchen she poured herself some wine and fixed a plate of crackers and cheese. In the living room she sat in the easy chair, arranged the skirt of her robe to cover her ankles, and called Lorraine.

"I have to get a job," she said, "in a few months."

"Mmmm," said Lorraine. "You're okay for money for now, though? Because I could help, if you need it."

"I've got sixteen thousand dollars in cash. That'll do me until the fall. I don't know what kind of a job I can get, though." She put some Brie on a piece of melba toast. "I never used my damn degree. I don't have any damn experience."

"Mmmm," said Lorraine.

Emma munched on the cheese and cracker. "Charlie screwed around on me. Did you know that?"

"Emma, come on," Lorraine sputtered into the phone.

"Well?" said Emma, smiling. "You knew him. Did you think he was screwing around?" She cut off a chunk of white cheddar and popped it into her mouth.

"I never liked the guy. Since long before he met you. What do you expect me to say? Sure, I think he was capable of screwing around on you. Whether he actually did or not, how would I know?"

"Why are you using the past tense? I'm pretty sure he isn't dead." Although, she thought, Charlie dead would have been infinitely preferable to Charlie having sneaked away on her. Emma swallowed some wine and selected another piece of cheese—Edam this time.

"He might as well be dead, as far as you're concerned."

"What else do you think he was capable of?"

"Emma, a man who deserts his wife instead of having the guts to say he wants out of his marriage—face it, Emma, the guy is a jerk. A dork. A no-nuts, wise ass, cretinous, fatheaded *jerk*. Capable of *anything*."

A few minutes later, Emma replaced the receiver and carried the plate and the glass into the kitchen. Then she went into the bedroom and opened the drawer in Charlie's night table. The gun was still there, along with the small box of ammunition. Satisfied, Emma closed the drawer.

She turned off the overhead light and climbed into bed, leaving the lamp on. She lay with her hands behind her head, remembering.

It was about a month after Emma had found out about Charlie's adultery that he'd brought it up again.

"Emma," he'd said, "I think we should talk." It was evening, and they were sitting in the living room watching the television news.

Immediately Emma felt under siege. Adrenaline surged to the rescue. How idiotic, she thought, that her body should blindly prepare itself for a physical confrontation that wasn't going to happen, while her beleaguered mind just lay there, defenseless and cringing. She reached for the remote-control device and switched off the TV set.

"You deserve better than this," said Charlie. He was sitting on the sofa, his long legs stretched out, his hands clasped in his lap.

"Better than what?"

"Better than a husband who—plays around."

Emma examined this sentence carefully, moving its component parts around in her head: the words and their potential meanings, and the several ways in which a person might react to what she'd heard.

"I'm really very sorry, Emma. I really am."

"I accept your apology, Charlie. And I appreciate it."

"It started—"

"No," said Emma sharply. "Really, Charlie, I think it's best if we don't go into it." She gave him a tentative smile. "We should go forward. Not backward."

"That's what I'm trying to do. But I don't want to plunge into the future thoughtlessly, Emma. I want to do things right."

Emma's love for him at that moment was so tender and poignant it brought tears to her eyes.

He got up and came over to the big stuffed chair and sat on the armrest. He put his arm around her. "This is not the first affair I've had, Emma. It just isn't working, hon. It'll be better for both of us if we get a divorce."

Of course, he had been wrong about that, Emma reflected, switching off her bedside lamp. But what a lot of time got wasted, what a lot of pain there'd been, before he came to see things her way.

As she prepared herself for sleep, Emma realized that she no longer traveled through her days as if Charlie were watching her.

Chapter
Thirty-Two

"Dear Kathy, Caroline, and Sandy." Eddie read the letter again, taking a bite of his ham and cheese sandwich. "You know how terribly sorry we all were to hear about Melanie."

One piece of bread had mustard on it, the other one had mayonnaise.

"We will all miss her dreadfully—although not nearly as much, I know, as you three will."

The bread was whole wheat, the cheese was Swiss, and the ham was Black Forest, sliced, not shaved.

"This must be an extremely difficult time for you."

Eddie tried to take small bites so the sandwich would last longer, but this was hard because he was very hungry. He read the next paragraph slowly, concentrating.

"I know you're rethinking your commitment to us, and I don't blame you. But I hope you'll allow me to suggest that to go ahead with your plans, even without Melanie, might be as good for you as it would be for us."

Eddie, chewing, still couldn't make sense of that part.

"You'd be kept extremely busy, of course. And I know you'd enjoy Sechelt a lot, especially in the summer."

He didn't like the sound of that one bit.

"I'm afraid I have to know one way or the other by the

end of the week."

Eddie licked mustard from his fingers, then put down the letter to wipe his hand on the paper towel he was using as a napkin."...the end of the week." That would be Saturday. More likely Friday, because this was a business-type letter—he could tell by the official paper with a name and address and every- thing—even though it was trying to sound so friendly. Today was Tuesday.

"I look forward to hearing from you."

He tore up the letter and the envelope it had come in and flushed the pieces down the toilet. Staking out the house had paid off, after all.

He'd been a little worried to find out that there were actually three apartments in the place, with two more girls living in the top part, and a guy in the bottom part. But they were out all day, every day. Not Melanie's roommates, though. He was hav- ing a hard time making head or tail out of their comings and goings—and this was necessary if he was going to end up with a foolproof plan.

He figured he'd better check out the place where she'd worked too. So yesterday he'd gone in there, bold as brass, and sat down at the counter and ordered a coffee. He was eyeing the owner of the place and trying to get up his nerve to ask about her, casual-like. He had it all worked out and had prac- ticed it at home: "Say, where's the blonde girl who used to work here?" he would say, and if the guy looked at him suspi- ciously, Eddie planned to add, "She's a real good waitress," or something like that. Well, he was working up to this when all of a sudden the door opened and this girl walked in who lived in the house, the one with her hair cut uneven. Eddie damn near choked on his coffee. He huddled into his jacket, holding up the newspaper that lay on the counter, hiding his face behind it, and then trying to hear their conversation. But the guy was whispering, for some damn reason. Eddie peered over the top of the paper to see if they were looking at him, but they weren't.

And then he saw the guy hand her a box, a small cardboard box. And Eddie *knew* that this box had to do with Melanie, and he was absolutely sure that at least one of his notes was in there: he'd delivered the second one here, to the café, in the middle of the night, slipped it through the mail slot in the door.

She must have told her boss about it too, he thought all of a sudden: but he changed his mind about that right away, because it was plain as plain the guy had never seen Eddie in his life before. When he looked at him, Eddie could tell that. For sure. So even if she'd told him what happened, she couldn't have told him what Eddie looked like, and so he was safe there.

When the girl left the café, he had put money on the counter and hurried out after her. He made sure to turn in the opposite direction, though, and stand a ways down the street and count slowly to thirty before turning around to follow her; this was in case the guy in the café got suspicious, but Eddie sneaked a glance in there as he passed, and the guy was leaning on the counter with his chin on his hand reading the paper.

He followed her all the way home, and once, she spotted him, but she didn't really notice him. Which usually was a thing that made Eddie mad, but not this time.

Up the street from her house was one with a FOR SALE sign out in front, and it was empty. So Eddie strolled around, looking at this house, staring in the windows, checking this and that, like he was interested in buying it. He even wrote stuff in his notebook about it, in case somebody was watching him. And all the time, of course, he was keeping an eagle eye on the roommates' house, trying to think what to do about that box.

Eventually, he'd had to stop pretending he wanted to buy this place—which was a falling down piece of shit, anyway, when you looked at it close up—and he just sat down on the lawn with his back against a tree trunk and watched the roommates' house and worked on his problem.

After a long time two of the girls came out of the house together. Which left inside only the one with the box. Eddie waited tensely, hoping she'd leave too.

And then the mailman came.

And as soon as he'd moved on down the street Eddie, without even thinking about it, ran across the road, snatched the mail from the box, and hurried away, around the corner and into a little park, where he looked through the mail as if it were his, and stuck two envelopes into his jacket pocket.

Next, he had to go back there and return the rest of it, the bills and advertising junk and whatnot. He was a lot more nervous doing this than he'd been when he'd taken it in the first place. Then, he'd watched himself as if from a distance, amazed and horrified, watched himself dart slick as a bug across the street, up the steps, and whip the mail out of the box and whirl around to scurry away. But when he had to put it back, he felt palpably there, all right, big and lumbering and cumbersome and *noisy*, Jesus but he was *loud* clambering up those steps.

Eddie put his plate in the kitchen sink, got himself a beer, and sat down to have another look at the second letter. This one was addressed to Melanie Franklin: that was her last name—Franklin. It, too, was a typewritten, businesslike-looking letter, and it was from the university. Eddie had whooped out loud when he first read it, because it was the library telling her off because she had a book overdue.

But then he thought about how he'd seen her lying on the pavement and the only thing moving was the pages of her book, and he wondered if that was the book they meant, and for a minute he felt sick and sad.

But there wasn't any future in feeling sick and sad.

Now he tore up that letter too and its envelope and flushed it down the john like the other one.

He opened his notebook to see all that he'd learned, but when he got to the end of what he'd written there, only one thing really stuck in his mind.

His job was going to be a lot easier now, once he got in there. A box was a lot easier to find than a little piece of paper.

But there was some urgency about everything because of the letter. He was going to have to do it really really soon. He hadn't worked it all out perfectly in his mind yet, though. He was still doing the planning part. But he'd have to put some speed on, that was for sure.

He thought and thought, but his thoughts ran around and

around in his head like frantic little rabbits and led him nowhere, nowhere at all.

Eddie put the notebook on the coffee table, took a drink of beer, and leaned back on the sofa. He wondered if you could get that seeing-yourself-from-a-distance feeling on purpose. He thought it would come in very handy sometimes, when you had stuff you didn't want to do, you were *afraid* to do, but you absolutely for sure *had* to do, like get in there and get that box.

Chapter
Thirty-Three

*A*lberg telephoned Emma on Wednesday morning to tell her he'd gotten more information from the woman in the leather shop.

"When she said he paid in cash," he told her, "she meant travelers' checks. He's got another bank account—at least he did have. In Vancouver."

Emma was stirring porridge in a small pot. She'd decided to start eating well again, building up her strength. "Had one? You mean he doesn't have it anymore?"

"Yeah. He closed it. A month ago. Left no forwarding address. Also, his car's turned up."

Emma stopped stirring. She looked intently at the face of the clock in the stove's accessory panel. It was nine seventeen. "Where?"

"In a parking lot at the Vancouver airport."

"But I thought you told me he didn't take a plane anywhere."

"I told you he wasn't booked out on any flights under his own name."

"Right. I remember," she said dully.

"Don't give up yet," said Alberg. "I've got a couple of things I'm working on."

"What things?" She gripped the phone between ear and

shoulder while she spooned the porridge into a cereal bowl.

"I'll tell you about it next time I see you."

When she'd hung up, Emma sat down at the kitchen table to eat. On the table in front of her, next to a glass of orange juice, lay her weapon.

It was a Smith & Wesson .38 with a five-inch barrel. Charlie had had it for years, ever since his father died. He should have gone down to the police station and gotten a permit for it, but he hadn't bothered. He never fired it—it was just a keepsake. "A 1945 issue," he'd told her once, and she'd exclaimed, politely.

Emma hadn't even known he had ammunition for it. And then, looking into its dull gray muzzle that night, she'd heard him say, "It's loaded." She hadn't been able to tell, looking at it, if it was loaded or not. He might have been lying. But then she looked up at his face and saw that he wasn't.

She pushed her porridge aside and picked up the revolver, cautiously, feeling the weight of it. Not a very big gun, really. She had several purses that were big enough to carry it; several coats and jackets with pockets big enough to accommodate it. It wasn't loaded now—she checked the cylinder to make sure.

Although Emma still felt somewhat hesitant while handling it, she'd come to realize that it was really a very straightforward device. There was the cylinder, and when it was released (and it had been easy enough to figure out how to accomplish that), there were the six chambers for the bullets, and here was the hammer—but you didn't have to worry about doing anything with that after all. Emma had always thought you had to cock a gun before you fired it, pull back on the hammer first, but apparently that wasn't necessary, at least not with this gun.

She'd practiced loading and unloading it, and she'd practiced firing it while it was unloaded. Next, she was going to find a place somewhere out in the woods where she could fire it loaded.

The cloth in which it was wrapped smelled of oil. Probably it ought to be cleaned from time to time, this weapon.

There was some printing on the top of the barrel. "Smith & Wesson Springfield Massachusetts," she read. "Patented... "

and several dates she couldn't make out.

The revolver was less ugly than she had at first thought. It had wooden grips and a sleek barrel, and it fitted into her hand quite naturally.

Emma was developing a plan, several aspects of which were still vague in her mind. Whenever she thought about this plan, her body felt as if it were sheathed in electric sparks.

A cardboard box sat on the table. "Dominion Centrefire Cartridges," it said on the lid. Emma took off the lid and examined the bullets inside.

Every time she visualized herself acting on her plan, instantly it was as if her skin were made of fire. She could feel it in her eyes, too, and thought that would be enough to do the job all by itself, her eyes filled with sparks and fire.

But the gun was necessary. For symmetry.

She removed a cartridge from the box and slipped it into a chamber, and snapped the cylinder into place. She raised the revolver and pointed it at the front of the stove. She didn't know whether she'd load it or not when the time came.

...her throat had burned; her mouth was dry; she tried to speak but words wouldn't come, tried to open her eyes but could not, heard sounds but couldn't make sense of them, moved her hand—"Emma? Emma?" a worried voice, an anxious voice. She tried again—eyelids, lift, she told them, and they did. And she saw Charlie and saw that he was holding her hand. There was one second in which she saw relief on his face, felt loved and cosseted. Then memory spilled into her mind, and tears spilled from her eyes. She had turned away from him then and said into the pillow, despite her shame, "I'll do it again if you leave me. I'll do it again..."

"No more," said Emma out loud in her kitchen.

Really, she had been an awful fool.

But no more.

Chapter Thirty-Four

"I want you to cut it," said Cassandra, who had gone to Vancouver for the day.

Lenore, standing behind her, gazed intently into the mirror. She lifted Cassandra's hair and pulled it up and back. "How short?"

"I don't know. What do you think?"

Lenore considered. "You got quite a lot of gray. You want some color? Highlights?"

"No color. No highlights. Only short."

"You go short, you're gonna get more curl. Right now, the weight of it, it pulls at your natural curl, straightening it somewhat. Cut it short, it's gonna frizz right up."

"I know that. I don't care. I want a change."

"Color's a nice change."

"Lenore. Please. Could we talk about length first? Then maybe—*maybe*—I'll listen to color."

"Not frizz. I shouldn'ta said frizz. It's gonna curl more, though. For sure. But if you don't mind that—okay." She stared at Cassandra in the mirror, playing with her hair, concentrating. "I'd say, if you're gonna do it, do it good and proper. Get rid of all this, keep the fullness around here, do the bangs thing—whaddya think?"

"Okay," said Cassandra. "Let's do it."

"I see you lost a lot of weight," said Lenore, leading her to the sinks. "You quit eating or what?"

"I got the flu," said Cassandra.

"That's handy. You gonna keep it off?"

"I haven't decided," said Cassandra, leaning back in the chair, breathing in the fragrances of shampoos and conditioners and gels and mousses and perm solution and hair-coloring preparations. "I might."

Alberg sat in his sun porch on Wednesday evening, wearing his reading glasses, studying his notebook, absorbed in the puzzle that was Charlie O'Brea.

He made a note to check the cabs operating out of the airport the day Charlie disappeared, in case Charlie had just used the long-term lot as a place to dump his vehicle and hadn't gotten on a plane at all.

So far he'd called seventy-five numbers from Nola King's collection of business cards, which represented everything from hairdressers' establishments to a piano tuner, from photographers to a health-care worker, from car dealerships to florist shops. Several of the people he'd talked to knew Charlie, but only casually, and only in connection with the insurance business.

Alberg put his glasses away and went outside into the backyard. It was ludicrous to be spending time on this thing. They guy had had months to get himself some false I.D. He'd probably done the obvious, flown out of Vancouver Saturday evening, right after getting rid of his car. Alberg would never run him down. Nobody would ever run him down.

He'd stick with it, though, until his leave ran out. Which gave him less than a week.

He found himself looking at the rioting rosebushes, the towering hydrangeas, the cherry trees run rampant. Jesus, he'd better hire somebody fast, he thought, hands in his pockets, eyeing the climbing roses waving three feet above the top of the fence. The hydrangeas were massive. He'd had no idea something called a shrub could grow that big.

He walked around the house, which when studied closely revealed itself to be in need of a new coat of paint. Why hadn't he noticed that when he gave in and bought the place? He saw that the front porch had progressed from rickety to sagging, and that the sidewalk leading to it was cracked. What he ought to do, he thought, crossing his arms, was a substantial renovation. Could he afford that and a sailboat too?

His mind wandered back to Charlie O'Brea. What if Charlie hadn't had anything exotic in mind, like fleeing to a warm beach somewhere? Apparently he hadn't been all that enthused about either his wife or his job. So what *had* he liked about his life? Maybe, Albert thought, if he could figure that out, he could make some progress.

He was mulling this over when a car pulled up in front of his house. He turned, only mildly curious, and saw that it was an almost-new Toyota, a four-door, red. He'd never seen this car before. He'd never seen the woman who got out of it either—at least he didn't think he had, until she turned around to face him, shading her eyes against the setting sun.

"My god," said Alberg. "What did you do?"

"I cleaned out my savings account," said Cassandra, "and put myself in hock again, too. Bought me a new car." She pushed the door closed. "And some new duds." She walked around the front of the car and through his broken gate and onto his cracked sidewalk. She held out her arms and turned, slowly.

"I've always admired your legs," said Alberg.

"Never mind the legs. How about the suit?"

"I like the suit very much indeed. Because it shows so much of your legs. What did you do to your hair?"

She threw back her head and shook it from side to side. Then she stepped closer to him, running her hands through her hair. "I got it cut."

"You sure did."

"I'm a whole new woman."

He put his hands on her waist. "I hope not," he said, bending to kiss her temple, her cheek, her neck. He felt her shiver. "What are you up to?" he said into her ear, kissing her. "What are you up to, Cassandra?"

She hugged him, pressing herself tightly against him. "I'm attempting," she said, "to alleviate my restlessness."

"Let me help," said Albert.

183

"Come to my house, then. I'll make you some dinner. And then we can—you know. Do stuff."

That night, Alberg edged past the overloaded bookcases in Cassandra's bedroom and stepped out into a net of luminous curiosity cast through her window by the moon: a tall, broad-shouldered figure, hair thick and tousled, his naked belly protruding, relaxed and vulnerable. Cassandra smiled to see this. She was a little surprised that he was fumbling his way through the darkness of her bedroom naked. He was usually quick to cover himself when they'd made love.

"You're a sexy man, Karl Alberg," she said, watching his belly, and sure enough he promptly sucked it in. She laughed out loud, and he pretended not to know why.

Cassandra pulled the covers up to her chin and gazed at the moonlight, bright and substantive, and after a while Alberg returned with two squat glasses containing scotch over ice cubes.

"Did the whole thing without turning on a light," he said. He settled himself on the bed, on top of the covers, with a bunched up pillow behind his head, his legs crossed at the ankles.

"Oh look at that," said Cassandra tenderly. "Look at your private parts, snoozing away there, all worn out—aren't they sweet."

"Hey, hey," said Alberg uncomfortably. He pulled a chunk of bedspread over his genitals. "Get your eyes off my private parts." He slurped scotch with a clear conscience, knowing he was staying the night.

"Karl," said Cassandra. "I have to tell you something." She'd figured she'd know when it was time. And now, suddenly, the time seemed to have come. Part of her wanted to balk, and for a moment she hesitated. "I really do," she said firmly, more to herself than to him.

She hadn't told her mother yet; shouldn't her mother be the first to know?

She hadn't told her brother, either.

Screw this, she thought. Just get on with it.

"I've been thinking," she said. "Quite seriously. And—"

Alberg had put down his glass, and now he turned to her. "Look at me."

She looked at him.

"Will you please marry me?"

Cassandra stared at him, his face half in moonlight, half in shadow. She reached out and smoothed his pale hair away from his forehead. Such a tranquil face. Unlined. Unreadable. But his eyes sometimes gave him away. "What are you doing, Karl?"

"I'm saying I want us to get married."

"Why?" She realized that they were whispering—no, not both of them, just her. She said it again, louder. "Why?"

"I want us to be together."

He was quite tense, she realized. "Why now, Karl?"

"I don't know why now. Why not now? If you mean why not earlier, I don't know." He took her hand and stroked it, looking at it attentively, as if it were her hand that would answer him. "I want us to have a porch swing."

She pulled her hand away, threw back the covers, and swung her legs over the side of the bed. "Fuck," said Cassandra. She reached for her robe, lying in a heap on the floor, and put it on. Then she stood up and stalked out of the room.

In the kitchen she stood, fuming, looking out the window toward the Indian cemetary across the highway: she could see some of its white crosses glowing in the dark like fireflies. Would he get up, hurt and bewildered, and get dressed and quietly leave the house and quietly drive away? Or would he wait reproachfully in her bed for her to return and explain herself.

She felt his arms slip around her from behind. He was still naked.

"I don't want you to go," he said quietly.

"What are you talking about?"

"I don't want you to leave town."

"I don't know what you're talking about. And even if you were right," she said, furious, "even if I *was* thinking about it— you've got no right to do something like this."

"Sure I have," said Alberg, his arms firmly

around her waist.

"It's my life," said Cassandra.

"And mine. Your life is my life too. And my life is your life. That's what's happened to us." He turned her around. "That's why I'm asking you now, instead of earlier. I didn't figure it out earlier."

She pulled her robe more tightly around her. "This is a ridiculous conversation."

"It's a very important conversation," said Alberg resolutely.

Her eyes flickered down his body. "You look pretty stupid, standing there buck naked, trying to have an important conversation." She turned away. "Ah, Karl. Don't complicate things." She tore a piece of paper toweling off the roll that hung under the cabinet and dabbed at her eyes. "Ah, shit."

"So what do you say?"

Cassandra opened the cupboard under the sink and tossed the paper towel into the garbage. "I've never been married before, Karl. It's a very big deal, to me."

"It's a big deal to me, too, for Christ's sake."

She turned and leaned against the sink. "We could try it out, I guess."

"Try it out?" He sounded indignant.

"We could, you know, live together. For a while. And see how it works out."

This possibility clearly had not occurred to him. "I don't know," he said reluctantly.

Cassandra raised her eyebrows. "You don't know if you want to live with me? I thought you wanted to *marry* me, and now you don't know if you want to *live* with me?"

"I want to, I want to. It's just that—well, shit, how the hell would it look for god's sake?"

Cassandra stared at him. "You mean—because you're a cop?"

"Oh, for Christ's sake—"

"Aren't cops allowed to live with people? Is there something in 'Rules and and Regulations' about not living with people? Does the R.C.M.P. tell you who you can bloody live with?"

"All right, all right!" The cold had seeped up through his body from his feet, bare on the tile floor of the kitchen. He shivered. "Shit." He wanted his robe. "All right. We'll live together."

"Good," said Cassandra briskly. "I'm glad that's settled." She looked at him with a certain amount of fondness. "You go get your robe. I'm going to make us a sandwich."

Alberg plodded off to the bedroom. His good mood had vanished. He'd thought they'd buy a house together, he and Cassandra. He had even had his eyes on a couple. It seemed that was no go, at least for the moment.

He picked up his robe from the end of the bed and put it on and slid his cold feet into his slippers. He gazed resentfully at the bookcases and wondered where the hell he'd find room in his small house for Cassandra's things. He tied the robe around his waist and headed back toward the kitchen. Maybe she could sublet, he thought. Bring only personal stuff with her. Still, even then, he only had the one closest.

He went into the kitchen, where Cassandra had turned on the light and was peering into the fridge, looking for sandwich fixings. She turned to smile at him, and her smile was so open, so loving, her mouth so soft and inviting, that he felt himself stirring and wondered if maybe instead of eating—

"When do you want to move in?" said Cassandra.

Chapter
Thirty-Five

The next morning, Alberg was sitting on the stool in his kitchen, waiting for the lawyer in Phoenix to come back to the telephone.

The weather had changed again—back to cold and gray and blustery. Alberg was in a snarly mood. It had something to do with Cassandra, of course, and something to do with his mother. He felt set upon by females, and wished that at least one of his offspring had been male.

While he waited, he looked within himself for that dispassionate crystalline substance that he thought of as his soul, as the essence of him. It wasn't very reliable. It was always coming and going.

"Here I am back," said the lawyer.

"Hi, again," said Alberg politely.

"You ever been down here?" said the lawyer, shuffling papers.

"I've been to Tucson," said Alberg.

"How'dja like it?"

"I liked it."

"Pretty nice up where you are, so I hear."

"Yeah, it's pretty nice, all right," said Alberg, looking out at the broody gray sky, flicked with rain.

"Okay, I found it," said the lawyer. "Here it is. She passed away on June thirteenth, ninety hundred and ninety-one, aged sixty-eight. Poor woman. Sixty-eight isn't old. Not anymore."

He said this with such firmness that Alberg was touched. "You're right," he agreed, smiling.

"She got a blood clot on the brain, and poof, that was it. Well, it can happen. Now, let's see..."

Alberg drank some coffee.

"Okay, right, yeah, that's what I thought. She had an estate worth a hundred thousand dollars, left the whole shebang to her only son, Charles Madison O'Brea."

"Has Mr. O'Brea claimed his inheritance?"

"You betcha. Came down for the funeral, stayed a week or so, tied up all the loose ends, arranged for the sale of the real estate, transfer of the funds—I guess it was, lemme see, yeah, about six months, early in December when he actually got the money. Just in time for Christmas. Probably got his wife one hell of a present, huh?"

"You'd think so, wouldn't you?" said Alberg. "Where was it sent? To his account in Vancouver, I guess."

"Right. Vancouver. To a bank in Vancouver."

Alberg hung up and made some notes in his book. Then he pulled another handful of business cards from Nola King's fishbowl and started dialing. An hour later no further ahead, he left his house, got into his car, and headed for the ferry terminal at Langdale.

"I'm Karl Alberg," he said when she answered the door. "We spoke on the phone." He felt her hostility immediately.

At first she didn't even ask him in. But Alberg was perfectly willing to conduct the interview standing in the hallway, and when she realized that, she stalked into the living room and sat down. But not in the chair that was obviously her favorite. That was a bizarrely shaped contraption designed to fit the reclining body, and Ms. McAllister had no intention of relaxing in the presence of a cop, even one who wasn't on duty. There was a table next to this odd-looking chair, on which sat a lamp, a library book, an overflowing ashtray, a package of cigarettes, and a lighter, also the remote-control device for the television set. She scooped up the cigarettes and lighter before sitting in an easy chair next to the TV. Alberg settled onto the loveseat.

He felt weary, contemplating the effort it was clearly going to take to persuade this unfriendly woman to talk to him. He thought irritably about the long trip home, an hour or more to the ferry terminal, half an hour on the boat...Why the hell was he doing this, anyway, looking for a sonofabitch who didn't want to be found: a runaway husband who, what with his dead mother's legacy and various bonds and things, had scooted off with more than two hundred thousand dollars—enough to get him anywhere he wanted to go, a hell of a lot more than Emma could expect to get for the house he'd signed over to her.

And now here he was having to deal with this antagonistic woman.

He struggled for patience.

Then, fuck it, he thought.

"Why did you agree to see me?" he asked her.

"Because Emma asked me to see you."

"Do you think you have anything useful to tell me?"

"Probably not," she said with satisfaction. She was wearing black-and-white-checked pants, a white sweater, and a black jacket. Her hair was dark brown, and so were her eyes. She was in her late twenties.

"Okay." Alberg gave his thighs a light slap and stood up.

"Okay what?"

Alberg headed for the door.

"Hey," she said, getting up to follow him.

He opened the door.

"What's up? I thought you had things to ask me?"

"See," said Alberg, conversationally, "I'm not on duty. This isn't my job I'm doing. It's a favor to a friend. And so I don't have to put up with any attitude I don't like. I don't have to put up with people who don't like cops."

She leaned her hand on the edge of the door. "Emma's your friend?"

"No, a guy named Sid Sokolowski's my friend."

"Is he Emma's friend?"

"No, he's Emma's neighbor."

"Why are you really doing it? Trying to find Charlie."

Alberg looked into the hallway, which had pale green walls that needed painting and indoor-outdoor carpeting in a peculiar shade of bronze. "I'm curious about him."

"What so odd about a guy leaving his wife?"

"Nothing. That's the point. It happens all the time. So why make such a big deal out of it? Why cause yourself to vanish? Why not just say, 'Emma, I'm outta here'?"

Lorraine stepped back from the door. "You want a drink?"

They went back into the apartment. Lorraine poured herself a scotch and water and gave Alberg a Coke.

"I've been thinking about it, of course," she said, settling into her recliner chair.

"Why do you think he did it?" Alberg, on the loveseat, pulled out his notebook and pen.

She shrugged. "I guess he figured it was about time he did something for himself."

"What do you mean by that?"

"In all the years they were married, the only thing Charlie ever did that was for him and not for Emma was to decide they'd live in Sechelt." She drank some of her scotch. "Emma did not want to live in Sechelt. Oh, no."

"You know Charlie pretty well, do you?"

"Yeah. Pretty well. We grew up in the same neighborhood."

"Did he confide in you?"

"You mean, did he tell me he was leaving Emma." She was shaking her head. "No. Absolutely not."

"Were you close?"

"Uh uh," she said, shaking her head again. "He was my oldest brother's friend. And when my brother died in a car crash, about six years ago, Charlie got into the habit of calling me up now and then."

"Tell me about him."

"Tell you what?"

"Anything. Whatever comes to your mind."

"What's the point of this, anyway?" she said impatiently, lighting a cigarette.

"I want to get to know him."

"Yeah, but, okay, so you get to know him, so you—detect, or whatever you do, and, hey, maybe you even find him. Then what? He'll just disappear again, I bet."

Alberg looked at her thoughtfully. "You've got a point. But I'm looking for him anyway."

She dropped her lighter on the table next to the ashtray. "Okay, okay. I told Emma I'd cooperate. So I'll cooperate."

Charlie O'Brea was an only child, Alberg learned, the son of an architect who had died before Charlie got into his teens. His mother kept herself busy with an eclectic assortment of activities, including the Conservative Party. "My parents were Liberals," Lorraine McAllister told Alberg, "and they used to hate to see her marching up the walk at election time. But between elections, my mom and Mrs. O'Brea were quite friendly—mostly because of Charlie and my brother Simon being friends.

"Okay, so anyway, we used to have this open house on Boxing Day. And this one year—I was about twelve—I remember my mother was looking over the buffet table, making sure there was enough food and stuff there, and Mrs. O'Brea came up and started talking to her about Charlie. And she told Mom that Charlie had a girlfriend. 'And I think this time it's serious, Myrna,' she tells my mom. And it turns out she's right. This woman—Joan, her name was—she ends up marrying Charlie a year later."

"Wait a minute."

"Emma didn't tell you Charlie was divorced?"

"Emma didn't tell me that, no," said Alberg, and Lorraine laughed.

"That's typical of Emma. What you don't think about doesn't exist. She's probably forgotten all about her. Seriously." She took another drink. "Okay, like I said, her name was Joan. I forget her last name. She was a doctor. Well, *is*, I guess. Mrs. O'Brea didn't know how to take that, exactly. Pretty nontraditional, for Charlie O'Brea's mom, to have a daughter-in-law who's a doctor. It didn't last long, though. They were divorced about the time I graduated from high school, so that's—let's see, no more than five or six years, they were married."

"Do you know why they got divorced?"

"Nope."

"Any kids?"

"Nope."

"Okay. What then?"

"I didn't see Charlie again for ages. Years. I was at U.B.C., in fourth-year education, when I ran into him in the Student Union Building. He used to have a little business—he redid people's furniture for them, you know? People would bring him in old stuff, and he'd strip the wood bare and refinish it. He always liked working with his hands, Charlie did. Anyhow, so he got pretty depressed when his marriage broke up, I guess, and his mother was after him and after him to go back to school, and finally he went. I don't think he wanted to, really. But it was something different to do. And it got his mother off his back."

"Did you know his mother well?"

"I didn't like her much. Never wanted to get to know her well."

"Why didn't you like her?"

"Oh, she was kinda pushy. And she gossiped a lot. Nothing serious." She stubbed out her cigarette. "She moved to the States a few years ago. California, I think. Someplace warm, anyway."

"Okay, go on. You ran into Charlie when he went back to university, right?"

"Right. He was in the M.B.A. program, of all things. And I ended up introducing him to Emma. I guess that's why he figured he could complain to me about her, later."

"What did he complain about?"

"Oh, Charlie's a wimp," said Lorraine impatiently, getting another cigarette out of the package. "He got exactly what he said he wanted, and then he found out he didn't want it after all, and so he complained all the time. Finally I told him to take his damn whining somewhere else." She grinned and lit the cigarette. "It worked, too. Haven't heard from him now in more than a year."

"What did he get, that he decided he didn't want after all?"

"You know that song. 'Someone to Watch Over Me'? Well, that's what he got. In spades."

Alberg thought about the living room in Emma's house, in which he could sense nobody's presence. He remembered the rage in Emma's face that day at the Sokolowskis', when she'd watched him kissing Cassandra.

"Why didn't she want to live in Sechelt?" he asked.

"Emma doesn't like small towns. She doesn't like boats, or fishing, or camping. Why the hell would she want to live on the Sunshine Coast?"

"But Charlie did."

"Yeah. He loved it over there."

"I didn't see any fishing gear. Or camping stuff. No boat."

"Oh, they had all that once. He persuaded her to try it. Didn't work, though. So he sold it all. To Emma's great relief." She got up, cigarette in her mouth, squinting against the smoke, and took the overflowing ashtray into the kitchen to empty it. Then she sat down again.

"If he could afford to go anywhere in the world," said Alberg, "where do you think Charlie would go?"

She meditated on this for a couple of minutes. "You know, that's the sad part of it—for Charlie. He loved being right where he was. And in order to get Emma out of his life, he has to give it up." She looked at Alberg. "I don't have any idea where he'd go."

Alberg closed his notebook and got to his feet. "Thanks for talking to me. I appreciate it."

"It's okay. You're not so bad, for a cop."

At the door, Alberg turned. "I still don't understand why he didn't just ask her for a divorce."

"He probably did. But she'd never have given him one. Emma would never have let Charlie divorce her."

"But why?"

She held her cigarette behind her, so the smoke wouldn't drift into his face. "It would have meant she'd failed. Emma hates to fail."

"Maybe it would have meant Charlie had failed. Or both of them together."

"Yeah," said Lorraine, nodding. "But there's no way Emma would see it that way."

Back in his car, Alberg contemplated heading out to the airport with Charlie's photo. But that would be a waste of time, he decided, without checking around first, finding out who was driving cabs and limos that day. He glanced at his watch. Too late to start digging into Charlie's first marriage.

So he went home. He'd drop in to see Emma, give her hell about not mentioning Joan-the-doctor. And try to find out how many other things she wasn't revealing.

But by the time he got back to Gibsons he was too tired to drive on to Sechelt. So he sat down at the phone with another handful of business cards.

An hour later, he got lucky.

"Coastal Flying."

"Brad Watson, please," said Alberg.

"You got him."

"My name is Karl Alberg, Mr. Watson. I'm trying to locate a Charles O'Brea. I've got one of your business cards here. Do you—"

"Charlie? Do I know Charlie O'Brea? Hell, yes. What do you mean, you're trying to locate him?"

Chapter Thirty-Six

"Mother, I don't want to discuss it here."

"You're the one who brought it up, Cassandra." Mrs. Mitchell took a pink dress from the rack and held it up to the light.

"I didn't bring it up in here."

"They don't make clothes for women my age anymore. You brought it up on the way over here, and you knew this is where we were coming. What do you think?"

"I think it's a perfectly fine dress."

"Maybe they never did make dresses for women my age. After all, I never looked for them, before I got to this age." She replaced the pink dress and pushed hangers aside, looking critically at another dress, then another. "Once burned, twice shy. I guess that's his reasoning, is it?"

"How about this?" Cassandra held up a pair of walking shorts.

Her mother glanced at them. "Don't be ridiculous. His first marriage didn't work out, and he's afraid to try again. That's it, isn't it?" She shook her head reproachfully. "You can do better, Cassandra."

"I told you, Mother, it's my idea. Not his."

"How're you doing there, Helen?" said the owner of the dress shop, approaching with a smile. She was a tall, buxom woman with jet black hair and extremely long fingernails. "Can

I help you find something?"

"Thank you, Margaret, but I'm just browsing."

"Well, you just let me know if you need anything."

Cassandra watched as her mother flicked her way through several racks of clothing. Cassandra had decided it would be wise to have this conversation in public, where her mother couldn't make too much of it. But it was occurring to her now that if she'd broken the news in the privacy of her mother's apartment, she'd at least be able to leave when she felt like it.

"I can't concentrate on this," said Mrs. Mitchell abruptly. "My mind's wandering like a stray dog. Let's go have some tea."

They crossed the street and entered a small café that Mrs. Mitchell favored because of its white tableclothes. She chose a table by the window and ordered tea and scones.

"I wish you didn't disapprove of practically everything I do," said Cassandra.

"Don't bother to tell me what you do," said her mother crossly, "if you aren't interested in getting my honest opinion."

"You're my mother," said Cassandra. "What am I going to do, let you find out from somebody else?"

"The whole town's going to be talking about this, that's for sure."

"I doubt it. It's not a big deal, Mother."

Mrs. Mitchell fixed an unseeing gaze beyond Cassandra out to the street. She was looking well, despite the pain Cassandra knew she suffered from her arthritis. Her hair was almost completely white now, still worn in a pageboy, with bangs. "I do not understand why you're doing it," she said after a minute, shaking her head.

"Oh god, Mother." Cassandra rummaged through her handbag, looking for aspirin. "I told you. I don't know if I want to marry him or not."

"Oh I understand that part of it." Mrs. Mitchell paused while the waitress set down cups and saucers, a small brown teapot, and a plate of hot buttered scones.

"Enjoy," said the waitress.

"Thank you," said Mrs. Mitchell. "What are you looking for?" she said to Cassandra.

"Aspirin."

"What I don't understand is what you think you're going to find out living with him that you don't already know." Mrs. Mitchell leaned closer and lowered her voice. "You two must have—you know—slept together by now. Haven't you?"

Cassandra set down her water glass and felt herself flush. "It's not that."

Mrs. Mitchell poured a little tea into one of the cups. "Then what is it?"

"Mother, I've lived alone for years. It might be too late for me to live with someone else. Aren't you going to pour that tea?"

"It's still too weak."

"I like mine weak." She reached for the pot and filled her cup. She wouldn't have anything to eat. She didn't need it. Fortunately, she wasn't even hungry.

Mrs. Mitchell stared out the window. Finally, she sighed and picked up half a scone. "I know it's a commonplace thing now, people living together without benefit of clergy. But it's a thing I will never get used to." She began eating. "He lives in Gibsons, doesn't he? So I won't see as much of you, in the future."

"You'll see as much of me as you ever did. I work here, after all," said Cassandra. Butter had dripped from the scones and was pooling on the plate. "And besides, I want us to live in my house."

Her mother looked at her in amazement. "That tiny place?"

"It's not a tiny place. There's plenty of room in it."

"How does he feel about it?"

"He's got a name, Mother," said Cassandra sharply.

"How does Karl feel about it? Living in your house?"

"He's a bit—he—he's thinking about it." She picked up a scone, put it down again.

"Is his place any bigger?"

"No."

Her mother examined Cassandra thoughtfully. "I like your hair short like that. And you've certainly lost a lot of weight."

"I'm feeling good these days," Cassandra confessed.

"It's steady work, being a policeman," her mother went on.

"And it's true you aren't getting any younger."
"We're none of us getting any younger, Mom."
Cassandra picked up the scone again and took a bite.

Chapter
Thirty-Seven

ddie's sister, Sylvia, was a single mom with two little kids, a boy and a girl, who were five and four and looked a lot alike. She cut their hair the same, which Eddie didn't approve of. He thought boys should look like boys and girls should look like girls, and the way they did their hair had a lot to do with this. Sylvia was too casual about stuff like that. She parted their hair on the side and cut them bangs and then evened it up around the bottom, just below their ears. They looked like twins. People on the street always figured they were twins. And usually people thought they were the same sex, too. So whenever Eddie took them anywhere, he always put a barrette in Edith's hair and messed up Will's. Will was named after the prince who might be king of England one day. Eddie didn't know who Edith was named after.

Sylvia was working days this week, at the gas station on Tenth where she'd had a job for a couple of years now. She had an arrangement with a friend; Sylvia looked after the friend's kids and the friend looked after hers. But sometimes this wasn't possible because they were both working at the same time. Then she had a list of babysitters she used, but today it turned out they were all busy doing something else, so she'd asked Eddie to pitch in. She hardly ever asked him to help out, but he didn't mind it when she did. She'd done a lot for him in his life, Sylvia had, and besides, he kind of liked her kids. Well, no, he actually loved her kids.

He tried to find a skirt for Edith to wear, but she didn't seem to have any. "Edith," he called out from inside the kids' closet, "where are your skirts?"

Edith just laughed.

So he left her in her jeans, but he found the orange barrette he'd brought one day about a month ago and stuck that in her hair, and then he took the kids by the hand and walked down to the end of Sylvia's block to a Big Scoop and bought them an ice cream sundae. They thought this was pretty exciting, in the middle of the morning.

"How about going for a little walk, fellas?" he said when they were back out on the street.

"Okay," said Will.

Edith let go of his hand and ran a few steps ahead. "Where to? Where to?"

"Only a little ways," said Eddie, "because then we've gotta get back and make us some lunch." He'd found that the best way to entertain Sylvia's kids was to keep them eating all the time.

"What are we having? What are we having?" said Edith, hopping backward down the street in front of him.

"Come on back here, hold my hand," said Eddie sternly.

"Can we have Chef Boy-ar-dee?" said Edith.

"We don't got any," said Will.

"Can we get some?" said Edith.

"You get over here and hold on to my hand," said Eddie, "and then maybe we'll go to the store and get some Chef Boy-ar-dee. Otherwise, you are outta luck, Edith."

Edith slipped her hand into his and skipped along next to him. He steered the kids around the next corner; it was in his mind to wander past Melanie's house, a few blocks away.

He couldn't spend any more time doing surveillance, because even in an indifferent neighborhood like that one, somebody was going to notice if the same guy was there every day. He had to get busy and take action, he knew that. But he was having a hard time working up his nerve. He longed to confer again with Gardiner—except that he was reluctant to face more of Gardiner's impatient contempt for the way he, Eddie, was handling things.

He'd looked her up in the phone book because she hadn't been—that is, the accident only happened ten days ago and so she'd still be in it, and she was. And he started phoning every so often, like several times a day, to make sure the girls were still there. He'd been sorely tempted sometimes when they answered just to blurt it out: "Where's the box?" he might say, and, who knows, they might blurt out where it was right back to him. But he never did this, naturally. He just listened. "Hello? Hello?" And then they'd hang up. After he'd phoned a few times, they started swearing at him, though they didn't know who they were swearing at, and then after that he just got the stupid answering machine, so he stopped phoning then.

"Where are we going?" said Will, sounding worried.

"Just to the end of this block," said Eddie. He'd herded them across the street, and now they were approaching the house on the opposite sidewalk. The old gray Reliant was parked out in front, wedged in between a Honda Civic and a Ford pickup, and the Reliant's roof rack was piled with luggage.

"Come on, Eddie," said Edith, pulling at his hand. "Hurry up you slowpoke you."

The dark-haired roommate burst through the hole in the hedge, carrying a carton that had printed on the top, in big red letters, "MELANIE." She was followed by the other two girls, and each of *them* had a box marked "MELANIE" too.

"Oh, shit," said Eddie under his breath, but Edith heard him and made a big to-do about his bad language. He hustled them along, his head averted, and he didn't sneak a glance back until they'd gotten to the corner. They were tying the luggage onto the roof rack and shoving more stuff into the backseat. "Oh, shit," said Eddie again. He hurried the kids around the corner and along the adjacent street to Fourth Avenue, where they stopped at a store to get Chef Boy-ar-dee and a package of cake doughnuts.

When they got back to Sylvia's house, he called Gardiner, who took a long time getting to the phone and then sounded sullen and unfriendly. But he agreed to come over.

Eddie let the kids play out in the backyard while he and Gardiner talked on the porch, keeping their voices low so the kids couldn't hear them.

"Okay, so gimme the story," said Gardiner, whose spirits had improved. "Tell me the tale."

"So it says in the letter," Eddie told him, while Will played with his toy marines in the sandbox, and Edith swung on the tire Eddie had hung last summer from the bottom branch of the big maple tree, "it says they've been offered these jobs, see, in Sechelt, and it says they gotta make up their minds by the end of the week if they're gonna go or not. So today I see them loading up their car, see, and I damn know that's what they're doing; they're going to damn Sechelt, and they're taking her stuff with them in those cartons, and my notes are in there, they gotta be."

"What the fuck's a Sechelt?" said Gardiner, digging at ear-wax with his little finger.

"It's a place," said Eddie. "Up the coast. You gotta get a ferry."

"Oh shit, ferries, I hate ferries."

"Watch your language, willya?" said Eddie, pointing with his thumb to the kids.

Gardiner yawned and stretched, standing up. He leaned on the porch railing. "Hey, kid," he called out. Will, who was squatting in the sandbox with his back to them, looked at Gardiner over his shoulder. Edith, hanging upside down, peered at him through the hole in the tire.

"What?" said Harry finally.

Gardiner shrugged. "I forget." He sat down again, next to Eddie on the top step.

"What the hell's the matter with you?" said Eddie.

"If they were gonna give you trouble with those fucking notes, they woulda done it by now. Shit, they probably burned them. Tore them up. No way they'd keep them. Why the fuck would they keep them?"

Eddie shook his head worriedly. "I don't trust them. Maybe they're waiting till they get outta town to give me trouble. Maybe they saw me watching the house and got scared.

Whatever. Gardiner—I just don't trust the bitches. You know?"

"Okay. Okay. Lemme think," said Gardiner, leaning on his knees, his hands loosely clasped between them.

Edith had gotten off the tire and was now scratching letters in the dirt with a stick. Eddie, watching, remembered doing that himself when he was a kid. He wished there was some lawn back here for Sylvia's kids to play on. But the maple tree was so big that the whole yard was in shadow most of the time, and what with that and kids playing on it, the ground just didn't let grass grow there.

"Well the way I see it," said Gardiner, "it's gotta be easy pickings."

"Oh yeah, sure," said Eddie sarcastically. "Right. Easy pickings. Sure."

"Well, shit, there's fucking cartons with her fucking name on them in red letters, right? You can't hardly miss the fucking things."

Eddie stared at him, exasperated. "They're on their damn way to Sechelt, Gardiner, didn't you hear me?"

Gardiner grinned at him. He grabbed Eddie's cheeks in his hands. "So are we, weasel. So are we."

"Shit," said Eddie, knocking his hands away. "Quit that."

Gardiner got to his feet. "I wouldn't do this for just anybody," he said, sticking his hands in his pockets. "Fucking ferries. I hate ferries. Hey, kid," he said, ambling down the steps toward the sandbox, "can I play?"

Chapter Thirty-Eight

*A*lberg set out from his house in Gibsons the next morning filled with expectation, focused and exhilarated. He drove up the highway from Gibsons on a day that was cool and sunny with a good breeze off the ocean. His life had for the moment stepped back from him, and he was not intruded upon by thoughts of living with Cassandra, or trading in his car, or buying a boat, or renovating his small house, or caring better for his aging body. He drove north in a state of controlled excitement, thinking only about Charlie O'Brea.

He wasn't angry with Charlie. But he had decided that Charlie must explain himself to Emma. There was usually nothing at all judgmental in the way Alberg went about doing his work. Judgment was other people's business, he always said; the court's business. But of course he had opinions. And this time, since he wasn't operating as a police officer, he was allowing his opinions to assume a greater importance in his decision making.

He drove the familiar road to Sechelt, through the town and out the other side, and then north to Halfmoon Bay and beyond. Eventually the road turned and descended, and below lay Ruby Lake. There was a motel and restaurant on the right side of the road, next to a pond, and the lake proper was on the left. As he drove toward it down the curving highway he saw a float plane moored snugly against the shore. Alberg slowed and pulled off the road. He parked in the empty lot in front of the restaurant, walked across the highway, and sat for a while on a large rock next to the water. He studied the float plane, white with red markings, and noticed that moorages were scattered along the shoreline as far as he could see.

The rock on which he sat was shale, and it extended beneath the clear, green water. There was a small round island out there, and a larger one, more oval in shape, beyond it. The breeze was soft and soundless.

After a while Alberg got up, crossed the highway again, and went into the restaurant. He sat at the counter and ordered a coffee. The proprietor was wearing jeans and a plaid flannel shirt. He put the coffee in front of Alberg, placed his palms on the countertop, and stared into Alberg's face. Alberg smiled at him.

"I keep a packed suitcase in my car," said Charlie O'Brea, "and I know the ferry schedules by heart."

"You probably wouldn't take a ferry, though," said Alberg. "You'd probably fly out of here, in your float plane over there."

Charlie had been severely jolted by the sight of Alberg trudging across the gravel. He caught sight of him when Alberg was still several yards from the door. He thought about running. He could ease out the back way, tell Paula in the kitchen that he was feeling sick. Yeah, that was a perfectly good workable idea. But he didn't do it. A powerful lethargy seized him, and he found himself watching almost calmly as Alberg got nearer and nearer, opened the screen door, and came inside. And when Charlie got a look at Alberg's expression, he knew it wouldn't have done him any good to run. The guy wasn't here on some kind of highway patrol coffee break. The guy wasn't accidentally discovering Charlie here. The guy had known right where to look for him.

Charlie asked Paula to keep an eye open for customers, and he and Alberg went outside.

"Why didn't you just divorce her?"

Charlie almost laughed. "Well, I tried that, Officer," he said. "But she wouldn't let me."

"Why?"

"Oh, Jesus, Alberg—" Furious, Charlie rubbed at his hair with both hands.

They were sitting outdoors on iron chairs from which the white paint was flecking. The cushions were stained and damp. Charlie loved the tired-looking chairs. He loved the rain-marked cushions. He loved the whole miserable, falling-down place. He was going to make it beautiful again. And profitable too. But he wondered if he'd be able to keep it now. He glanced at the off-duty cop who'd made it his business to find Emma's errant husband.

"I'm a simple man," he told Alberg earnestly. "I like simple pleasures."

"Uh huh."

"I've got simple dreams," said Charlie, warming to his tale, and to Alberg's attentiveness. "Always have had. The insurance business? That was a deviation from the norm. All my life," he said, crossing his arms, enjoying the tinge of grief in his voice, "I've been buffeted by the aims and ambitions of women."

"Bullshit."

Charlie winced. He looked out at the pond and the highway that wound down toward them from the south. The two men sat in silence for a while. The willow trees by the edge of the water were green-gold with new leaves. "I almost killed her," he said heavily. "That's why I left her."

"What do you mean?"

"I mean I held a Smith & Wesson to her head and damn near pulled the trigger, that's what I mean. And then I knew I had to get out of there, out of the house, the job, the marriage." He leaned forward, hands clasped, elbows resting on his knees. "I was unfaithful to her. And she still wouldn't let me go. I was her career. I was her damn life's work." He sat up. "She's very sweet, Emma is. But she's wrong about a lot of things."

"When did this happen, this incident with the firearm?"

Charlie stared at him disbelievingly. "This 'incident with the firearm'? Is that how you guys really talk?" He shook his head. "A year ago."

"Why didn't you leave right away?"

"I wanted to know where I was going and what I was

209

going to do when I got there," Charlie snapped. "I had to have some kind of a plan." He slumped back in his chair. "And then my mother died. All of a sudden, about six months ago, I had money. It sounds crass, I know..."

"How did you keep Emma from finding out your mother was dead?"

"I just didn't tell her. They never got along anyway. So it's not as though I had to worry about Emma writing to her or calling her up."

"What then?" said Alberg. "What did you do next?"

"You know what I did. I took flying lessons. And then I bought that float plane. And I put a down payment on this place." He looked at Alberg curiously. "How did you know to come here?"

"You filed a flight plan."

"Yeah." Charlie sighed, and laughed. "So I did."

"How come you didn't get yourself new I.D.?"

"I wouldn't have known how to go about it," said Charlie, gazing across the highway at the lake, sunlight sparking from its blue-green surface.

"You could have found out, though."

"Yeah. Well, I didn't want to be anybody else. I wanted to be me again. Finally."

"Were you you," said Alberg dryly, "with your first wife?"

Charlie laughed again. "I tried to be. But we were just too different to make things work. I wanted a home and kids, but Joan—there was no way she was going to take a year out of her life to have a kid. To her, marriage was like—it was like something she kept in her purse, you know? Like a book you haul out to read when you're stuck in traffic. Something to do when her career slowed down for a minute."

"But Emma wasn't like that."

"No," said Charlie softly. "No, Emma wasn't like that." He remembered the first time he'd seen her, on the stage at U.B.C. in a play. He couldn't remember anything about the play except Emma, who was so beautiful he'd found himself unable to take deep breaths. "Emma really wanted to be married." And she was sexy too, as well as beautiful and smart. No, more than sexy. She was wanton, she was seductive, she was insatiable. At least, so it had seemed.

Charlie stood up and went to the rickety pier that led out into the pond. "Someday all this is going to be landscaped," he said, with a gesture that took in the weedy, scrabbly terrain that stretched between the pond and the motel units. "I'm going to do it all myself."

They'd made love under a blanket on the ferry and on a gravel beach and in the back of the car. They'd done it on the kitchen table and in the shower and on the floor in front of the fireplace. Emma said she loved sex. Emma couldn't get enough sex.

"She didn't want to do anything else except be married," he said dreamily to Alberg. "Just wanted to be married. Just wanted to take care of the house and the garden and the household finances and me." He looked up the hill to the south. There wasn't much traffic this time of year. Things would get busier in a few weeks, though. He had a lot to do to get ready for the tourist season. Cleaning. Repairs. Gardening.

"And that was exactly what you wanted, right?" said Alberg irritably.

"Yeah," said Charlie.

He knew the exact moment in which his marriage had started to die. It happened eighteen months after the wedding. He and Emma were coming out of a restaurant in Vancouver. He'd taken Emma's hand and glanced at her, and he'd seen desire in her face, shimmering from her skin, which was pale, diaphanous. He was tremendously excited. Out on the street he'd taken her around the corner into an alley and pushed her against the wall. He pulled up her dress, she undid his fly. She bent her knees and thrust herself forward, and Charlie pinned her arms against the wall. Her mouth opened for his tongue as he entered her.

When they were finished, Emma adjusted her clothing and combed her hair with her fingers and leaned down to brush at the toe of her shoe—Charlie, gazing unseeingly at Alberg, remembered that she had been wearing black patent-leather pumps. Light from the streetlamp at the corner caught on her face. It was utterly blank. Dispassionate. And Charlie realized that it wasn't desire he'd seen on her face: it was hot in the restaurant; she was just sweating a little.

"Yeah, she was exactly what I thought I wanted." He shoved his hands in the pockets of his jeans. A car pulled off the highway onto the gravel and parked next to Alberg's.

She had been presenting herself to him, he'd realized in the coming days and months, like a series of portraits. Each one charming—delightful—but one-dimensional.

Charlie shrugged. "Emma got too enthusiastic about being a wife, that's all," he said, watching a couple with two small children go through the screen door into the restaurant.

After the incident in the alley, Charlie had started talking to himself in the bathroom mirror. He'd wipe away the steam from his shower and stare at his reflection, making faces, and babble away at himself. This shook him up quite a lot.

"What do you mean?" said Alberg.

Charlie looked at him for a moment. "Why the hell am I talking to you, anyway?"

Alberg grinned at him. "I've been wondering that myself."

Charlie studied him. Alberg looked like an easygoing type of guy. A little wary, but that must go with the job.

"You probably needed to talk," said Alberg. "And I'm probably the first likely candidate that's come along."

"How much is she paying you?"

Alberg looked surprised. "Nothing."

"You're doing this as a favor? For somebody you barely know?"

Now the cop looked uncomfortable. "Not exactly. I'm on leave. It was—something to do. And then I got interested."

Charlie nodded slowly. "Okay. I don't think I've got anything more to say, though."

They say quietly for a while, looking at the water, listening to the birds and the far-off sound of a powerboat. Alberg thought there was probably a lot more to Charlie's story.

He got up and began walking toward the parking area, Charlie following. "The revolver," he said. "Is it registered?"

"No," said Charlie. "I never got around to it." He glanced at Alberg. "Hell, I've had it for years, it was my dad's. It was just a keepsake, you know?"

"You brought it to Ruby Lake with you?"

"No. I left it behind."

They reached the car. Alberg unlocked the driver's door and opened it.

"Listen—are you going to tell her where I am?"

"Not right away," said Alberg. He looked at Charlie. "But I want you to get in touch with her. She deserves some kind of explanation."

"I planned to write her a letter. Every time I sit down to do it..." He rubbed his hands together. "I will, though."

"You've got a week." Alberg started to get into the car, then stopped and turned back to Charlie. "Is there ammunition too? For the Smith & Wesson?"

"Yeah," said Charlie after a minute. "Why?"

"I think I'll drop in," said Alberg, getting into his car, "and talk to her about permits."

Chapter
Thirty-Nine

S uch a short time ago, thought Emma, sitting in her kitchen, marveling; only two weeks ago, in fact, she would have been sitting here planning the evening meal, pondering momentous decisions like pasta versus pot roast, salad versus soup; shall we eat at the dining room table or in front of the TV set? That would have depended on whether there was a hockey game or something important on the news. Charlie always got home in time for the six o'clock news. He was as regular as clockwork, as dependable as the sunrise.

He hadn't always been regular and dependable.

He'd become so, though. After Helena.

Emma hadn't known the names of the others. And she didn't think Helena was any more important to him than the others had been. But Emma had met Helena, who had been the last. So of course she had known her name.

Emma had been much taken aback by the look of her. She was a skinny young woman with hair so short it made her head look the size of a marble. She wasn't at all attractive.

Emma had found her easily, by following Charlie. She was surprised at how easy it was to follow Charlie. It didn't seem to have occurred to him that she might do this. But she did.

Helena worked in a chiropractor's office, in the building that also housed Charlie's consulting firm.

Emma followed Helena, then, and learned all sorts of things about her. She went to church most Sundays—her hypocrisy, thought Emma, was limitless. She visited her parents in Surrey once or twice a month. She sang in one of the city's major choirs.

Emma followed her several times over several months, working on a plan.

One day Emma followed her home from work and went to a nearby restaurant and had a sandwich. At about six-thirty she went to Helena's apartment in the house on West Seventh Avenue and knocked on the door.

"Hello," she said warmly when Helena answered. She held up a clipboard and a file folder. "I'm doing a survey for city hall," she said, "on the importance of municipal funding to cultural organizations. Could I possibly have a few moments of your time?"

Yes, Charlie had changed, all right, after Helena, thought Emma. The revolver lay on the kitchen table in front of her. She pushed it away from her, using the index finger of her right hand, then hooked her finger inside the trigger guard and pulled it back toward her.

What if I had a dinner party? she thought, and began composing a guest list. She'd invite Lorraine. And the Sokolowskis next door. She could invite Karl Alberg too. She got up and went into the bedroom and looked through the glass doors into the backyard, hands shoved into the pockets of the oversize cardigan she was wearing over jeans and a denim shirt. She'd recreate the menu from the anniversary dinner, she decided. She'd use the best china, and the silver. She saw herself setting six places, one for Charlie. She saw crystal glittering in candlelight, white linen glowing, silver gleaming...and this image led to thoughts of Charlie's mother, who had given them silverware as a wedding gift.

Charlie's mother would know by now of his disappearance, thought Emma, hurrying back to the kitchen: Alberg would have told her. She wondered why she hadn't yet heard from Alberg about this, since he'd reported to her promptly about everything else.

And she would have expected a call from her mother-in-law too, she thought, reaching for the phone...

An image popped into her head, full-blown, like a photograph hung suddenly in the air before her. Charlie and his mother were sitting side by side on a long sofa upholstered in fabric with a dark background—maroon—with large flowers splashed on it. There were lace antimacassars on its back and arms. Charlie's head was resting on his mother's shoulder. She was sitting tall and straight, with her right arm around him. Charlie's hands were in his lap. Mrs. O'Brea, knees primly together, had on a white dress with small blue polka dots, and her white hair was soft and wavy. On her feet were dark blue shoes with low heels. Charlie's dark hair gleamed. He was wearing a white shirt, open at the throat, and an apple green pullover vest and a pair of pants the color of butterscotch. They were both looking directly at Emma, unsmiling, unmoving.

Emma, rattled, quickly dialed her mother-in-law's number.

"I'm sorry," said a recorded female voice. "That number is no longer in service." Emma wondered if the voice was a real person or a computer.

She sat down, heavily, convinced that Charlie was in Arizona. She thought about what she ought to do. She wanted to rush directly to the Vancouver airport and climb onto the first available flight to Phoenix.

But the number was out of service. What did that mean?

Maybe they've gone, she thought. Scuttled away from there. Gone to South America or Tanzania or New Zealand or someplace.

Emma hurried upstairs to Charlie's desk and started rummaging through the drawers. Someday she'd have to dispose of all this stuff. She imagined setting it on fire, right here—making a big pile of all this paper right on top of the desk and putting a match to it. To hell with him, she thought, feeling reckless; he isn't the only one who can start all over again.

She slammed the bottom desk drawer shut and turned to the filing cabinet. There wasn't much there. "CATALOGS," said one folder. "DOCUMENTS," said another. In there was their marriage license and birth certificates and Charlie's expired passport. "HOUSE," said another folder. "INSURANCE." Emma had been through all of them. Finally, "MOTH-

ER." She took this folder into the kitchen and dumped the contents out on the table—a pile of letters written over several years—and started reading them, looking for clues.

She found references to her mother-in-law's sister and remembered that the woman lived in Brandon, Manitoba.

Emma dialed 1-204-555-1212. "Operator? I'd like a number in Brandon, please."

Chapter
Forty

*S*anducci was enjoying his thirties. He acknowledged this
to himself, somewhat surprised about it, as he turned off
Roberts Creek Road onto the highway. He was even
beginning to give serious thought to finding a nice girl and settling down. Unbelievable.

He was returning to the detachment in Sechelt from a rou-
tine investigation into a car theft. The victim was a single mother whose ten-year-old Toyota had vanished from her driveway
during the night.

The corporal was feeling pretty good about life, all things
considered. He was due to be transferred, and he didn't like
that much; he would miss the Sunshine Coast. But the move
would provide a smooth, tidy way to end things with Roxanne,
so he wasn't entirely unhappy about it. Roxanne Baker had
been his steady girlfriend for a year now. And although it had
at times been excruciatingly difficult, he had actually managed
to remain faithful to her. He was proud of himself.

There was a dearth of public transportation in Sechelt, and
that single mom was really going to feel the absence of her
vehicle. She needed it every day, she'd told Sanducci, to take
her kid to daycare and to get herself back and forth to work.
She had veered during the interview between despair and a
rage so towering that Sanducci had become alarmed.

He'd never been serious about Roxanne, but he was serious about getting serious about somebody. The relationship had been invaluable preparation. What a relief, to know that monogamy was actually possible. For a year, anyway. And a year was a very long time, he told himself.

He'd see if he couldn't rustle up some wheels for the single mother, he thought, pulling out to pass a heavy-laden logging truck laboring along at thirty kilometers per hour. He figured they'd find the Toyota, all right—some kids had probably gone joyriding in it, and they'd leave it in the bush somewhere when they were done or maybe in the shopping center parking lot if they were cocky enough—but the woman couldn't put her life on hold in the meantime.

He'd had a good year with Roxanne. He hadn't spent so much time with one particular female person since he'd gone steady with Angela Giovando, way back in high school. When you saw that much of somebody, you couldn't spend all your time in the sack. He'd learned all kinds of things in conversations with Roxanne, who was a medical secretary.

The trees on either side of the highway were a green color so bright it glowed almost like neon, thought Sanducci, as he came up behind a gray Plymouth Reliant, even on a day like this, when the sun kept disappearing.

The Reliant had a roof rack that was laden with suitcases. He couldn't make out how many people were inside. In the back window was a pile of flowers.

Sanducci grinned to himself because the Reliant slowed down in a hurry when the driver saw his patrol car. He decided to just sit there for a while, two car-lengths back, doing a steady sixty K. He loved it that traffic slowed to the limit whenever they spotted a patrol car. And he got royally pissed off every time some macho-stud-jerk-shitrat got all defiant at the sight of him and gunned it, giving Sanducci the metaphorical finger. Usually he managed to restrain himself when this happened. He'd radio the guy's plate up ahead. But sometimes he wanted so badly to take off after the sonofabitch...

The flowers bouncing around in the back window of the Reliant looked familiar. One kind looked like fruit tree blossoms of some sort. Little flowers, dark pink ones, in clusters along branches— "Flowering quince," he said aloud, snapping his fingers. He beamed behind his sunglasses. Roxanne's folks had a big bush of it in their front yard. Flowering quince. He leaned toward the windshield, peering more closely into the Reliant, trying to see what the other flowers were, big yellow ones—oh, boy, he thought.

He turned on the light bar and punched a brief howl out of the siren, pulling the Reliant over.

He picked up his peaked service cap and fitted it on over his thick, curly hair, opened his door, and ambled over to the small gray car, which had come to a stop on the shoulder of the highway.

The driver had rolled down her window and was looking at him impatiently. "What's your problem?" she said.

There were three women in the car and a lot of luggage. The women, all in their early twenties, were dressed casually in jeans and sweaters. The one in the backseat had been lying down, but she sat up now, observing Sanducci with suspicion.

"Good afternoon, ma'am," said Sanducci with a wide smile. He wished he'd left his dark glasses in the patrol car. The sun had gone away again.

"What is it?" said the driver. "You've been following us for five miles, you know damn well we haven't exceeded the limit."

"You're right," he said, still smiling.

The person in the seat next to the driver was red-haired, with very pale skin. Sanducci figured she'd have to be real careful of the sun. The woman in the back had light brown hair that was a mass of waves falling down upon her shoulders.

"Well what the hell do you want, then?" said the driver. Her dark hair fell to her jaw on one side and was clipped above her ear on the other. Sanducci liked this effect very much. He decided she was by far the most attractive of the three.

"Actually, ma'am, I pulled you over because of those flowers back there."

"I told you, Kathy," said the young woman in the backseat. "I told you we shouldn't have taken them!" She looked strong and capable, and Sanducci was amazed when she burst into tears.

Sanducci, dumbfounded, looked from one young woman to another. "Hey, it's okay. Really." He looked left and right along the highway, thinking about police harassment.

The girl next to the driver turned to look into the backseat. "Oh stop it, Caroline," she said wearily, brushing at the strands of hair that had come loose from her ponytail.

"We'll pay the fine," the driver said to Sanducci. "Just give me the damn ticket."

"Ma'am, there isn't any fine," said Sanducci. "There isn't any ticket. Listen, I only stopped you because—those yellow ones, see them?"

"They're water lilies," she said. "Caroline, please." The sobbing abated. "She—we get upset, sometimes. Can't seem to do anything about it." The driver rubbed her forehead as if she had a headache.

"A friend of ours," said the redhead, "our roommate—"

"Shhh," said the driver impatiently. She looked up at the corporal. "So? Can we go, or what?"

"Well, see, the trouble is, those aren't water lilies. They're skunk cabbages."

All three of them looked at him as if he were deranged.

"They're what?" said the driver.

"Skunk cabbages. I know they're very pretty, but believe me, if you leave them back there, your car's going to stink like hell in a little while."

The driver stared at him. Then, "Caroline," she said, "hand over those water lilies." The girl in the back collected the bulbous yellow blooms and handed them to the driver, who started to open her door.

"I'll take care of them," said the corporal.

She thrust the skunk cabbages through the window, into his outstretched hands. "Thanks."

There came an angry outburst from the redhead in the passenger seat. "What are you doing, anyway? Pulling people over. Skunk cabbages for god's sake. Haven't you got better things to do?" Her face was flushed, and her hands had curled themselves into fists. "I *know* you've got better things to do. So go and do it."

"Sandy," said the driver. "Don't." She turned back to the

corporal. "What's your name, Officer?"

He noticed that a wind had come up. "Sanducci."

"Your first name, I mean."

Sanducci hesitated. "Eduardo."

The driver tilted her head to study him; her hair fell away from her face like a dark, curved wing. "Eduardo." She nodded. "It suits you."

Sanducci smelled blossoms on the wind. Or maybe it was the girl's perfume, drifting toward him through the cool spring day.

"We've had a bad thing happen in our lives, Eduardo. A calamity." The other two were watching her as if hypnotized.

"I'm very sorry to hear that."

"And as a result, we aren't ourselves these days." She glanced into the backseat. "That's Caroline back there." She indicated the girl sitting next to her. "This is Sandra." She pointed to herself. "I'm Kathy."

"How do you do," said Sanducci. A few raindrops spattered onto the car.

"We go to U.B.C. We've got summer jobs over here."

Sanducci found himself listening intently, awaiting epiphany or at least revelation. But if she'd been about to confide in him or request his assistance, she changed her mind.

"Thank you again," said Kathy abruptly, and she cranked up the window, started the car, and moved off onto the highway, leaving Sanducci standing by the side of the road with a heart full of wonder and an armful of skunk cabbages.

Chapter
Forty-One

On Saturday morning, Emma awoke early. She got dressed quickly and sat in front of the TV set watching *Newsworld* until she thought it was late enough to go looking for Alberg. But when she opened the front door, he was standing on her porch, about to ring the bell.

"I was just going to see you," said Emma severely.

"And here I am." He wasn't smiling. He looked quite grim and not a bit guilty.

She led him into the living room. "Why didn't you tell me she was dead?"

"I've got a question for you, too," said Alberg.

"Why didn't you tell me?" Emma insisted. "I felt like an idiot, on the phone to that woman, a person I've never met, who'll be wondering forever why on earth I didn't know my own mother-in-law had died."

"Can we sit down?" said Alberg.

"I don't want to sit down."

Alberg studied her for a moment, and Emma didn't like that at all. His pale blue gaze swept across her face like a cold breeze, and she became uncertain of his capacity for compassion.

"Where's the revolver, Emma?" he said.

Instantly, she looked behind him, toward the front door.

She thought about the gun, in the night table drawer. She pressed her hand against her chest to calm her heart. "You've found him," Emma said finally.

Alberg watched her and said nothing.

"Where is he?"

He shook his head.

"Where is he? My god, you've got to tell me, you can't— you can't do all this work and *find* him and then not to tell me where he is!"

"He's going to get in touch with you."

Emma's entire body was shaking. It felt extremely violent. "Where is he?"

"I told you, he'll be in touch."

"Oh, to tell with that. To hell with him. To hell with him. To hell with *you*." She looked around for something to throw at him. "'He'll be in touch.' 'He'll be in touch.'" She wanted to heave the bookcase at him, squashing him underneath it, but it was too heavy, and she was too weak because of the trembling.

She whirled around and hurried out of the house. He was calling her name, but she ignored him. She got to her car before she realized she didn't have her purse and therefore didn't have her car keys. He caught up with her there.

"Emma, I'm sorry. I promise you, he *will* be calling you, or writing. If you haven't heard from him in a week, I'll tell you where he is."

She needed time to calm herself, to think, to work things out. She took a deep breath and smoothed her hair with both hands. "Okay."

"Emma. The revolver. It's an unregistered, restricted firearm."

"Oh, I don't have that damn thing." She turned to look at him, keeping her face relaxed. "I assume Charlie told you about—well? Did he? About when he pointed the damn thing at me?"

"Yes. He did."

"I couldn't possibly have it in my house." She shuddered. "I found it, and I chucked it out with the trash."

She could tell that he didn't know whether to believe her or not and that, in either case, he was not happy.

"I have to know exactly when you did this," he said quietly. "We have to try to recover it."

"Really," said Emma with interest.

"I take firearms extremely seriously, Emma."

"My goodness, Karl," she said, looking him in the face. "So do I."

Chapter
Forty-Two

L ater that day Emma, wearing old jeans and a sweat-shirt, marched outside and pawed aimlessly in the garden with a three-pronged fork for a while.

Then she dragged out the lawnmower and cut the grass. Wiped off the outdoor furniture. Swept the patio. Watered the hanging baskets. When there was nothing more to do, she went to the back of the yard and leaned on the cedar fence.

It was a mild day, a benevolent day. Emma could see the ocean two blocks away and smell it in the spring breeze that blew gently from the west. The lilac in the corner of the yard was fragrant with deep purple blossoms. Emma, exhausted, rested her head on the top of the fence. She heard the familiar birdsong again—two notes, which she'd identified as the first two notes of "Swing Low, Sweet Chariot"—and felt herself begin to cry.

Then she heard the neighbors' screen door open and bang closed.

Emma lifted her head and looked eastward to see Sid Sokolowski in the middle of his back lawn, surveying his property with a critical eye.

At last, she thought, swiping tears from her eyes. At last.

Emma moved quickly to the fence that separated the O'Breas' property from the Sokolowskis'. She took hold of the top of it and with an effort produced a smile. "Hi!" she called out.

Sid turned, and his face brightened. "I heard the good news last night," he said, heading toward her.

"Yes, isn't it wonderful?" said Emma enthusiastically. "Of course, it doesn't mean the end of my troubles," she said, casting a sigh. She looked up at Sid bravely. "But it's the beginning of the end of them. I'm very grateful to Mr. Alberg."

"Karl's a good man," said Sid. "A good police officer too. I was pretty sure he could help you."

"Did he tell you how Charlie reacted?" said Emma. She laughed. "I was so excited, I didn't think to ask him."

Sid leaned on the fence. "He was pretty calm, I guess. You heard from him yet?"

"Not yet," said Emma, with an effort. "He—maybe he needs more time."

"Yeah," said Sid. "Well, I don't hold with that, myself."

Emma was staring at the fence, trying to calm herself. It had rained earlier in the day, and the cedar was still wet, a deep glowing red. "I don't know what's going to happen," she said.

Sid shifted his weight from one foot to the other. "You're the one needs the time," he said.

"I do. I probably do," said Emma.

"I hope to hell the guy doesn't take it into his head to just show up here."

She looked at him quickly. "Well," she said cautiously, "it would take him a while, though—wouldn't it? To get here?"

"No, it's not that far—about an hour and half by car, I guess," said Sid Sokolowski. "Of course, he's got that float plane. He could just drop it in over at Porpoise Bay. That'd be real quick."

Emma pored over the highway map of the Sunshine Coast. An hour and a half south—you couldn't drive south for an hour and a half without ending up in the ocean. An hour and a half north, then, and near water, because of the float plane. . . .

Late that afternoon Emma sat in her car on the gravel shoulder of Highway 1, looking down the hill at the Ruby Lake Motel and Restaurant, about half a mile away.

It was a somewhat ramshackle place, a one-story building that had spread in apparent aimlessness from its original structure and now encompassed four or five small motel units as well as the café. The lake itself was on the other side of the highway, a narrow piece of water bearing several small, thickly treed islands upon its blue-green surface; it looked small and crowded, but Emma knew from the map that, although narrow, Ruby Lake was also long.

Every so often she raised to her eyes a pair of opera glasses given to her by her mother for her eighteenth birthday and studied the large smudged window in the front of the restaurant. She wasn't able to see much more than an occasional vague shadow.

This had to be the place. It was the right distance from Sechelt. And she could see a float plane moored next to the lakeshore.

The opera glasses were very old; her mother had found them, she had told Emma, in an antiques shop. The leather case was worn, and so were the glasses themselves. But they worked well, and Emma liked the feel of them against her eyes.

She put them on her lap and looked distractedly around her car's interior. She was surprised to notice on the seat next to her an empty glass bottle that had once held a fruit juice and mineral water combination, on the floor, a couple of scrunched up gum wrappers and what looked to be a used Kleenex, on the dashboard a coating of dust. She looked over her shoulder into the backseat and saw a white sweater and several library books. These things were evidence of preoccupation; Emma kept her car, in normal times, as clean and tidy as she and Bernie kept the house. But never mind, she told herself, raising the glasses to her eyes: the end of the thing is in sight.

The glasses were aimed at the door, and as she looked, it opened and a couple of tourists came through and made for the parking lot. The screen door slapped closed behind them— and then it opened again, and a man wearing jeans emerged, striding toward the motel rooms.

Charlie.

Emma kept the glasses trained upon the back of his head and realized that she was half crouched over the steering wheel as if attempting to hide herself—but if he did stop, and turn, and look up the hill, he'd recognize the car anyway, wouldn't he?

It seemed that she didn't care. She watched him intently through the opera glasses and felt this to be her due, that she was able to watch him, unseen. Her mouth was dry, and her hands clasping the glasses were wet with sudden perspiration. She saw him reach with his right hand under his plaid shirt, to scratch the top of his shoulder. She saw that he was wearing hiking boots. She watched him go through a door, leaving it open, and emerge carrying a mop and a pail full of what Emma assumed were cleaning supplies. She lowered the glasses for a moment, blinking in disbelief, and raised them again to see him pull a ring of keys from his pocket. He unlocked a door with the number 1 upon it and disappeared inside with his mop and pail. Emma sank back in her seat.

Did he have any idea how ludicrous he looked? Wearing jeans and a loudly colored shirt and carrying that mop, for heaven's sake, and a pail full of Windex and Mr. Clean and SaniFlush toilet bowl cleaner or whatever he had in there. Her eyes had filled with tears, and there was a great ache in her chest, as if something had her in a vise.

Emma bent her head and put the opera glasses back in their case. Whatever had possessed her mother to give her such a thing? She thought there were probably people in the world—somewhere in the world, in the farthest reaches of someplace—who believed that the opera glasses, when presented to her, already contained all the images she would see through them. She brushed tears away, blew her nose, and sat upright again, her hands on the steering wheel.

Who the hell knew why he'd done it.

Who the hell cared.

She turned on the motor and waited for a Winnebago with Ontario license plates to lumber past. Then she made a U-turn and headed south, back toward Sechelt.

It occurred to her that there was no longer any reason for her to be living on the Sunshine Coast. She tried thinking of jobs she might like to do, of areas in Vancouver where she might like to live. She even wondered if she might not decide to live for a while in another part of the country—Calgary, maybe, or Winnipeg, or Halifax. And she named these cities, speaking out loud in the car, trying them out...but it was no use. It was too soon. Because it wasn't over yet, the thing with Charlie.

"I understand why you don't believe me," she had said to him on the night of their fifth wedding anniversary. "But it's true. A person can do almost anything, if she's resolute and reasonably intelligent. And I'm both. Plus, I'm organized."

"And crazy," said Charlie, who she could tell was having a hard time controlling his temper.

"Not at all crazy. Determined not to let you make a fool of yourself, that's all."

"You can't change my mind, Emma. I don't know why you want to hang on like this. Christ, where's your pride? Where's your dignity? Why are you telling me such stupid lies?'

"Her living room is small," said Emma. "There's a window that overlooks the street. The floor is oak, with a rug in the middle. There's a long sofa, two armchairs, a coffee table, two end tables."

"Jesus Christ, Emma, who do you think you're kidding? You've just described half the living rooms in Vancouver."

"And there's a rather amazing collection of objects—they're from Mexico, she told me. She was there for a couple of weeks last winter."

Charlie's expression had changed.

"The most amazing of them all," said Emma, "is a class-room of little devils, twenty little desks occupied by twenty little devils, with a great big devil up at the front, teaching them. Helena said it's made of plaster of paris. Helena has very strange tastes, hasn't she." She cocked her head at Charlie. "Now, truly, is that something I could have made up?"

"Why the hell did you do it?" said Charlie hoarsely.

"She's completely unsuitable for you, Charlie. I know your mother would agree."

He looked at her for a long moment. "Emma—I don't know

233

what to say to you. It's over. And I'm moving on."

"I'm warning you, Charlie—"

"It won't work anymore, Emma."

He stood up, and Emma knew this was because he wanted to tower over her. She looked straight ahead, into the leaves of the schefflera on the other side of the living room. She wasn't going to crane her neck and peer up at him. Emma's submissive days were over. Submissiveness didn't work. None of it worked. Not flirtatiousness, not submissiveness, not seduction, not hanging on his every word, not making sure his suits were pressed and his shoes were cleaned, not stocking cupboards and freezer and refrigerator with things that were good for him and things he liked as well, not cleaning the damn toilet and sponging out the damn sink and doing the damn vacuuming, not taking damn courses and reading things she didn't care about, just so she'd be interesting to Charlie—none of it worked, none of it, none of it. . . .

"So don't threaten me," he said, "because if you try to kill yourself again, I'll let you do it. So help me god this time I'll let you die."

"I'll do it there," she said, jam-packed with grief and rage.

"I won't listen to this," said Charlie, and he turned to head for the door.

"I'll do it right there," Emma shouted, "in Helena's living room, on Helena's couch, in front of Helena's devils."

Charlie spun around and moved swiftly toward her.

"I'll splash my red blood," said Emma, "all over Helena's steel-gray sofa."

Charlie almost hit her. She could see it in his eyes.

"I will," said Emma quietly. "I will."

Chapter
Forty-Three

"*M*ove move move move move!"

"Settle down, Gardiner."

"Get us the fuck offa here." He was practically bug-eyed, and Eddie was pretty sure he was sweating.

"You got two eyes in your head, Gardiner; you can see there's no way I can move until the guy ahead of me moves, and no way he can move until—for god's sake, Gardiner, we're in a *lineup*, here. Have a smoke. Relax. Shut your eyes."

He was surprised Gardiner was that scared, even though he knew Gardiner didn't like ferries; well, it wasn't ferries, actually or even boats that he didn't like—it was water, deep water like you find in oceans or lakes or rivers. He didn't even like going over it on a bridge. And some bridges were worse than others. He'd go miles to avoid the new one south of Vancouver, the Alex Fraser Bridge. "It's so fucking high," he'd told Eddie, "you might as well be up in the fucking clouds."

Finally, they were docked, and the ferry guys started directing the lines of cars and trucks off the boat, and then they were on the road to Sechelt.

"Okay, so pull over," said Gardiner.

Reluctantly, Eddie pulled over, and they switched places.

"I'd like to know what you think we're gonna do when we get there," said Eddie, feeling irritated. He wanted to be in his Camaro, not in Gardiner's beat-up Olds Delta 88, and if he did have to sit in Gardiner's beat-up Olds, he'd at least like to be able to drive it. But Gardiner would only let him drive onto the ferry and off it. Eddie, looking out the window at the green trees, didn't really blame him. It was hard for anybody who knew how to drive to be a passenger.

"We find the bitches," said Gardiner. "Where they live. And we break in and get your fucking letters." He'd been driving with only the fingertips of his right hand on the steering wheel, his left elbow on the open window, but suddenly as he steered around a corner the road went practically straight up, and then around in a hairpin curve. "Holy shit," said Gardiner, concentrating on his driving for a while.

Once they were on the straight and narrow again—and it was certainly narrow, all right, thought Eddie, this road was nothing that deserved the word highway attached to it— Gardiner said, "How big is this fucking town we're going to, anyway?"

Eddie shook his head. "I don't know. Not big, I think."

About half an hour later they got there, and Eddie had been right, it wasn't big.

"Jesus," said Gardiner, cackling, striking the flat of his hand against the steering wheel. "I never seen a place this small before."

Eddie looked at him in disgust. It was nothing to brag about, never having been out of Vancouver in your entire life, not in Eddie's opinion, anyway.

"There sure aren't gonna be a hell of a lot of people doing plays in this burg," said Gardiner.

"So what do we do, cruise around looking in windows until we find them?" said Eddie.

"We stop and look in a phone book," said Gardiner. "Theaters have phones like everything else."

But they didn't even have to do that. They parked on the main street, in front of a fish-and-chip shop done up to look English, and went into the drugstore on the corner to buy Gardiner some smokes. The ferry fare had just about wiped out Eddie's PROJECTS envelope, and he wouldn't get to put any more money in there until the end of the month, almost three whole weeks away. So he watched enviously while Gardiner stuck the package of Craven A in his shirt pocket, and then he turned away so Gardiner wouldn't see him eyeing the smokes—and there right in front of his eyes was a pink poster that said, "SUNSHINE COAST THEATRE COMPANY PRE-SENTS....40" And then there was a bunch of information: dates and times and names of plays and on and on.

Eddie poked Gardiner with his elbow, and they both studied the poster intently.

"Okay," said Gardiner decisively. "Got it."

Back in the car he revved the motor until Eddie winced. "Hey, let's not call attention to ourselves, okay?"

Gardiner was cackling his head off. "A tent. A tent. For fuck's sake, a *tent*."

They sat around a big table on the platform that would be their stage, doing the first read-through of the play that was to open in two weeks' time. People loved Agatha Christie. Kathy didn't pretend to understand why.

She glanced around frequently as the cast worked its collective way through act one; her character didn't make her appearance until shortly before the first curtain.

They were in a huge, red-and-white-striped tent that had been set up in a meadow three miles north of town. Through the open flaps at the other end, Kathy could see the ocean across the highway, beyond a grove of trees.

"Ainswick!" cried Caroline, as "Midge." "Lovely, lovely Ainswick!" She had the best part of any of them, at least in this play—*The Hollow*. They'd be doing two more, but the casting for these hadn't been finalized.

Kathy rested her chin on her hand, fingering the pages of her script, daydreaming.

The side flaps were open too, and every so often kids peered in at them.

She heard, "My dad says I ought to call myself a domestic help," and realized they'd gotten to Sandy's first scene. Sandy was playing Doris, the maid, who was supposed to be a little bit half-witted and terrified of the butler.

Kathy thumbed ahead in the script, looking for her entrance.

A dog appeared in the opening at the far end of the tent. He observed them for a moment, tail wagging hesitantly, and then padded in their direction.

"Muffy!" A boy of about eight stuck his head around the corner.

Kathy caught Sandy's eye. "'Muffy'?" she mouthed, silently.

"Muffy!" The boy emitted a piercing whistle, and the cast, as one, lifted their faces from their scripts in time to see the dog run toward the boy and vanish with him around the corner.

Oh, god, and here was "Gerda," thought Kathy, wincing, straightening in her chair.

"Oh, John, you don't mean that," said "Gerda," and Kathy didn't dare look at Sandy or Caroline, because Gerda was the part Melanie was to have played. She tried not to listen, but that was neither fair nor wise, because, after all, they were going to be working with this woman the whole damn summer—they'd made their decision, here they were—she hissed at herself furiously, causing the guy playing John, who was sitting next to her, to glance at her uneasily.

Every so often someone darted across one of the gaps created by the swung-back tent flaps or sat down on the grass to listen for a while.

Kathy heard somebody trip, swearing, over one of the guy wires. She glanced over to see a big fellow with reddish hair start picking himself up from the ground.

"Veronica," said the director.

Those wires were damn dangerous, she thought indignantly, watching him limp quickly out of sight.

"Veronica," said the director, more sharply.

Kathy's heart lurched. "Oh, god, sorry," she said, scanning the page. "Uh...'You must forgive me,'" she said, "'for bursting in upon you this way...'"

"Christ, Eddie, you stupid weasel." Gardiner had grabbed him by the sleeve of his denim shirt and was literally dragging him across the grass to where the car was parked by the side of the highway. But he was laughing as he said it. "Ass over teakettle, shit, you got the brains of a fat-ass toad."

They climbed into the car, and Eddie waited to catch his breath before shutting his door, but Gardiner didn't wait; he started the motor and got the broken-down Oldsmobile heading down the road, and Eddie, grabbing at the door handle, almost fell on his face, right out of the car, which just made Gardiner laugh harder.

They found a place where they could get a hamburger and a beer, and they took the food back to the car and drove back to nearby the tent so they could watch people coming and going.

"Did you hear any of that crap?" said Gardiner, munching.

"Some of it."

"I never heard such boring shit in my life."

They finished eating, and they drank their beers, and they waited and waited. After a while Eddie got out of the car and sat on the grass. Gardiner wandered across the highway and disappeared among the trees. "Fuck this," he muttered, when he got back. "The fucking ocean's over there."

They'd been waiting for more than two hours when people started dribbling out of the tent, heading for cars parked on a road that went off the highway along the side of the meadow. They climbed quickly back into Gardiner's car and waited another few minutes. Eddie, just to be safe, slid down in the passenger seat so he couldn't be seen. He stayed there on the floor, his head bumping against the bottom of the glove compartment, his legs cramping, while Gardiner watched for the girls; Eddie had told him what they looked like.

"Okeydokey," said Gardiner, firing up the Olds. "Here we go."

He could be a good driver when he wanted to, Gardiner. He moved them along smooth as silk, whistling softly to himself.

"We're leaving the highway here, going up this here road; it's looking good, my man, not much civilization up this way— okay, they're turning off. I'm following, they're pulling into a driveway here, and I'm keeping right on going; looking over at me, they are; I'm giving them a friendly little wave—"

"Jesus, don't," said Eddie, horrified.

"—Hi, bitches, hi there," said Gardiner, waving. "Going going going...okay, can't see them anymore."

Eddie hauled himself off the floor and onto the seat. He was panting a little bit, as if he'd been working out.

"Okay, I'm gonna cruise by one more time, sport," said Gardiner, getting the car turned around, "to get the lay of the land."

They were on a very narrow road with no yellow line down the middle of it. On one side was a thick forest. On the other were some dug-up places where new houses were going to be built. Every so often there was an old house set in the middle of a huge lot that Eddie figured was probably actually a small farm: most of them had other buildings on them besides the house—barns and henhouses and things. They drove slowly past some more land cleared for building and approached a small white house with big flowering bushes at the front door.

"That's her," said Gardiner, pointing. "That's the place." He stopped the car, motor running.

"Shit, Gardiner, don't let them see you," said Eddie, ducking.

Gardiner had a big smile on his face. "No problem," he said. "Duck soup." He turned to Eddie and gave him a playful punch in the shoulder. "Your troubles are nearly over, Ed." He revved the motor and sped away, laying rubber.

"Christ, Gardiner," said Eddie, craning to watch the small white house as it rapidly got smaller and then disappeared.

"Now we get ourselves some more food," said Gardiner, "and a six-pack, and we tilt ourselves a couple 'til it gets dark."

They sped down the hill, back onto the highway, and through town, heading south. They picked up hamburgers and French fries at a take-out place and found the liquor store, where Gardiner sprang for a case of beer. They discovered a logging road and drove along it a couple of miles inland— Gardiner didn't want to be too close to the ocean. Gardiner turned on the radio and seemed surprised to find the same station coming through that he listened to in Vancouver. He sang along in his twangy voice and Eddie, so as not to get irritated with the country music and not to get nervous at the thought of breaking into somebody's house, which he'd never done before and which he could just hear Sylvia yelling at him about, drank one beer after another. So did Gardiner.

When it got dark, Eddie said, "Should we go do it now?"

Gardiner shook his head. "Gotta wait till they're asleep."

"How long?"

"I don't know. What do you think?"

"I don't know when bitches go to sleep."

"When it's midnight we'll drive past the place, see if there are any lights on."

When midnight came, they did, and saw no lights.

But they drove past and waited a while longer, just to be sure. It was getting cold, and they'd run out of beer.

And then they went back to the small white house. Gardiner switched off the lights before they got there, and turned off the motor, too, and the car drifted to a stop a little way past the house, on the other side of the road. For a few minutes nothing happened. Then both doors opened, and Eddie and Gardiner got out.

Chapter
Forty-Four

*T*here was a moon that night, and wind, and the wind tossed trees around, creating shadows to roam in Kathy's bedroom. She lay sleepless in her single bed, watching the shadows flicker across the wall. The room was so depressing, filled with boxes she'd been too tired to unpack before falling into bed.

There were altogether too many things to worry about, that was the problem, she thought, turning over, tossing her pillow on the floor. First, she was pretty sure she'd been badly cast in *The Hollow*. Second, she didn't like Sechelt—it looked like a very boring place. Third, she missed Melanie. And fourth, she wondered if she shouldn't have stayed in Vancouver after all and looked for non-theater work that would have paid some real money.

Kathy heard one of her roommates moving around somewhere in the house, sleepless like herself, moving quietly so as not to disturb anyone. It must be Sandy. It wouldn't occur to Caroline that anything she did could possibly bother anybody.

Oh, don't be a bitch, Kathy told herself impatiently and turned over again.

There was a thin strip of light around the blind covering the open window. Every so often it widened, as the blind shivered and moved into the room on a puff of wind, and nar-

rowed again when the wind subsided. There was a faint clatter-
ing sound as the slat at the bottom of the blind struck the windowsill.

Maybe if she went through her problems one at a time,
looking at each one clearly, they'd turn out not to be so bad
after all. She knew that worries attracted other worries like
magnets, glomming together to create something intolerably
heavy, and that when she was able to grab them and deal with
them one at a time, life was a lot more manageable. Kathy
retrieved her pillow, propped it against the headboard, and
leaned back, her arms crossed under her breasts. First, the casting. She was playing Veronica Craye, an actress who was
incredible beautiful and knew it. Kathy winced whenever she
thought about it. There was no *way* she could, believably, play
"incredibly beautiful."

"Trust me," the director had said.

But this was always a problem for Kathy. She hated relin-
quishing control—though she knew this was an essential part
of learning a role. She'd just have to grit her teeth and do it, she
thought. Let herself go, make herself try everything Doreen
suggested. If it didn't work, if it turned out that she really *had*
been miscast, this would be quickly obvious to everybody.

The wind caused the blind to flutter again, and Kathy felt a
gust of nighttime caress her face, bringing with it the scent of
the lilacs that grew at the front of the house. She'd been very
glad to see the lilacs; they reminded her of her parents' house
in Richmond.

Next, Sechelt. She admitted that it was pretty. But there was
absolutely nothing to do here. She punched at her pillow,
which was thin and knobbly, and arranged it behind her head.
Of course, she'd only just arrived, just barely met the rest of the
company. As soon as they began to know one another, they'd
start exploring the town together, and eventually they'd settle
on a place—a café or a bar—that would become "their" place
for the remainder of the summer. Kathy's common sense told
her this, and she knew it was true.

Down the hall the toilet flushed, and she heard the hall
floor squeak, and the sound of Sandy's door softly closing.
Kathy knew Sandy was lonely in there, although she hadn't

said so. It was the biggest of the bedrooms, with twin beds and two chests of drawers and a huge closet. Sandy and Melanie had been going to share it.

She groped for the travel alarm clock on her bedside table. One-thirty. Shit. She still wasn't a bit sleepy, and she had to get up in five hours.

She lay on her back, hands behind her head. Her mother always said that if you couldn't sleep, you might as well get up and do something. Read or watch TV or bake bread or something. Go for a walk, maybe.

A swath of bright light swept suddenly, unexpectedly, through her room, which was a corner room at the back of the house. Kathy felt for a moment as if she were on a ship that had come too close to a lighthouse—she experienced a strong sense of motion because of the shifting shadows on her bedroom walls and the beam of light flashing its warning...but almost immediately she heard the sound of automobile tires and realized that what she'd seen was the headlights of a passing car.

At least she had transportation. Thank god, she had transportation. If she got totally fed up with being in this rinky-dink town, sharing a house all summer with the same people she lived with the rest of the year, depressed at not doing well enough in the show—she'd hop in her car and get the hell out of here for the day, go back to Vancouver, see her family, get free food and some TLC from her parents.

It was too depressing to consider her fourth worry, which was money. There wasn't a damn thing she could do except plummet deeper and deeper into debt. Maybe when she graduated she'd work for a year at something other than the theater, something that paid well, so she could knock off at least part of her loan real fast.

Or maybe, she thought, smiling to herself, she'd be lucky. Maybe she'd get some television work or a film and make a lot of bucks quickly. Who knows? she thought. Anything's possible.

At this point Kathy heard something. But it was a sound not immediately identifiable—a foreign sound, unconnected to anything she was thinking about. And so she ignored it. Her brain, preoccupied with worrying, absently stashed it away somewhere: Kathy could consider the nature and significance of this sound later, if necessary; assuming, of course, that she could remember, later, just where in her brain she'd put it.

She looked again at her clock and, to her dismay, saw that only seven minutes had passed. She was going to have to get up and do something, all right.

Baking bread seemed a bit much. And she didn't want to go for a walk, because that would mean getting dressed, and probably by the time she'd gotten dressed, she'd be tired, and then she'd just have to get undressed again. But that's what she wanted, right? To feel tired? Tired enough to sleep...

She wondered what was on TV. Some old series, probably. Maybe an old movie or two.

Now she was hungry. Christ, she said to herself. This was getting ridiculous.

Down the hall she heard the floor squeak again and Sandy's door opening.

Fuck this, thought Kathy, and she flung back her covers. She'd drag Sandy into the kitchen, and they'd make themselves a snack and then go watch TV, and so what if she didn't get any sleep the whole fucking night...

She was halfway to the door when the world exploded.

The next minutes passed like a dream in which flight is imperative but fleeing is impossible. Kathy moved as if swimming through a sea of molasses. She turned, aimed herself at the open bedroom window and propelled herself through it to the hard-packed ground below. It felt to her as though she'd bounced, lightly, like a feather, but later she saw that she'd skinned both her knees. Kathy, the feather, strained across the grass toward the forest, weightless, insubstantial, blown by small desultory puffs of a careless breeze, moving with agonizing slowness—but when she touched the trunk of the first tree, the world snapped back into its proper rhythm, and Kathy, released, ran.

She pelted through the forest, barefoot, sobbing, her hands flung out in front of her to catch branches before they whipped at her face. She stumbled, fell, scrambled to her feet, ran, fell again, staggered up again, ran again. And she heard him behind her, and maybe she imagined this, but it made her run harder and faster, and finally she erupted from the woods onto the highway.

It was sleek and black, and the yellow line down the centre was garish in the moonlight. The wind tossed restlessly in the trees and sent bits of woodland skittering across the road. There wasn't a car in sight. Nor a building, either.

Kathy stood on the highway, panting, looking from left to right, trying not to listen to the sounds in the forest behind her. And when a car did finally appear, from the left, she flattened herself in the ditch and gripped the weeds that grew there; she felt the soft flesh of dandelions dying in her hands. As the car drew closer she forced herself to peer over the shoulder of the road. It was an R.C.M.P. patrol car. Kathy struggled to her feet and began screaming.

Chapter
Forty-Five

*T*he white cat had one hazel eye and one blue one. He sat in the sun on the narrow stone walk that led to the small white house and cleaned himself; his tongue had backward-curving spines like the teeth of a comb. The sun warmed him while he licked—industriously, thoroughly. When it was time to do his face and ears, he licked the inner surfaces of his forepaws and used them as a washcloth.

The cat had been outside for several hours now: he had been frightened from his customary sleeping place on the living room sofa and had fled outdoors to find shelter in a woodshed at the bottom of the yard. He'd emerged just when the sky was beginning to lighten, when a silver sheen hung over the world and the dew was thick on the grass.

The cat had crept back to the house when he saw signs of activity there. From within the screen of lilac bushes by the front door he had observed several people coming and going; none was familiar, so he had backed away, to groom himself in the sun.

Now he sidled along the walk and peered through the doorway. After a moment's hesitation, he edged around the open door into the house.

There were two men at the end of the hall with their backs to the front door. One was standing, the other was kneeling.

They were looking down at the floor. The cat padded near and tried to see around the kneeling man but couldn't.

He slid into the nearest of the bedrooms, where one of the blinds was still down, outlined thinly in sunlight. But the other blind had been raised, and the sun had burst through, falling upon another man who was crouched beside the bed.

The cat crept to the other side of the bed, away from the man. He saw the limp arm that dangled over the edge of the mattress and swatted it with his paw. This attracted the attention of the man, who said, "Get out of here," and made a swift, threatening gesture.

The cat loped away to seek refuge in the living room, where he leapt silently onto the sofa, then the sofa back, and then the open shelving that held books and knickknacks and plants in pots. He stood on his hind legs and reached up, stretching, to sharpen his claws on the heavy cedar from which the bookcase was constructed. Then he sat, front paws close together, and he curled his tail around his body and yawned. Unblinking, he watched the doorway. None of the voices he heard was yet familiar.

A few minutes later he descended from the bookcase and ambled out of the living room, across the hall, and into the kitchen. He lapped some water from one of his dishes and sniffed at the other, which was empty. He went to the doorway and peeked around in time to see the kneeling man stand up.

The cat edged out of the kitchen and slithered along the wall until he got to the inert shape on the floor. Delicately, he sniffed the outflung arm and the large wet spot on the wooden floor.

"Beat it," said one of the men.

The cat ran into one of the other bedrooms and sprang onto the empty, rumpled bed and then onto the windowsill. He sat there in the wide-open window holding his face into the warm, fragrance-laden breeze. Then he leapt down and returned to the kitchen, to sniff again at his food dish.

"You hungry, cat?" said Alberg as he entered the room. The cat uttered a creaky meow. Alberg opened cupboards, hooking his ballpoint pen behind the chrome pulls, until he found a box of dry food. He poured some into the cat's dish.

Sanducci came into the kitchen. "The hospital says you can talk to her now, Staff."

"You okay?" said Alberg. Sanducci's olive skin had an alarming layer of white beneath it.

"Yeah. I'm okay." He hesitated. "Her name's Kathy."

"Kathy," Alberg repeated. He looked closely at the corporal. "You better come with me, Sanducci." They went into the hall. "Alex. Are you finished?"

The doctor leaned, dizzy, against the wall. "Yeah. Jesus."

Alberg went out onto the porch and gestured to the ambulance attendants waiting by their vehicle. When they reached him, he said, "There's one at the end of the hall and one in the first bedroom."

He stood on the porch looking toward the small crowd of people that had gathered on the street in front of the house. It was a relief to get out into the fresh air. He had turned his eyes into a camera, but there was nothing he could do about his other senses, and he was sick from the smell of blood.

"You want to go now, Staff?" said Sanducci.

Alberg glanced back down the hall and quickly away into the living room. He saw blossoms filling a vase that had been set upon a wooden table, branches of deep pink flowers whose petals had begun to fall, scattering themselves over the tabletop and upon the floor.

"Yeah," said Alberg. He put a hand on Sanducci's shoulder. "Let's go talk to Kathy."

Chapter
Forty-Six

A'll Eddie could think of was that they were going to get up, the two of them, what was left of them, all red and dripping, and come after him and Gardiner. He wasn't afraid of the cops or the girl that got away; he was only afraid of the dead girls. He could see them getting onto their dead feet, wobbly and shaken, with blood on their faces, blood on their chests, big chunks of flesh gone, accusation in their eyes. Already he could see this. He'd barely turned away from the open window the girl had gone through when he saw it. Staring down at the one lying dead in the hallway, he'd seen it even in her stillness, her blood-spattered inertness. Even as he saw that she would never move again, he saw her begin to move—to stand, to raise a hand, to point. He leapt over her and ran down the hall after Gardiner, who was already halfway to the car.

Gardiner scuttled across the lawn, across the road, and it looked to Eddie like Gardiner's legs had suddenly become too long for him to manipulate. He was covering ground fast, though, clutching at it, pulling it toward him, like a spider skittering or a person swimming. Eddie was moving fast too. He got to the car just as Gardiner cranked up the motor; he flung himself inside and slammed the door shut.

"Oh god oh jesus," Gardiner kept saying, over and over

again: "Oh god oh jesus."

Eddie didn't say anything. He just looked out the window into the darkness and waited for his heart to stop pounding, waited for his chest to stop hurting, waited for what had happened not to be true. He stared intently at the world Gardiner was rushing them through, seeing it awash in light from the moon. The few houses they sped past were dark; there were no cars on the road, and even when they reached the town, he saw streetlights but no sign of life: it was as if they were all dead, everybody in Sechelt, as if every single person had died when those two girls died.

Except, of course, the girl that got away. But maybe she was dead by now too, Eddie thought, lying dead in the forest, scared to death.

Gardiner took the winding, hilly road to the ferry terminal so fast Eddie felt like he was on a roller coaster. When they got there, a sign told them the first ferry didn't leave until six o'clock.

Gardiner turned to Eddie. "What do we do?"

"Go back in the bush, I guess."

Eddie thought about Sylvia for a minute. He wanted to call her up, so he could hear her talking to him. It wouldn't matter what she said or even if she was mad at him for calling her so early; it would be very good to hear her voice.

Gardiner turned around and drove back to town, and through it, and along the highway for a while, and off onto the logging road, and he parked in the same place they'd spent the evening, waiting for it to be night. "What are we gonna do, Eddie?" he said, when he'd turned off the motor.

Eddie shrugged, feeling immensely weary.

"Do you think she saw us?"

"I don't know."

"We've gotta get outta here. Isn't there another way? Isn't there a goddamn road somewhere?"

"There's another ferry. Up at the other end. It goes over to Vancouver Island."

"And then what, for fuck's sake—we'd have to take another ferry, right? Back to Vancouver? So one way we take one ferry, and the other way we take two ferries—is that right?"

"Right."

Gardiner sank back in his seat. "Fuck. What a fucking mess."

Maybe if they stayed here long enough, Eddie thought, looking at the squashed beer cans and the empty potato chip bags cluttering up the moonlight, time would go back to when it hadn't happened yet. The bends in the beer cans would go away, and they'd fill up with beer again, and the potato chip bags would get smoothed out and fill up with potato chips, and it would be last night again, and he and Gardiner could change their minds and take the last ferry home.

"We gotta disguise ourselves," Gardiner had said—only a few hours ago, although it seemed like years.

"What?" said Eddie, dismayed. "How?"

"Bags over our heads." Gardiner, tossing a can out the window, started cackling. "Or socks. Or those nylon stocking things. Panty hose."

"I'm not wearing a bag on my head," said Eddie sullenly. "And what're you talking about, socks; you couldn't get a sock to go over your head. And I'm not wearing any damn nylon stocking on my face, either."

Gardiner was hooting with laughter now, clutching at his stomach, banging his forehead against the steering wheel.

"We don't need disguises," Eddie insisted loudly. "We're going in there in the middle of the night; they're gonna be asleep."

"No, but we gotta," said Gardiner, sobering up. "You never know; one of them might wake up; maybe a car drives by and backfires or something, and somebody wakes up; it happens, Ed, believe me." He was shaking his head and looking like he knew stuff that Eddie didn't. He started the car and drove them back down to Sechelt.

"Okay," he said to Eddie, parking outside a drugstore, "go in there and get us some panty hose."

"Fuck you," said Eddie promptly.

Gardiner leaned back and sighed. "Look, weasel. Why am I here, eh? Outta friendship. I'm doing you a big favor, here, helping you get yourself out've a big horse trough of shit."

Eddie sat there for a long time. Then he got out of the car and went into the drugstore.

He came out fifteen minutes late carrying a plastic shopping bag.

"What the fuck you got in there?"

"Never mind. Just drive."

"What's in there?" Gardiner said again, pulling out into the traffic.

"Stuff."

"What stuff? Did you get them or not?"

"I got them, I got them."

When they were parked off the logging road in the bush again, Gardiner snatched the bag from Eddie's lap and dumped the contents onto the seat between them. Two pairs of black panty hose, queen size. "Queen size? *Queen* size?" Gardiner sniggered. He pawed through the rest of the stuff: a *Road and Track* magazine, two packages of sugarless gum, an alarm clock in a cardboard box, a bottle of aspirin, and a box of Kleenex. "Why'd you get all this other crap?"

"I couldn't go in there and just get the panty hose," Eddie snapped. "It'd look suspicious."

Gardiner tore open one of the packages, shook the hose free from a piece of cardboard, took hold of the waistband, and pulled it over his head. "Whaddya think?" he said to Eddie. Eddie put up his hand to hide his face. "What do I do with these?" said Gardiner, fingering the legs, which hung down on either side of his head like two enormous rabbit ears.

"You're the expert," said Eddie, smiling behind his hand. "Tie them on top of your head," he suggested, "like they were shoelaces."

So Gardiner did. Eddie laughed out loud.

Gardiner yanked the rearview mirror around so he could get a look at himself. "Fuck," he said, staring. "I'll cut them off."

Eddie unwrapped the second package. Cautiously, he pulled the panty hose over his head. Gardiner, who had removed his mask, looked closely at Eddie. "Jesus, Ed. It really works." He pushed the mirror toward him.

Eddie studied himself. Behind the fabric—which was not

really black, but dark gray—he was unrecognizable, even to himself. His nose was pushed slightly to one side. There were blackish spots where his eyes were, and as he breathed he made a small wet spot. His ears were pushed flat against his head. He had no hair. His whole head looked like a nonhuman thing made of something like rubber.

"Yeah," he said to Gardiner. "It really works. It really does."

And now they were back here again, and the intervening hours had changed their lives forever. The beer cans lay where they'd thrown them, and the potato chip bags too, maybe blown around a little by the wind, but basically right where they'd tossed them. The magazine was on the car floor, and the aspirin bottle was down there too and also the alarm clock in its box. The gum was in Eddie's pocket. The Kleenex was next to him on the seat. Eddie stared at these things. He could give the alarm clock to Harry, he thought.

"What happened, Eddie? What the fuck happened, anyway?" Gardiner asked him in a whisper. Gardiner's eyes were huge.

Eddie just shook his head again. "I don't know," he said, and he was surprised that there wasn't any expression in his voice. It felt like something had cracked to death in his chest and he would have thought this would be obvious in his voice, but it wasn't.

In the car, parked across the road from the house, they'd pulled the panty hose over their heads and made sure the interior light wouldn't come on when they opened the doors.

"Okay, man, let's go for it," said Gardiner, and they got out of the car. "Wait a minute," he'd said, pushing the driver's door softly closed. He went around to the back, unlocked the trunk, and hauled out the shotgun.

"What's that for?" said Eddie, alarmed.

"Just in case they wake up. We'd need it, you know,"—he pointed the shotgun at Eddie—"to keep them under control. 'Til we get them tied up and gagged." He walked across the road and onto the lawn.

"They're not gonna wake up," said Eddie in a furious whisper, following him.

"How the fuck do we get in?" said Gardiner, keeping his voice low. "Maybe they don't lock their doors." He jiggled the handle.

"Shhh!" said Eddie.

Gardiner began tiptoeing along the front of the house.

Eddie pulled nervously at the waistband of the panty hose around his neck. He could see tufts of Gardiner's hair sticking through the holes were the legs had been, and he fumbled at the top of his head to see if that was happening to his hair, too.

"Look at this!" Gardiner whispered excitedly, and he pointed to a window that had been left open about three inches.

Eddie pushed it up and climbed through, and took the shotgun from Gardiner while he climbed in.

They stood still for a moment, listening intently. Eddie blinked frequently behind his mask; it felt like he was keeping his eyes open underwater.

Once they were sure nobody had heard them, they looked cautiously around. They were in a small dining room. Straight ahead, there was a kitchen. Off to the right, across a hallway, a lot of moonlight was pouring into what looked like a living room. The moon was so bright that it lit up the whole front part of the house, which was full of stuff, boxes and bags and piles of clothes. Eddie couldn't see any sign of boxes with MELANIE on them.

"Okay, let's get going," whispered Gardiner. "What does this box look like?" Before Eddie could answer, he went on: "It's probably in the bedroom. We're probably gonna have to go in the bedroom, wake them up. Whaddya say we locate some rope?" he said, still whispering, and he started opening cupboards and drawers.

"Shhh!" Eddie hissed.

And all of a sudden it was like some kind of dream, being there. He couldn't believe he was standing there in some stranger's kitchen. I've done breaking and entering, he kept thinking: breaking and entering—breaking and entering—it repeated itself over and over in his head.

"No," he said to Gardiner, and pulled off his mask. "This is crazy. No." He felt dazed and stupid and terrified. And when he heard noises down the hall it wasn't a surprise to him: it felt to him like thunder does; first you see the lightning, and then comes the thunder—you might not like it much; it might scare the hell out of you; but you knew it was coming; it's no surprise.

Eddie moved two steps to his right and looked down the hall and saw her come out of one of the rooms down there. She looked at him for a split second, and he saw that she had carroty-colored hair, like him. And then Eddie raised the shotgun and fired.

She dropped to the floor amazingly fast, as if he'd shot her legs right out from under her. And behind where she'd been standing, the wall was sprayed red.

Eddie started down the hall toward her—he didn't know what he planned to do when he got there—and heard a sound coming from behind a door on his left. He pushed it open and saw another girl, sitting up in bed, wearing something white, and he lifted the shotgun and fired again. Gardiner was shrieking at him, clawing at his arm. Eddie's only thought was that there were three of them, three girls. He went down the hall to the third bedroom and found an empty bed and an open window. The blind had been whacked upward so hard and so fast that it was still bouncing.

Eddie and Gardiner saw the third girl pause at the edge of the woods, look back toward the house, and disappear into the trees. Gardiner tore his mask off.

"Eddie—Christ—" He was crying and shaking. "—What the fuck—why? why? why?"

Chapter
Forty-Seven

"I heard there was a witness," said Sokolowski from the doorway.

"Yeah. Come on in, Sid."

The sergeant entered Alberg's office and sat down. "What do you figure, Karl?"

Alberg picked up his notebook and flipped back the pages. "Two guys. Amateurs. We know there were two of them because they left footprints, for Christ's sake. Under the window. They climbed in through an open window. An open window," he repeated, looking at Sokolowski, who just shook his head.

"They come in through the window, wearing nylon masks—which they left behind, by the way—and they blow two of the three girls away, and they leave." He tossed the notebook down on his desk. "We got roadblocks at both ferry terminals and the airport. The victims lived in Vancouver— they'd only just arrived here. If it was a premeditated thing, it's got to be somebody they knew over there."

"Why didn't they do the witness, too?"

"Because she happened to be awake and on her feet when the shooting started. She got away. Out the window. Christ. They come in a front window, she goes out a back window, what a farce. Except that in between, two girls get splattered all over the walls. Christ."

261

"What's she got to say?"

"She heard the first shot and ran. That's what she told Sanducci—he picked her up on the highway. I just got back from the hospital, but now she's in shock, and she's not saying anything at all." He went over to the window and raised the venetian blind. "She told him something else too. Originally there were four of them. Four roommates. Sharing a house in Vancouver. A week and a half ago one of them was the victim of a hit-and-run." He looked quizzically at Sid.

"Are you—are you connecting that with this?" said Sokolowski doubtfully.

"I don't know yet. I've got a call in to Vancouver."

"When can you talk to the witness?"

"They say maybe by noon." He leaned toward the sergeant. "If she can give us suspects, we've got the masks, footprints—maybe enough evidence already to nail the bastards."

"But if they went in there to kill them, and not to rob them, then why bother with the masks?"

Alberg shrugged. "In case somebody saw them going in or coming out, maybe."

"Okay. Another alternative. Maybe we got us a couple of local looney-tunes here."

"It's possible," said Alberg. "But I don't think so. We know all the crazies on the Coast. I can't think of one of them who'd pull something like this."

"I gotta get something to eat," said Eddie, talking loudly over the sound of the wind rushing in through the open window.

"Fuck that. Wait 'til we're on the ferry—then eat," said Gardiner, maneuvering the Olds pell-mell along the road toward Sechelt.

"I gotta eat now. Or I'm gonna pass out or something. I need something on my stomach right now. Stop at the next place. I mean it, Gardiner. I'm gonna be sick, or die, or something." If he'd been in Vancouver, he could have gone to Sylvia's house for a lettuce and tomato sandwich and a beer. But he wasn't in Vancouver, and it scared him not to be there because it was making Sylvia's house get hazy in his mind—it was like he was running away from it, backward, watching it get smaller and smaller.

Gardiner was shrieking at him. "What are you, crazy? We gotta get outta here!"

"No, I gotta eat first," said Eddie doggedly. Gardiner was sweating a lot. He kept wiping the sweat off his face with his shirt-sleeve, but it just popped out again, and it must've been pouring into his armpits too. The smell of it was making Eddie nauseous.

"Shut the damn window," Gardiner yelled, and Eddie was shivering with the cold by now, so he rolled up the window, which made the smell a whole lot worse.

"I gotta eat," said Eddie. "Right now."

"Shit!" said Gardiner. But he swerved off the road to park in front of a café with a sign out front that said "Earl's."

From the car, they peered in through the big front window.

"This is crazy, man, crazy," said Gardiner.

Eddie opened the passenger door and got out. All of his bones ached. He'd always been convinced that when he got pain, it was more pain than most people would suffer from exactly the same ailment. Eddie was bigger than most people, and therefore so was his pain.

They sidled into the café—that is, Gardiner sidled in; Eddie just walked in as if everything was normal, thinking about nothing but the pain in his bones and his hunger. Gardiner led the way to the table that was farthest from the door. He slithered into a chair and immediately opened the menu, crouching down behind it.

Eddie didn't look at the menu. He already knew what he wanted. "Pancakes and sausages," he said to the Chinese man who took their order. "And a large glass of orange juice. And coffee."

"Just coffee," said Gardiner. "I want to look at this some more," he said, hanging on to the menu.

Eddie took a few cautious looks around. There weren't many people in the place. A big guy with a beard sat at a table near the window; there was a young brown-and-white dog at his feet, which kind of surprised Eddie, who thought there was some kind of law against letting animals into restaurants. Unless they were Seeing Eye dogs, of course, which this one wasn't. And a tired-looking woman sat at another table, drinking coffee and smoking and reading a paperback book. And there was a young guy at the counter. He was wearing the kind of coveralls that mechanics wear and eating what looked to be bacon and eggs.

Gardiner continued to hide behind the menu.

The Chinese man set down the orange juice and two mugs of coffee.

A little later he returned with Eddie's pancakes.

"Put down the menu, Gardiner," said Eddie, just as a young guy with longish hair came in.

"Hi, Warren," said the young guy, sitting down next to the mechanic.

"Yo, Bentley," said the mechanic.

"I'll have a coffee, Earl," said Bentley.

Eddie, eating his pancakes, listened to them at first idly and then intently. Gardiner, once he clued in to what they were saying, started giving Eddie urgent little kicks under the table, which Eddie ignored.

"Who is this you're talking about?" said Warren, the mechanic.

"Girls from Vancouver. Over here for the summer. They were renting the Lester place up on Anchor Road," said Bentley, who, it turned out, was an ambulance driver.

"And somebody killed them?" said the mechanic, sounding incredulous. "Why?"

"How do I know why? They're dead, that's all I know. Shot to death. Two of them. What a mess. You never saw anything like it." He drank almost his entire cup of coffee in one gulp. "The other one's in the hospital. Shock. Jesus. No wonder."

"Who did it?" said the proprietor.

"Jesus, Earl, I don't know who did it. The cops don't know who did it—how the hell would *I* know who did it? Gimme an order of brown toast too, will you?"

"Eddie!" hissed Gardiner.

Eddie forked pancakes and maple syrup into his mouth.

"And you know," Bentley went on, "this is weird, but it turns out they used to live with Melanie Franklin. Now, is that weird, or is that weird?"

"Eddie, we gotta get going," said Gardiner, who was sweating even more now and wiping it off his face with serviettes from the metal container on the table.

I could pretend I worked in the hospital, thought Eddie, trying to plan. A janitor. Or I could pretend to be her brother or something.

"Eddie!" said Gardiner, more loudly. But nobody else heard him. Everybody in the café was listening, transfixed, to Bentley, the ambulance driver.

"Her folks moved up to Lund, I think," said Earl, setting a plate of brown toast on the counter in front of the ambulance driver. "Last summer."

Eddie pulled his wallet out of his back pocket. It was thin, because there was hardly anything in it, and curved, because he sat on it so much. He pulled out a five. Earl spotted this and came over to the table with a coffeepot. "Just the bill," said Eddie.

Gardiner was wiping the palms of his hands on his knees. He was pale and continued to sweat, watching Earl write out their bill.

Eddie knew from movies that's what he ought to do, all right. Sneak into the hospital in disguise and—and what? Do what? He slapped the five down on top of the bill. "Come on," he said to Gardiner, and plodded from the restaurant, Gardiner skittering in his wake.

Chapter
Forty-Eight

"**W**e're trying to see if there's a connection," said Alberg gently, "between what happened to Melanie and what happened here last night."
Norah Gibbons sat in a chair next to Kathy Schofield's bed, taking notes. But Sanducci, standing at the foot, was taking notes too. Constable Gibbons was mostly keeping an eye on Kathy.

"Yes," said Kathy. "I see."

Sanducci thought she had shrunk since he'd first seen her in the gray Reliant, with her roommates and the skunk cabbages. And every bit of color had been bleached from her face. Her eyes were unnaturally round—sometimes he could see an edging of white all the way around the pupil. Only her hair looked as he remembered it, thick and dark, cut away behind one ear, falling softly across the opposite cheek. He chastised himself halfheartedly for having lustful thoughts about a person still suffering a severe case of shock.

"Well, actually," said Kathy, "no, I don't see."

She was in a hospital bed, wearing a hospital gown. When he had stopped the patrol car for her, she'd had on a pair of cotton Jockey shorts made for women and a sleeveless cotton undershirt. She was scratched, scraped, dirty, and hysterical.

"I mean, if you're saying maybe Melanie was—that it wasn't really an accident...the police came, you know. And talked to us." She began nodding her head, her conviction

267

growing. "It was definitely an accident. Definitely."

"I think we have to consider the alternative, though. Even if it's just to be thorough."

Sanducci actually saw her heartbeat accelerate. He happened to be looking at her throat, at the small, pale hollow at the base of her elegant neck, and he saw the beating of her heart cause the skin there to shudder and vibrate. He looked quickly at Alberg, who was leaning forward, his hands clasped lightly between his knees; he looked completely relaxed, as if he had all the time in the world and absolutely nothing on his mind but Kathy.

From the other side of the bed, Norah Gibbons said firmly, "It's all right, Kathy. You're perfectly safe. Your parents are on their way. And we'll be with you every minute until they get here." She reached to touch the back of Kathy's hand. Kathy squeezed her eyes tightly closed, and grabbed Norah's hand in both of hers, holding it so tightly that Sanducci saw it whiten in Kathy's grip. Norah Gibbons and Alberg exchanged a glance. Alberg gave an almost imperceptible shake of his head. Kathy had begun to weep. Tears washed down her cheeks and flooded the tiny lines on either side of her mouth and splashed from the edge of her jaw. Alberg got a handful of tissues from a box on the table next to the bed and tucked it into the clasping of Kathy's hands with Norah's.

Sanducci was acutely aware of himself. It was cruelly difficult to stand here doing nothing. He was at his best when he was physically active. He felt confident, then, and purposeful. He hated standing still. He hated taking notes.

He looked through the small window in the top of the door and saw a figure hurrying past along the corridor, a female figure wearing a white hat; and he could hear brief, muted messages being relayed over an intercom system. But it seemed to him that the world out there was ephemeral, that the only reality was here, that it was a false and treacherous reality that could be blown apart in an instant with a single shotgun blast, and that there ought to be something he could do to prevent this.

Kathy let go of Norah's hand and rubbed at her face with the tissues. She blew her nose and opened her eyes, blinking furiously, gazing straight into Sanducci's face. He felt his heart soar into his throat.

"Yeah. But it's a hard thing to wrap your mind around. That somebody—" She turned to look at Alberg. "I don't know how to do this. I don't know what you want me to do."

"I want you to think hard and make a list of anybody you can think of who might have had a grudge against Melanie or Sandy or Caroline or—"

"Or me."

Alberg nodded. "Or you."

She was already shaking her head. "There's nobody. I'm telling you. There isn't anybody."

"We're looking for anything—anything at all," said Alberg. "Somebody one of you stood up. Jilted. Wronged in some way. Or who could have thought he'd been wronged."

"'He,'" said Kathy.

"Yeah. Definitely a *he*." Alberg stood up. "Wrack your brains, okay, Kathy? Constable Gibbons and Corporal Sanducci will help you."

Chapter
Forty-Nine

*E*mma felt the need to seek advice—but from whom would she seek it? She sat in her living room and looked around her and wondered at the smallness of the world she'd made for herself. There were really only two people in it. Herself and Charlie.

She went outdoors and observed the cedar trees and the hanging baskets and the lush green lawn and the tulips, a splash of red against the house—but she wasn't touched by these things, not the way she'd been touched when she was seeing for Charlie. There'd been a sweetness to the surface of her then that she'd reveled in. And everything that came bubbling out through that surface was also sweet—had a sweet taste to it—and she'd given it to Charlie lovingly, unstintingly. And now it was gone, that layer of sweetness. She was like a face stripped bare of makeup. And beneath it Emma found herself raw and unpredictable.

She went back inside, thinking that there was nothing to give shape to her days, now. No responsibilities. No obligations. No assignment, anymore, to see the world for Charlie, to be a wife for Charlie. She had given herself to him as a gift, and it had never occurred to her that this was a gift he might have grown not to want.

"My mother was right. There's something unnatural about

me," she said to herself, regarding her face in the bathroom mirror. Yet she didn't look particularly unusual.

"I'm at the very beginning of my life," she said to herself. But this was only theoretically true.

She banged around inside her house for a while, feeling like somebody's caged-up budgie.

And then Emma went into the bedroom and took the gun from the drawer—which opened soundlessly—and once more she acknowledged that this was the only truly personal thing he had left behind, and that he'd placed it where she could be sure to find it. So, she thought, removing the oily cloth in which it was wrapped, it shouldn't surprise him that she'd adopted it as her own.

She put the revolver on the bed and took out the box of cartridges. She selected six, and loaded the cylinder. She put the cloth and the box back in the drawer and closed it.

Emma put the opera glasses in her left-hand jacket pocket and the revolver in her right-hand jacket pocket, picked up her handbag, left the house, got in her car, and headed north, back toward Ruby Lake.

Chapter
Fifty

"ook, man," said Gardiner. "I'm pleading with you, I'm begging you, we gotta get outta here *now*, right *now*, Eddie. Eddie. Eddie! Do you hear me? Do you hear me, man?"

"I hear you, Gardiner," said Eddie, who was buried in a highway map of the Sunshine Coast. "We're gonna get outta here, all right. We're just going to go the long way."

Gardiner, clutching the top of the steering wheel, let his face fall forward. Eddie thought he might be bawling.

"We're gonna go up there to Lund," Eddie said stubbornly, "because that's where those boxes are. No question about it. They're up there with her folks," he told Gardiner with conviction. "No place else they could be."

"I want to go home, Eddie. Now." Gardiner lifted up his head, and Eddie was relieved to see that he hadn't been bawling after all.

Reluctantly, Eddie shook his head. "I told you, I'm not driving this heap onto any ferry until I got those notes in my hand."

"Eddie, Eddie," Gardiner pleaded, "the fuckin' boxes were in one of the fuckin' bedrooms, they had to be."

"No," said Eddie, shaking his head. "They would've been out in the living room part, if they'd been there. Nobody'd keep a dead person's stuff in the bedroom with them. I told you, it's at her folks' place. And that's where we're headed."

"Fuck you, Eddie." Gardiner sounded like he was at the end of his rope. Eddie thought he might be near the end of his, too.

"Lund is a very small place," said Eddie, studying the map. "No way there's gonna be more than one Franklin family there. We wait 'til it's dark, we break in, we find the boxes, I get my notes—and that's it. We're homeward bound."

"You wanna steal us a shotgun first?" said Gardiner bitterly. "Or a rifle, maybe? There ought to be some hunter types living away to hell and gone out here. Then, if the dudes wake up while you're rippin' 'em off, you can just blow them away too."

Eddie sank back in his seat. He raised a hand and wiped his face with it, then gripped his forehead between his thumb and middle finger, rubbing his temples, pressing his forehead. He stared out the window, brooding. They were parked at a roadside rest stop next to a big jeezly motor home with Minnesota plates. The people from the motor home had spread their lunch out on a nearby picnic table. Eddie looked through his window at their food and thought he might have to throw up before long. "It won't be ripping them off," he said. "I only want to get back what's mine."

"But Jesus Christ, Eddie, is it worth going around wasting people for?"

Eddie started folding up the map. "The cops don't know nothin' about us. There's no way they can know we did it."

"'We'? What the fuck's this 'we'?"

Eddie stared out through the windshield. "You're right," he said painfully. "Me. They can't know it was me who did it."

"Yeah. Right. They'll find the fucking shotgun, and it's me they'll come after."

Eddie turned to him. "They won't find the shotgun. Why would they find the shotgun? But if by any chance they do, you just tell them you lent it to me."

Gardiner snatched a glance at him. "You bet I'll do that, too," he said in a mutter.

"But they won't find it. The only thing they could find that would be bad for us is those notes."

"Stupid weasel," Gardiner grumbled. "I told you how dumb that was."

"Yeah, yeah, yeah." Eddie slapped the folded map on the dashboard. "Come on. Let's get outta here. Let's get it over with."

"She's doing real well," said Constable Gibbons with a smile as Alberg entered Kathy's room.

"It's very depressing," said Kathy, "to actually face the fact that there are definitely people in the world who don't like you."

"Not many, I'll bet," said Alberg, looking over Sanducci's shoulder at his notebook. "No. Not many at all. Don't get up, Corporal."

"I also remembered a couple of weird things that happened," said Kathy, and she told him about the day somebody had taken their mail and then put it back. "And we found out later there was a letter missing—from the theater company that hired us."

"What did it say?"

"That they hoped we wouldn't change our minds about coming to Sechelt."

Alberg nodded. "What was the other thing?"

"There's a woman who lives across the street from us . . . " She broke off suddenly. "This doesn't feel real. None of this feels real."

"Go on, Kathy," said Norah Gibbons. "What about her? What's her name?"

"Her name—it's Garber. Mrs. Garber."

"And what do you want to tell us about her?"

Kathy was staring into Constable Gibbons's face. "I'm the only one left."

"I know, Kathy. I know. Now, tell us about Mrs. Garber."

"She—she came over. The night before we left. To tell us—"

"What?" said Alberg gently.

"—somebody—she'd seen somebody—lurking, she said. Lurking around her house, but she said he seemed to be interested in our house." She reached for Norah Gibbons's hand. "I am really scared. I don't know what's going on."

"I know. But hang in there, Kathy. We need you. Okay?"

"I'll try. Okay."

"Tell me about this list of names," said Alberg.

"This first part," said Sanducci, pointing, "these people date from before the four girls started sharing a house."

"Women," said Kathy.

Sanducci looked startled. Then, "Oh, sorry, women, the four women."

"Uh huh," said Alberg. "Good. Okay, Kathy. Tell me about them. And let's start with the most recent and work our way back."

"The first one was—well, it was still going on when we came over here," said Kathy. She reached for a glass of water. "It was a guy Caroline was going out with. He gave her a bad time for a while." She took a long drink.

"What kind of a bad time?" said Constable Gibbons.

"She told him she didn't want to see him anymore, but he couldn't take no for an answer, you know? At least at first. So he sent her these, like, voluminous letters. And later he'd send her taped ones. She played them for us. There was nothing really bad in them. They were just—vaguely threatening."

"Did she keep them?" said Alberg.

Kathy shook her head. "She burned the letters and sent the tapes back to him."

"And he's the first name here?"

"Yeah. The next guy—this is reaching pretty far, I have to tell you. It's somebody Melanie had some trouble with. I don't know exactly what."

"'Drugstore guy,'" said Alberg, reading from Sanducci's list.

"Yeah," said Kathy. "I don't know his name. She had some kind of a run-in with him." She hesitated. "Melanie could be a little—haughty. You know? So sometimes she offended people. But this time, whatever it was, she was kinda shaken up."

"Okay. And the third one—Sam Peterson."

"Yeah," said Kathy glumly. "He's mine. You know, I really don't like this. I feel like I'm slandering people."

"I know," said Alberg, smiling at her.

"Sam Peterson. It was last fall. He wanted me to be in a student film he was directing, and I said no. But I'd said yes first, so he got pretty mad. Really mad. Raged around throwing things and stuff."

"Have you heard from him since?"

"He called me up when he'd finished his film and told me the actress who'd done it was a lot better than I'd ever be." She shrugged. "That's all."

"Okay. Sam. Who's next?" said Alberg, glancing at his watch.

Back at the detachment, he got a call from Vancouver about the hit-and-run. "Did you do a background check on the victim?" he asked.

"We did the whole nine yards. Sure we did a background check."

"What do you know?"

"Why are you interested, Staff Sergeant?"

"She had three roommates."

"Yeah."

"They came up here for the summer."

"Yeah?"

"Two of them got blown away last night."

There was silence from Vancouver.

"The third one would have got it too," said Alberg. "Except she dived out her bedroom window and got away."

He heard the shuffling of papers. Then, "Vehicle's a '81 Camaro, bronze over original red. We're working on an area vehicle check through Motor Vehicles."

"Thanks," said Alberg.

Chapter
Fifty-One

Eddie would have laughed about it, except for the situation they were in. He ought to have known better than to go anywhere in a car belonging to Gardiner without checking the thing out himself. "I never heard of anybody," he said heavily, gazing at the useless Oldsmobile, "who didn't carry an extra fan belt with him."

"Well you've heard of him now," said Gardiner defensively. He kicked the right front tire, which to Eddie didn't make much sense. "So what the fuck do we do now?"

"It's your car, Gardiner."

"And it's your fucking neck, Ed," Gardiner snapped.

Eddie lumbered over to the edge of the gravel shoulder and leaned against a big tree. He was very tired. He thought about his apartment, his bedroom: it had a little window high up in the wall, and there was a flowerbed on the other side of it. In the summertime the leaves of the dahlias were all that he could see. Eddie never bothered to close the curtains in the summertime because the dahlias kept out the sun and nobody could see through them into his bedroom. They were up now, the dahlias. Summer had already started really, even though the weather wasn't good yet. There was lots of stuff growing, and blooming.

Inside Eddie's bedroom was his bed, which was a three-quarter-size bed, and he had a wooden table next to it with a lamp on top and an ashtray just in case he felt like having a smoke in the middle of the night. There was a small chest of drawers too, but he had to keep it inside the closet because there wasn't room for it anywhere else.

Through the open door of his bedroom when he lay in his bed waiting to go to sleep, he could see pretty clearly into the living room because of the light from the streetlamp that fell in through the window out there.

He wished he were home right now. Making himself some dinner or watching TV or going through his envelopes or talking to Sylvia on the phone. His longing to be home was like a big ache. And this ache, in addition to hurting him, made him terribly sad.

Gardiner was slouched against the fender of the Oldsmobile, lighting a cigarette. Eddie watched him wave the match in the air until it went out and then drop it on the ground. It was still too wet to worry about forest fires.

They were on a deserted stretch of the highway. There was some traffic now and then, but no other sign of life at all. All Eddie could see, north and south, was the highway, narrow and curving, with forest crowding close on both sides.

He figured they were about half an hour from Earl's Cove, which the map said was the name of the place where they'd take a ferry over to the other side of Jervis Inlet, where Powell River was, and then Lund.

"So what do you want to do?" said Gardiner. "Hitchhike?" He cackled, and Eddie thought that was probably a good sign: he was getting back to normal. "Or maybe there's buses come along here," said Gardiner, and he cackled again.

"No," said Eddie, who must have been thinking about it, because here he was with an idea. "We're gonna have to flag somebody down, get him to take us somewhere, to a town somewhere, where we can find a car to take."

"Take?"

"Take. Borrow."

"Borrow?" Gardiner was cackling again.

"For a while," said Eddie. "Just until we get home."

"Why don't we just 'borrow' the one the guy's in

that we flag down?"

"Because he'll be looking right at us," said Eddie patiently. "And as soon as we take off, he'll call the cops." He glanced left and right at the unfriendly woods. "It might take him a while to find a phone, but sooner or later, we'd be dead meat."

They poised themselves expectantly on the highway side of Gardiner's Olds and began to wait.

Gardiner finished his cigarette and lit up another one.

A car appeared, a speck in the distance, and got big enough to reveal itself as a station wagon, and Eddie and Gardiner waved vigorously, but the wagon shot by without anybody in it even giving them a glance.

This happened several times.

Finally, Eddie took a good look at Gardiner.

"You look like shit," he said disapprovingly.

Gardiner's denim overalls were oil-splotched and food-stained. His work boots were scuffed and dusty. The flannel shirt was frayed at the collar. Most of his hair was standing straight up, forced upward when he pulled off the nylon mask, frozen there by dirt and vestiges of mousse. Also he needed a shave, as usual. So did Eddie, of course, but in every other way his appearance was an improvement over Gardiner's.

"Stand over there," he ordered Gardiner. "Behind the car."

Gardiner protested, and lit another smoke.

"Can I have one of those?" said Eddie irritably. He shouldn't have had to ask. Gardiner should have noticed that he'd run out hours ago.

281

Chapter
Fifty-Two

E mma, driving, let memory flood unchecked and examined with scrupulous deliberation the recollection that emerged. It was Charlie laughing. She couldn't remember the occasion, but it was a real memory, all right, and there was such love in his eyes, such openness in his face, that she felt an eager surge of hope.

Reminiscence is not a good idea, she thought, driving, her hands tight on the wheel. She was being careful to keep strictly to the speed limit. She couldn't allow herself to get pulled over with a loaded gun in her pocket.

She'd park at the top of the hill and wait until it got dark, wait until there were no lights burning in the café or in any of the motel units, and then she'd drive down the hill and park across the highway, and then she'd walk over there, around the café and back where the motel was, and she'd find Charlie. She was going to scare the hell out of Charlie O'Brea. She had it all planned.

She had to be angry, though, to do it. Where had all her anger gone? Chased away by that image of Charlie laughing.

She conjured up another.

I'll bleed all over her sofa, Emma had told him. He believed her too. He'd looked awful as it sunk in. So bug-eyed and sweaty that for a split second she almost changed her mind and let him have his damn divorce.

But she'd kept her mouth shut and just stood there, feeling very strong. Extremely strong. Victorious. Knowing this was a phase and there would be another one and another, straining in her mind to see beyond the present and all the intermediate phases to the last one—where there would be peace between them again, and they would stretch out their hands to one another—knowing they would get there but wondering how long it would take, and how much pain there would be.

Charlie's eyes bugged out more and more. Emma was fascinated. Is it possible, she wondered, is it physiologically possible that they might pop out altogether? And if that happens, what on earth can I do about it? She'd catch them in her hands, she decided, and slap them back into their sockets and hope for the best.

Then Charlie whirled around, looking for something, Emma couldn't imagine what. The vase? The big vase? He was striding to the corner table where it sat holding branches of bright yellow forsythia, and he picked it up and hurled it. Emma watched, astonished, as it soared across the room and crashed into the mirror above the fireplace.

And Charlie proceeded to demolish the living room.

Emma found her voice and shouted at him to stop. She ducked as books and heavy ashtrays flew through the air. She flung up her arms to shield her face from flying glass and china and crystal. It seemed to last forever, but finally it stopped. She heard a tinkling sound, window glass falling from its frame. She heard Charlie's harsh breath coming fast and faster. She stood with her head bowed, waiting, heard Charlie's feet crunch across the debris and down the hall, heard the front door open and slam shut.

Emma went into the kitchen after a while and made a pot of tea. She sat at the table drinking it and wondering what was going to happen next. Her life had been detonated. Its pieces had fallen willy-nilly around her head.

A long time later, Charlie came back. He'd brought an emergency-glass person with him. The glass man was chattering cheerfully when he came through the front door with Charlie. "Whoops," he said when he saw the inside of the house, and that was the last word he spoke the whole time he was there.

Charlie directed the glass man to the broken windows. Then he got some cardboard cartons from the garage and some garbage bags from under the kitchen sink and started working on the mess.

Good, thought Emma. And she went to bed.

She thought that was the worst of it. But it wasn't.

Now she realized that waking up and seeing the gun wasn't the worst of it either. Nor was involuntarily filling the bed with her own urine. The worst of it came after that. Now, only now, she knew this.

Charlie broke down and began sobbing, and she comforted him. Sitting in her pee, she comforted him. She could smell it, her pee, as she held Charlie's face tightly to her breasts and stroked the nape of his neck and said, "Shhh," over and over.

He calmed, gradually. She handed him some tissues. He took them and wiped his face. He looked like—well, Emma had heard the phrase, "like a beaten dog," but never having seen a beaten dog she hadn't known exactly what it meant, until this moment. Tears came into her eyes as she looked at him, her husband, the beaten dog.

Charlie looked back at her. And something changed in his face. "I'm sorry," he said.

At the time she'd thought the change in his expression was the reemerging of his love for her, the forging of a new resolve to live with her kindly and purposefully.

"I'm sorry," said Charlie.

Now she knew that he had been apologizing, not for what he'd done, but for what he was going to do. In that moment Charlie had decided that he would leave and *how* he would leave—furtively, stealthily, craftily, like the sneaking son-ofabitch he must have been all along.

And all that stuff he was to spew about starting over had been nothing but a lie. The whole last perfect year—one big lie. And how had this happened? How had she gotten from calmly deciding upon wifehood as a career, to attempted suicide? To threats of public blood-spilling? Is this what devotion is? Emma wondered. What love is? What madness is? Had she let

Charlie drive her into madness?

"Sonofabitch!" Emma shouted, pounding on the steering wheel, glancing skyward through the windshield—and she looked back at the road just as a large man appeared from nowhere to leap directly into the path of her car.

Emma wrenched the wheel to the right and trod hard on the brake pedal. The man was at her window before she came to a complete stop.

"Sorry," he said. "Sorry to scare you like that."

Emma rolled down the window. "What's the matter with you?" she said, shaking, her voice shaking too. "Don't you know I could've killed you?"

He gestured to a car about fifty feet away, sitting at the side of the road. "My car broke down."

"I'll get you some help," said Emma, starting to roll up the window.

"No, hey, we need a ride."

"'We'?"

"Yeah, me and my friend, there."

She saw another man appear from behind the parked car. He was wearing overalls. "It's out of the question," she said, watching the man with the overalls loping toward them.

"Hey, no, I'm sorry, but we gotta get to a town, see?"

"I told you," said Emma, "I'll call somebody for you. I'll get you some help."

"Open the fucking door," said the man in the overalls.

They were both crowding against the car now. Emma had managed to roll the window up halfway, but the big man had his arm inside, and she could smell dirt and sweat and strangeness.

"I will get you help!" she shouted. "Leave me alone! Get your arm out of my car!"

"Fuck this, I'm gettin' a rock," said the man in the overalls, and he half-turned away.

"No!" shouted Emma, and she pulled the revolver out of her pocket. "No!"

The man wearing overalls glanced back. When he saw the gun he turned a greeny-white color, his eyeballs rolled up, and he crashed to the ground.

286

Eddie, watching her, considered taking his arm out of the window. He felt pretty stupid with it stuck in there anyway. But then a whole lot of stuff went through his head, very fast. And the thing that stuck there, the thing that mattered, was that what he was seeing in the face of this person was his doom.

He gazed at Emma with extraordinary tenderness, and thrust his arm farther into the car, his hand, she thought, seeking the lock on the door.

"No," said Emma. "Please." And she shut her eyes, averted her face, and fired.

Chapter Fifty-Three

The window shattered, spraying Emma with hard-edged pieces of glass. The roar made by the firing of the revolver went on and on. Emma sat in the driver's seat shaking and weeping, her eyes still tightly closed. The revolver had flown out of her hand. She wiped that hand again and again on her jacket, crying out. She didn't know what she was saying. She couldn't hear herself; she couldn't hear anything but the roar. It was as if a bomb had gone off in the car. Maybe I'm hurt, she thought. Her eyes flew open, and she looked quickly down at herself but saw no sign of injury.

But, oh, God, what about the big man with the red hair...

Her heart was pounding so hard—maybe that's what's making the roaring noise, she thought, maybe it's my heart.

She scrabbled for the seat-belt release, her hands shaking so much she was afraid for a moment she wouldn't be able to do it, that she'd have to sit there for eternity, in hell or in purgatory, forever unable to flee the scene of her crime. But finally the seat belt popped free. Emma scrambled across the passenger seat, unlocked the door, and opened it, and fell out onto the ground.

She lay on the grass that met the shoulder of the road, facing the car. On the other side she could see two inert bodies. It was only right, she thought, that she lie there with them, separated from them only by the width of the car, until somebody came along who knew what to do in situations like this, somebody who could take charge of the bodies, all three of them. And the gun too. She felt her breath on her hand and the wetness of tears that continued to fall. She stared hard at the two bodies on the other side of the car, willing life into them.

And it worked too. One of them started moving. He got himself up on his hands and knees, leaning over the other one. And then through the roaring, Emma heard a shriek and saw him try to stand up and fall and try again—and this time he made it, and she saw him stagger away, moving unsteadily as if he were drunk. But the other man kept on lying there, still as a stone.

Finally, Emma pushed herself to her feet. She made herself go around the car and look down at the red-haired man. Then she started walking shakily along the edge of the highway.

It took her twenty minutes to get to the Ruby Lake café.

She pushed the door open and stood there with her back to the sun, and for a minute she couldn't see anything. She blinked several times, and shapes began to emerge: a long counter, several small tables each with four chairs, linoleum on the floor, a blackboard menu behind the counter.

And Charlie, standing very still and looking at her. He was the only person there. Emma was glad of that.

She saw that his mouth was open and he was saying something.

"I can't hear you," she said. Her voice sounded small and distant. "I can't hear you," she said loudly. "There's a big roaring; I can't hear anything." She started to move toward him. He slipped around the corner of the counter so that he was behind it. Oh, damn, I didn't bring the gun, Emma thought. She sat on one of the counter stools. Why had she wanted to bring the gun, anyway? She looked long and hard at Charlie and placed both hands on the countertop in front of her. She saw for the first time that there was blood on them. She took a napkin from the metal container in front of her and started brushing at her hands.

Charlie took one, too, and dampened it at the sink behind him. He reached out and put his left hand against the nape of

Emma's neck. She hoped very much that he wasn't planning to kiss her.

"I don't want you to kiss me, Charlie. I never liked being kissed by you, I'm afraid."

She couldn't tell what he was thinking. With his right hand he started wiping her face, very gently, and she saw blood stain the napkin and saw tiny chunks of glass falling as he wiped.

"I wouldn't have done it, Charlie, I think," she said. "I don't think I would have done that to Helena." She spoke loudly, pushing each word separately through the world of noise in which she was trapped. She didn't say anything more. She lived in the roar of noise and felt flicks of pain ripple across her face and looked into Charlie's eyes and didn't know him.

When he was finished, he leaned very close and said, "What happened?"

"I shot somebody." She started to shake again. "Dead." She pulled her jacket closely around her, causing her hands to sting. "It was an accident. You better call the police."

After he made the call, Charlie poured her some coffee and poured some for himself too. He came around the counter to sit next to her. He put his left hand over her right hand, and Emma looked curiously at this, her small pale hand covered almost completely by Charlie's larger brown one. She gazed into his face. She could ask him about her picture now. She was pretty sure he'd tell her just about anything she wanted to know. She could ask him why he'd put the gun in the night table drawer.

"I wonder if this roaring in my head will ever go away," she said. She withdrew her hand from under Charlie's and took off her wedding ring and her jade ring and her silver bracelet. She put them down in front of her. After a while she slid them along the countertop to Charlie. "I don't want these anymore."

Charlie started to protest, then he turned quickly to look out the window, and Emma did, too, and saw the police car. They stood up.

"Charlie," she said, and he turned back to her. "Please come to the house at your earliest convenience. And pack up all your things."

Chapter
Fifty-Four

"I'll do it for you," said Sanducci."

"What?" said Kathy, amazed. They were sitting in the hospital waiting room. Kathy was wearing clothes brought to her by Norah Gibbons—shorts and a T-shirt and a pair of thongs.

"Yeah," said Sanducci, who was keeping her company until her parents arrived. "I'll do it. I mean, somebody has to. It might as well be me."

"I thought—my mom and dad and I would..."

"Come on, Miss Schofield. You don't want to go back in that house."

"No, I don't *want* to—"

"So let me do it. I'm off duty in a couple of hours. I'll take care of it then." He watched her push her hair away from the side of her face. He was very relieved that she was no longer in danger.

"Corporal Sanducci—"

"Eduardo," said Sanducci, flushing. But this caused her to smile at him, so he didn't mind it. He thought she was the most beautiful woman he'd ever met.

"You call me Kathy, then, okay?"

"Kathy. Right." Maybe not beautiful. He couldn't tell. But he'd definitely never met anybody he liked looking at so much.

Her smile faded away. "When you go there—will

293

it be—cleaned up?"

"Not yet."

"Who does that?"

"The owner of the house. Or else he'll hire somebody."

They were sitting on a vinyl sofa near the door, next to a tall plant. Kathy reached out and brushed a layer of dust from one of its large, thick leaves. "I never thought about that before," she said. "I mean, when I read in the paper about things like this happening, I never thought about who'd be cleaning it up." She glanced at Sanducci. "I guess I kind of assumed it would be the police."

Sanducci shook his head.

"No," said Kathy. "I mean, it's bad enough you have to spend time there looking for evidence and stuff. You don't want to have to—clean it up, as well." She tucked her hands together in her lap. "I feel like doing it, you know? I don't mean I *want* to, exactly. But I just feel like I ought to do it."

"Because you got away, and they didn't?" He wanted to go to bed with her, sure, of course he did. But he thought that if he couldn't do that, he'd be happy to just sit here and look at her, and listen to her, for the rest of his life.

"Yeah, maybe," she said. "But also—it would be doing something for them, you know?"

"No," said Sanducci, "you're wrong about that. They wouldn't want you to do that for them. They definitely would not want that." Through the glass doors he saw a middle-aged couple hurrying from the parking lot toward the hospital. "I'll get Norah to help me," he said, turning his service cap in his hands. "We'll get your stuff and your roommates', too. And, uh, I could probably go over there in a day or so, take it to you over there in Richmond, at your folks' place. If you want."

"That would be great," said Kathy, smiling at him.

Her parents burst through the door, and Sanducci stood and watched while Kathy ran toward them and into their arms.

"Holed up there like a rat in a nest. I never did like that man," said Bernie, her arms crossed over her flat chest.

"I don't think I'm ever going to hear properly again," said Emma, banging her left temple with the heel of her hand. She was sitting at the kitchen table with a cup of coffee. "Sid Sokolowski told me that might happen."

"You just be happy you're alive, never mind you can't hear things right. You coulda been killed dead, like those poor girls."

"Will you go to court with me, Bernie? For moral support?"

"You just bet your life I will."

Self-defense, that was Emma's plea. Her lawyer was pretty confident. But there were weapons charges, too.

"At least I didn't have to stay in jail," she said with a shudder.

"I would've stopped doing for Mr. Alberg," said Bernie fiercely, "if he'd clapped you in jail."

She'd been released on recognizance, because she was known in the community, and not considered to be a danger to herself or others. Emma had found the whole process humiliating, but fascinating.

She was going to sell the house and move somewhere, just as soon as this business was over and she was free to go where she liked.

She looked out the window into the backyard. She thought about the red-haired man. It ought to make her feel better about shooting him, knowing he'd murdered two people. But it didn't. She couldn't get it out of her mind, the inexplicable gentleness on his face, just before she killed him.

"We don't know which one of them actually did the shooting," said Alberg. "The one that's alive blames the one that's dead, of course."

"Isn't there some way you can tell for sure?" said Cassandra.

"He showed us where they dropped the weapon, so we've got prints, but both of them handled the shotgun so that's no help. The dead guy is the one with the motive. And it's his car that ran down Melanie Franklin. So I'm inclined to think it was him, all right."

They were on the ferry that crosses Jervis Inlet, on their way to Lund. It was breezy and cold out on deck so they'd moved inside and were sitting in the cafeteria. Alberg looked across the table at Cassandra. "Thanks for coming with me."

"Thanks for asking me."

There was an awkward silence. They were supposed to be talking, trying to work out which one of them was going to move. But now neither of them wanted to be the one to bring it up.

Twenty minutes later they were driving off the ferry at Saltery Bay, heading up the highway toward Powell River. They passed through Westview and the Powell River townsite, where the pulp mill belched smoke into the air, and then they were on the road to Lund.

Cassandra, studying the map, followed the highway, a confident red line moving up the Coast from Langdale to Gibsons to Sechelt to Earl's Cove, and starting again across the Inlet at Saltery Bay, and going northwest to Powell River and through the hamlet of Sliammon and beyond to this place called Lund...where it simply stopped. There was no way to continue up the coastline except by boat.

What if it turned out that she didn't *like* living with Karl Alberg on a regular basis? Sharing housekeeping tasks, and the food bills, and the television set, and the bathroom. What if she didn't like sharing a *bed* with him, on a regular basis?

They drove through forests and past acreages, past signs directing them westward through the trees to oceanfront campsites—and then the road took a curve to the left, up a lilting little rise, and they drove around the curve and saw the village of Lund, clustered around a small but perfect harbor.

The highway ran straight toward that harbor and drowned itself in the waters of the Pacific Ocean.

Alberg parked across from the hotel, and they got out of the car.

Still, thought Cassandra, gazing out at the sea, she wasn't the only person getting into cohabitation in midlife. She'd have to learn to be flexible. That was the important thing.

They went into the hotel café, where they found a waitress, three townspeople, and two tourists waiting for the water taxi to Savary Island.

"What's on Savary Island?" Alberg asked over coffee.

"Sandy beaches," said Cassandra, "and the biggest arbutus

tree in the world."

He inquired about the Franklins and learned that they lived right behind the hotel. "Wait for me here, okay?" he said to Cassandra.

She could probably be flexible, she thought, watching him go. As long as he could, too.

Alberg knocked on the door of the brown-shingled house and looked down at the concrete step while he waited for somebody to answer. They had a boot scraper. Albert hadn't seen one of those for years.

He looked up as the door opened. "Mr. Franklin?" he said through the screen.

"That's right. You're Staff Sergeant Alberg?"

"Yes. My car's right here," said Alberg, stepping back.

Franklin pushed the screen door open and joined Alberg. "How many boxes did you say?"

"Four."

"I can't believe it," said Franklin heavily, watching Alberg open the trunk. "Any of it."

They transferred the cardboard cartons to the Franklins' living room.

"They were going to do this, you know," said Franklin. "The girls. Kathy and Caroline and Sandy. They were going to bring this stuff up here Saturday night. Had it in the car all ready to go. But then they put it off a day." He glanced at Alberg. "If they hadn't put it off, those girls might be alive now. Is that right?"

"It's hard to tell, Mr. Franklin."

Franklin looked at the boxes, lined up on the living room floor. "Her mom will want to go through them. I'll just leave them here." He turned to Alberg. "I thank you for this," he said, and they shook hands. "I appreciate your trouble."

"It was no trouble," said Alberg.

He collected Cassandra from the hotel café, and they went back to his car.

"That was the northern end of the road, back there at Lund," said Cassandra, as they headed for Powell River. "The southern end of it's in Chile."

"Maybe we should just keep on driving," said Alberg, smiling at her.

They drove a mile or so in silence.

"So what about it?" he said.

"I'll live in your house for a year," said Cassandra promptly. "That is, if we find that—that this whole thing is a good idea."

Alberg grinned, and a nice zinging sensation warmed his chest. "And then what?"

"And then we'll see," said Cassandra. She rested her hand on his thigh.

"Okay," said Alberg. "I can handle that." He covered her hand with his. "Jesus, I feel good."

"Me too," said Cassandra, laughing.